Ecodisasters.
Torture prisons.
Fire-breathing cows.

A love story.

Night Shade Books
San Francisco

Cover art and design by Cody Tilson
Interior layout and design by Ross E. Lockhart

First Edition

ISBN: 978-1-59780-233-8

Printed In Canada

Night Shade Books
Please visit us on the web at
http://www.nightshadebooks.com

REVOLUTION WORLD

KATY STAUBER

I'd like to thank Marie Stauber, Chester Hoster and Chris Roberson for for all their help and support.

CHAPTER ONE

Sometimes Lady Luck's idea of girlish decorum is to pull on a pair of jackboots and frog march you towards the jaws of destiny. She was in that kind of mood the night ninjas broke in to Clio Somata's genetics laboratory.

If Clio hadn't been working late on a strain of medicine grapes, she might never have known her lab had been raided at all. She had just finished splicing in the requested vaccines. Now she was waiting for the mutation tester to cough up its results. She had a hunch that this batch of grapes would come out with too many mutations.

Mutations were normal, of course. But too many mutations and she'd have to start all over again. If that was the case, she wanted to get a new strain growing tonight. The French had promised a huge bonus if they could have these plants in time for the next growing cycle. Plus, she thought it was hilarious that the French wanted to take their medicine in wine format. It was just so French. They'd requested something robustly flavored, like a Pinot Noir or Beaujolais.

"Who wouldn't be willing to work a little late for a cause like that?" she asked one of the rabbits she was playing with. The rabbit just wiggled its nose. Clio had decided to wait for the results in the Animal Lab One while playing with one of the bunnies she had been working on.

She worked at the Floracopia Co-op, an agricultural gene modification company started by her mother almost thirty years ago. The Co-op was now one of the most cutting edge genetech companies in the world and managed to employ almost everyone in their small Texas town. While they mostly developed plant species for their clients, they did occasionally get to do more interesting projects like endangered species tweaks or herbivore remodeling.

These particular bunnies had not been a success, but they had some interesting phenotypic traits that she wanted to figure out. Being the head gene splicer and one of the founder's daughters meant that people tended to look the other way for what her mother called 'Clio's silly little projects.'

"Which is good for you guys, isn't it?" Clio asked the rabbits. "Otherwise I would have had to incinerate you, no matter how cute you are." The rabbit ignored her in favor of the carrot she had given it. People also overlooked the fact that she talked to her work. She felt it made the plants and animals happy. And since she spent so much time in her lab, it was good to practice talking so she wouldn't be rusty the next time she had real people to converse with.

Her handheld twittered to indicate the tests had finished. A brief glance at the results confirmed her earlier fears. There were too many mutations. One of them was particularly bad.

"Oh great. I'm going to be here all night," she moaned. The Newpox vaccine and the heat-resistance splices combined to cause the vines to produce a low yield of grapes.

Clio blew an exasperated sigh and ran her hand through her chin-length blond curls. There wasn't much point to making vaccine grapes without the Newpox vaccine, but they had to have the heat resistance too. Since The Troubles, almost all the food crops needed extra help withstanding what had happened to the environment.

The UN kept promising that Global Cooling would start any year now, but until she actually saw a summer day that was less than one hundred twenty degrees, she was going to keep planning for scorching heat. She thought about moving the Newpox vaccine to a different chromosome, but then decided that it would make the grapes taste too bitter.

She got up to go back to the Plant Lab and get the next batch of grapes in the incubator. Her stomach rumbled and she wished she had eaten more for dinner than chips and queso.

I really ought to eat more protein, she thought. *It would be easier to eat healthy if cheese would stop tasting so good.* She stretched her back a bit and groaned inwardly at the thought of a few more hours of work before she could go home.

That's when she saw the light flickering in the hallway. Someone was walking around out there with the lights off, using a flashlight. No one who was supposed to be here would do that. No one was supposed to be here this late anyway. Clio noticed a loud pounding sound in her ears. She realized that it was her heart going into overdrive. She turned off the small lamp next to her and sat down behind a bench.

"What should I do?" she asked the bunnies. The bunnies were unconcerned with her issues.

She watched the shifting lights for a minute and decided that the intruders were at the far end of the building. She started creeping towards the door before smacking herself on the forehead for not doing the obvious. She sat back down, pulled out her handheld, and firing off urgent cries for help to her family and friends.

Now I'll just sit tight here in Animal Lab One and wait for the cavalry to come, she sighed after she had finished. She realized that it was pretty late and the labs were a few miles from their tiny hometown of Ambrosia Springs, so it might be a while before someone showed up.

But wait. What if it isn't an intruder? What if it's just one of my sisters playing a stupid joke on me? Or a lab tech sneaking in to impress a date? Clio wondered.

Now that she thought about it, she felt foolish for not checking it out before crying for help. The doors to all the labs had windows in them. She crept to the door and peered out of the window without opening it. There was no one in the hall, but she could see the door to Animal Lab Two was open and a flashlight was moving around in there.

She quietly nudged the door of Animal Lab One open and peered down the hallway. A crash and muted cursing ruled out her sisters or a lab tech. She felt a jolt of fear before the anger set in. Someone was breaking things in her lab! She snuck down the hall and cautiously looked in the open door. There were two masked figures dressed all in black standing in front of an ancient filing cabinet. They weren't really ninjas but they obviously had ninjas on the brain when choosing their attire for the evening.

These intruder guys kind of look like ninjas, she thought. *When I tell this story later, I'm going to say they were ninjas.*

One of the intruders was obviously a large man, a little on the pudgy side. The other was tall and very thin and could have been a woman or man. The large man was showing the other a folder while shaking his head with confusion. After watching for a minute, Clio realized they were looking over her lab notes and didn't understand what they were reading.

She almost smiled to herself. She'd been lectured far too many times about neglecting to post her lab notes in the company data files. Instead of being able to pull up her notes on a company handheld, anyone wanting to read her techniques had to come in here and find them. The few times she had remembered to scan her notes in, she'd been further criticized about her indecipherable shorthand. And now these intruders were having a hard time finding whatever it was they wanted because they couldn't read her notes.

Apparently, being a lazy slob with bad handwriting does come in useful on occasion, she thought.

The smaller intruder began rapidly scanning all the documents into a handheld. The large man appeared to be collecting samples from some of the cages. Clio tried to remember what they had in those cages right now.

There were some high methane cows they were engineering for an alternative fuel company. One normal cow produces enough methane to power a small house. Since The Troubles, fuel was always a problem. So even something as gross as fitting out cows with special devices to capture gaseous emissions from the parts of them that might emit gases was pretty lucrative. Fortunately, this company got the bright idea of converting old sports arenas into huge methane plants. So no one lit a match for a mile around the old Astrodome in Houston.

Especially now that grain was so expensive, the methane capture company wanted cows that made even more methane. Clio was not fond of this project. These cows stank. And all that methane made them a huge fire hazard. She had to make very sure the ventilators were working in this lab or else one spark and she'd have a room full of fire-breathing cows. It had happened a few times and it wasn't a good time for anyone involved.

There were also the pygmy pumas that had been born out of the pseudo-womb two weeks ago. They were wanted in Colorado as a more manageable solution to the state's current rat infestation. All the rodents had been out of control since The Troubles. The state agency requested that they make them easy to identify so she'd made them bioluminescent. She could see the glowing little balls of cuteness in their cages as the large man shuffled around. There were a few other specimens, but nothing worth stealing. At least that's what Clio thought.

She was almost tempted to storm in and give these guys a good telling off. They didn't look that tough. But there were two of them and they might decide to beat her up. She'd had some self defense classes but wasn't confident in her abilities to do more than knee the groin of a drunk date who was getting a little too free with his hands. Clio thought about trying to take a picture with her handheld, but her hands were shaking pretty bad. She decided that the best thing to do was to go back to Animal Lab One and wait until help arrived.

She turned and realized she had forgotten two things. One was to shut the door to Animal Lab One. The other was to shut the door to the bunny cage. She could see three of the huge beasts hopping down the hall towards her. Clio's rabbits were much bigger than normal rabbits, even the ones meant to be a meat source. They tended to be about the size of a large dog. One of them gave a piercing shriek and Clio's heart sank. This strain tended to do that when they were happy about something. The two intruders turned and instantly spotted her. The larger man froze, but the smaller one quickly produced a gun. That's all she saw before she bolted down the hall.

She could hear them coming after her and it gave her speed she never knew she had. She leapt over a rabbit like a champion hurdle jumper and was almost to the doorway before the first shot fired. She couldn't believe it. Clio had been bitten, kicked and cussed out, but she'd never been shot at before. She could barely see straight, she was so scared.

She heard a rabbit squeal in pain and terror as one of the bullets struck it. They really meant to kill her! She heard cursing down the hall.

"Jesus Christ, is that what I think it is?" said a man's surprised voice.

The rabbits had confused the auto-sighting on the gun. She

was thankful even as she worried about her poor bunnies. As more shots rang out, she slammed the lab door shut and locked it. Then she turned and looked through the window even though she knew she should probably run and hide.

The intruders were still at the end of the hall arguing over the twitching corpse of one of the rabbits. The other two bunnies were huddled against her door, obviously terrified.

The sympathetic nervous system is, among other things, in charge of the 'fight-or-flight response.' In times of stress, the sympathetic nervous system hijacks your higher brain functions and initiates a series of responses to help you survive. Responses such as raising your heart rate so that blood can rush to your muscles and give you speed. It dilates your pupils so that you can find your enemies and your escape routes with greater efficiency. It stops activity in non-essential areas like digestion so that every bit of reserve energy can be used for survival. Unfortunately, it also makes you do extremely stupid things. Like open the door to save your rabbits and let the bad guys know exactly where you are. That's what Clio did.

The smaller one with the gun started towards Clio while the larger turned back to Animal Lab Two. Clio slammed the door shut and re-locked it as another shot was buried into the door near her head. She raced to the corner farthest from the door and hid behind a lab bench.

Clio realized as the small intruder rattled the door, that she was repeating "Oh god oh god oh god oh god" quietly to herself like some sort of mantra. She forced herself to breathe slowly and think.

You are a rational creature so act like one, she told herself. She decided that while the stranger wouldn't be able to get through the door, he would be able shoot through the window. She could hide behind a lab bench, but would a bench stop a bullet? Probably not. Clio remembered the auto-sight. She crawled over and let the remaining bunnies out of their cages. She hoped this would confuse the auto-sight again. She also hoped that someone with an auto-sight had never learned to actually aim the gun.

As the glass on the window crashed and shots echoed through the room, she crawled into the lowest bunny cage and hugged that last and slowest rabbit to her like a child's toy. She did not fool herself with the thought that this was the act of a rational person. She just wanted comfort.

The bunnies did confuse the gun's internal computer. However, she was wrong to think the door would hold. After a moment it swung open, the digital lock released without a fuss. The intruder stormed in.

He knows the codes. They must have access to our network. How? Have we been betrayed or did someone manage to hack our security? Clio wondered, even as she tried to stop breathing.

Please don't let him hear me. I don't want to die, she thought as she buried her head in the soft fur of the huge rabbit. She felt its heart pound as frantically as her own.

Then something happened that made her inner scientist sit up and slap her inner human right in the face. The bunnies stopped acting like bunnies. She blinked hard when she realized she was watching the remaining half dozen rabbits take cover and slowly advance upon the intruder in a tight formation. They made a series of clicking noises with their teeth like chattering squirrels. The shooting stopped as the intruder searched the darkness.

Then there was a cloud of fur as the rabbits reared back their legs to reveal long fangs and yellowed claws.

"Holy Christ, monsters!" the intruder screamed as he or she floundering backwards, then wheeled, and fled back down the hall, shrieking the whole time. As the rabbit onslaught scrabbled down the hall after the shooter, Clio was lost in wondering how she had made fuzzy lettuce-eaters into ferocious attack beasts.

Was it in the protein folding? Post-translational modification? What could it be? she asked herself. Clio stumbled after them in a daze, just to see what would happen next.

That's when she heard the sirens. She looked through the hall windows and saw the flashing lights of the police cars, fire engines, and Uncle Bubba's tricked-out hunting truck pull into the parking lot. Her friends and family had taken her pleas for help seriously. She was so happy she could cry.

On the other side of the building, she saw the two intruders burst out of a door and slam it behind them. They were raining bullets and laser pulses in every direction. They dove into a black hovercar that was waiting there. The smaller one was bloody and gripping a bag of papers. The larger one limped, but clutched a bag large enough to contain a few specimens. The car shot off like only a nuclear-powered hovercar can. The police saw the car as it sped off. They were in hot pursuit within seconds.

Clio sighed with relief and staggered towards the lights and the sirens. She could see her mother and two of her sisters were running towards her as she got to the door.

CHAPTER TWO

"What are you doing?" the sheriff bellowed with exasperation forty minutes later. He'd ordered the women to stop touching evidence and go outside for the fourth time. After the initial hysterical hugging and questions, the women began compulsively tidying up the damage.

Harmony came over to soothe the sheriff's ruffled feathers. She understood his frustration, but she had no intention of letting the man get in her way tonight. Her daughter had been in danger tonight and, worse yet, it had happened inside Floracopia. If any place in this world should be safe, it was the little splicer company she had built with her own two hands.

The problem was that the Floracopia Co-op employed practically everybody in town in one way or another. So the Somata Sisters were the closest thing to local celebrities they had around here. Harmony did feel it was idle vanity to recognize that. The identical quadruplet sisters would have been local celebrities anywhere, though. Harmony smiled proudly when she thought of her daughters.

All four of them were short and curvy with blond curls, green eyes, and, unfortunately, a reckless disregard for the laws of reality. Harmony frequently wished she had spliced away that characteristic. It would have made their lives so much easier. Constantly getting mistaken for each other had stopped being funny when they were about eight years old, so now they went out of their way to look different. Harmony knew the townspeople really appreciated it. Although most people believed they could tell them apart anyway. It was a very small town.

Harmony remembered the day, over twenty years ago, that old Myrna Hix had finally asked the question everyone in town had been dying to ask.

"Missy, are you pregnant?" she rasped.

"Yes, ma'am," she'd answered, determinged to keep her voice level. She reflexively put a hand on her belly.

Myrna had sniffed. "Well it don't surprise me, what with all your people dead and you running that devilish gene business. It don't matter that it's all legal now, Jesus don't like it."

"I have to go now, ma'am," Harmony said politely and moved away.

Myrna was having none of that. This was the hottest gossip of the year. "And who's the daddy?"

Harmony had sighed. "That's my own business," she replied.

"Did you mix 'em up in one of your satanic gene buckets?" Myrna asked.

Harmony couldn't keep her voice level this time. "Human gene splicing is illegal, Myrna," she snapped. "Don't ever suggest my girls are strange. You know what would happen if the government thought they were spliced."

Myrna had paled and blinked hard. Harmony was kicking herself inside. She just knew the old lady would spend years making her pay for raising her voice to an elder. The subtle gossip in a small town can drive you mad.

"Well," sniffed Myrna. "Congratulations."

Harmony had watched the old woman scuttle off. And that was the last time anyone had asked her where her girls had come from. Which was good since she had no intention of telling. And they were all strange.

Clio, the splicer, spent most of her time in her lab so she usually wore loose, comfortable clothes like the cotton yoga pants, lab smock, and running shoes she had on this evening. Her sister, Terpsi, kept trying to make her sit in a corner and drink something warm, but every few minutes she erupted in outrage as more people pawed through her precious lab equipment.

Terpsi was what most people thought of as 'the responsible one.' She seemed far too young to be a married doctor with two little boys. Harmony felt much too young to have grandchildren, but she doted on them. Terpsi occasionally worked with the Co-op whenever they had a germ or medical project. Harmony did not like to take medical projects, so Terpsi maintained her own clinic in town as well. She always kept her long hair up in a smooth twist and wore sensible, conservative clothes. Tonight, she wore a soft plain shirt and matching loose cotton pants.

Kalliope was her wild little engineer. That girl always had tools and mad machines hidden in her pockets and grease smears on her face. She was given to wearing overalls, thick boots, and an ever-changing parade of party colors in her hair. Tonight she'd roared up on her homemade steamcycle with bright purple hair, sporting a thin nightgown over jeans. Harmony could see more tattoos on that girl than she'd known a person could have. She resisted lecturing her daughter, but it took effort.

Thalia was the only one of the Somata sisters not here. She was in California this week collecting samples for their next genetech project. Harmony was thankful. Thalia was too charming and persuasive for her own good. She just kept chattering until somehow she got what she wanted.

Harmony kept up a soothing litany as she gently steered the sheriff away from all those interesting cages. The man looked like he would very much enjoy poking around. Not all of the projects Floracopia took on were totally legitimate and she just didn't need any more complications tonight.

"Oh, sheriff, be reasonable. Half the town is tromping around in our parking lot. We've just had a major breech of security. We've got to make sure nobody else gets in," Harmony said sensibly as she patted the frustrated sheriff on the shoulder. She swept him out of a big lab room and into the hallway as graciously as she could. He craned his neck looking for the monsters the local kids always swore were in here.

"Now, it looks like the intruders opened the locks pretty easily, so either they had extremely good equipment or they had clearance to be here," Harmony said as she showed him the outer doors of the lab building. "Naturally, we prefer the employees do not come in after hours, steal specimens and shoot up the place, so we are looking into that aspect of it. We'll keep you updated with any information we have."

Harmony knew that if the girls were local celebrities, she herself was something like a minor deity around this town. She patted her hair to make sure it was still secured in a neat bun and checked her clothes for wrinkles or smudges. Although she always tried to dress and act in a way that was reserved, she couldn't avoid the looks her shining bronze hair drew, any more than she could avoid the whispers about her past.

Well, a single woman with four girls to raise and a cutting edge genetech business to run is sure to draw some comment. And if she was able to use her influence to direct local policy, it was only natural. She knew that any policy that helped Floracopia would help the locals. She grew up here too, after all.

"What are these scratches?" asked the sheriff, bringing Harmony back into the moment.

"What?" she asked innocently.

He pointed to the deep scratches along the walls of the hallway. "They look like they could have been made a pack of large dogs, maybe. But I don't know of any dog that could gouge concrete like that."

Harmony laughed nervously. "Oh look sheriff. I think your men need you." She quickly pulled him in to Animal Lab Two. The scratches were also at the base of the door. The sheriff continued to frown at them despite her attempts to draw him away.

"Is that blood in the corner?" he asked, but a police officer came up with questions that distracted him. Harmony slumped against a wall with relief.

Animal Lab Two was bursting with police and lab personnel sifting through things, taking pictures and bagging evidence. The sheriff smiled in appreciation.

"I do like a well-worked crime scene. Much better than monsters any day of the week," he said as he waded into scene. He looked with disappointment at some of the cages. "They look like normal animals to me."

Harmony decided to ignore his fascination with the specimens and filled him in on what she thought he should know. "It looks as though they made off with some specimens and some notes on our procedures for various techniques. Since the specimens themselves have no real value, we think perhaps a rival business or foreign government are looking to steal some of our intellectual property."

"Most likely it was *our* government," the sheriff remarked aloud. He was distracted. He had been watching a little mouse shoot out an impossibly long tongue and pull a loose pen into its cage. Its cage was labeled 'Garbage Mouse, Batch 42.' It gulped down the pen audibly and began eyeing the sheriff's shiny badge. The sheriff took a step back.

Harmony gave a tinkly little laugh and shook the sheriff's shoulder like she was trying to wake him from a dream. "Oh sweetie, why of course our government would never do such a thing. They'd ask for it nicely and we, as good patriots, would give it to them. Of course, poor little small business owners that we are, we have nothing worth the government's time," she said loudly.

She looked pointedly at the gaggle of uniforms behind him. He got flustered, realizing he'd slipped and criticized the government where others could hear him. These days, even a police chief could get snatched by Homeland Security and labeled as a terrorist. Harmony knew he had two kids in high school and couldn't afford to have everything he'd ever owned seized by the government as 'terrorist funds.'

"Of course, of course," he agreed hurriedly. He moved away from her to speak to the other police officers present.

"Good patriots are we, Mother?" chuckled Kalliope quietly. She had walked up behind her mother a minute before. Harmony hushed her with a look. Now that she was free of the sheriff, she could get some work done.

"What did you find?" she asked as she pulled her three daughters into a storage room, one of the few places free of outsiders right now.

"They took some of the Peruvian monkeys and the notes about that project," Clio said without preamble. Whatever Harmony had been expecting her to say, that wasn't it.

"What? Seriously? The monkeys? Are you sure they didn't make a mistake and mean to grab those stupid fire-breathing cows or the electric sheep?" Harmony asked in disbelief. "I could see industrial espionage for those guys, but Peruvian monkeys?" Clio shook her head. Harmony still couldn't wrap her head around it either.

Kalliope snickered, "Were they sea monkeys by any chance?" The others look at her blankly. Kalliope could never get her family interested in the finer points of twentieth century popular culture. They just weren't much on history.

Harmony shook her head and turned back to Clio. "They really took the monkeys? But we're releasing the stupid smelly monkeys into the wild to help rebuild their population. They could just go to Peru and pick some up and no one would ever know." She trailed off for a minute, lost in thought. Then she shot a sharp look at Clio.

"Did you do something to those monkeys, girl? Sweet Mother of God. Someday your tinkering is going to land us all in a maximum security torture jail," she said accusingly as she put her hands on her hips and used that tone only mothers can achieve.

Clio shrugged. "Nothing exciting. Had to get a little fancy and do a p-mod. Thalia was only able to bring back a few and they died so easily. I couldn't clone them any better than we could raise them in captivity. You remember? I don't understand how such a cute primate could be so difficult. Probably why they were going extinct before I got hold of them."

Harmony nodded thoughtfully. "A p-mod? Oh my baby girl, you are brilliant. Maybe that's it. A p-mod is awfully difficult and your method was very successful. I remember reading the outcomes. I was proud of you, honey." Clio brightened up a bit. Harmony knew she was not the best at overwhelming displays of affection so she did not try for a hug at this point.

"But next time you do something brilliant, do it for the paying customers and not the charity cases," Harmony added severely. She was a scientist first; a businesswoman second; and a mother third. Somewhere way down at the bottom of the list, she was a lonely middle-aged woman.

"OK, gene nerds, what's a p-mod?" Kalliope asked with the thinning patience of one who loves gears and pumps, but grew up in a house full of people chattering about biology and genetics. She'd never been interested in their consuming passion and they'd never listened to hers. But they were family, so what can you do? Part of the reason Terpsi was the only married one was the tightness of their family unit. It was hard for others to break into such a close-knit family and even harder to find someone willing to try.

"The Peruvian monkeys were almost completely wiped out. They live in the cloud forests of Peru and those are pretty thin these days," Clio explained patiently to her sister. "We could barely capture enough to get a full genomic work-up. That is, a complete library of their DNA. We had a terrible time cloning the eggs to test in the lab and totally failed to splice up a variant that would breed in captivity."

Kalliope looked at her blankly. Harmony quickly interjected, "P-modding, short for phenotype modification, is what we call it when we introduce a change in the genes of an adult. Imagine your genes are like a book of recipes for your life. Your body reads the various recipes when it wants to make something. So to make changes to the book of their life, we first need to know what it says. That's a complete genomic work up. You remember? We talked about that before?" She paused and looked at Kalliope, who nodded.

So Harmony continued, "Usually splicers have to work with eggs or seeds and cultivate modified species from there. In other words, we change the story in their book of life before it's printed. P-modding is trying to change the story of an individual who has already been born. That is, whose genetic book has already been printed. It's technically difficult, but not totally impossible. You see what I'm saying?"

Kalliope nodded slowly. "So your DNA is the recipe book for your life. It's easy to edit the book before it's printed, but really hard after it's been printed. Got it. Why is that? Because it will damage the book? Or just come out as nonsense?"

Clio gave her sister a big grin. After only a quarter of a century, some of it was finally sinking in. "Exactly. If it damages the book, who knows what happens? Usually something bad like cancer or heart attack. If it comes out as nonsense, your body will just ignore those pages. That's what usually happens. Nothing, in other words."

She gave her sister a minute to think about that as her mind wandered to the pollution fish in the Aquatics lab that she was developing for the Great Lakes. Clio just loved her job. She remembered how frustrated she'd been with the monkeys.

"So how did you do the p-mod in the monkeys then? What did you change?" asked Kalliope.

"I ended up modifying the genes of a fruit that wild monkeys loved to eat. The fruit produced chemicals and proteins that caused the desired changed in the adult monkeys. Plus, let's just say their libido got juiced up. Which made for a population explosion. They were able to survive at lower altitudes and eat a wider variety of foods." Clio thought it was funny that she had produced the primate equivalent of a goat. The spliced monkeys could and would eat almost anything.

The result was wild adult monkeys that reached maturity faster and produced more babies. Usually any changes you could manage to make to an adult were not likely to be passed on to their babies, but Clio had some techniques that ensured the babies possessed the same ability to grow up quickly and make lots of babies. The resulting population explosion brought the monkeys back from the brink of extinction.

Clio was now working on a subspecies that could be more easily raised in captivity. Those were the monkeys that the intruders took. Clio had added a few changes to the fruit that resulted in a greater proliferation of the Peruvian cloud forests as well.

Clio had slightly changed a few of the proteins in the fruit to break down as they passed through the monkey's digestive tract. The digested proteins enriched the local soil dramatically. Now monkey manure, by the pound, was worth more than gold in Peru. All in all, she was pretty proud of that project.

Harmony began pacing. "Gene research is so secretive now, it's hard to know where the other splicers are. The private labs don't publish their results for fear of a competitor using their own research to get an edge. The government has snatched anyone worth anything at university labs for their never-ending war projects and everything those guys even think about is classified. And that's assuming any of them have the funding or the brains to do anything really interesting in the first place. Maybe someone really did want the p-mod technique and thought this was an easy way to get it," Harmony concluded, turning to her daughters.

"But why would they get all in a lather about a primate splice? There are so few primates left and none of them are really commercially viable. I mean, there's not much you can do with primates that results in a profit," said Clio.

"Flinging poo and scratching fleas never did make anyone rich," laughed Kalliope.

"Humans are primates. Maybe they want to use the splice on humans," said Terpsi.

"Don't be silly. Human gene modification is so illegal it isn't even funny," Clio scoffed.

"If the war project labs had a useful p-mod technique like that, they'd use it to make zombie soldiers and human bombs and god knows what else. Do you think anyone in the military really cares about what the UN thinks is legal or illegal?" Terpsi asked. She had a point.

"Heck, it sounds like they could cause gene mutations in people through food with that technique thingy of yours. They could modify people who weren't even aware of what was going on. There are a lot of people in our government who would find some mighty nasty uses for that kind of tool," Kalliope exclaimed.

Clio scowled. Everything she did could be used for cruel purposes. She hated it, but it was something she'd come to terms with long ago. "Even with my notes, it would be difficult to take a technique that worked with monkeys and apply it to people. And that's assuming they could understand my notes," Clio replied.

"Back to the original issue," said Harmony. "Anyone with the power or money to get access to our lab like this could just have broken into our network to get the technique. So why didn't they?" She looked around the room as if the answer might be written on the walls.

Clio blushed and stammered. "I didn't upload my notes. It was laziness." The other women smiled, but didn't laugh. They knew Clio was monomaniacal about her work, but didn't care about much else.

"So let's say they wanted the p-mod. They must have gotten someone with access to help them. Even with all the money in the world to break the locks, they couldn't know exactly where Clio kept those notes unless they'd been here before. That's the scariest part." Harmony tried to maintain a brisk, business-like attitude. "Ruling out everyone still hanging around in the parking lot right now, we only have a handful of likely suspects for betrayal. I'll get working on that."

"It was lucky I was here tonight," remarked Clio.

Harmony gave an unladylike snort. "It was lucky you weren't shot."

At this point, Terpsi finally stopped scanning Clio with her palm-sized diagnoser. "So they came to steal a technique. Why take the monkeys and the notes? Why not just scan the notes into a handheld? It would take like five minutes and then no one would ever know they'd been here."

"I think that was the plan," Clio replied. "Only I was here and caught them. Oh, and the *Lepus* bunnies attacked them." She did not explain that her horrible handwriting had kept the intruders from figuring out exactly what they needed to steal. She could only hope that, however embarrassing, it might also keep the thieves from using the notes they had taken with them.

"So they panicked and grabbed everything they thought they might need. Then the rabbits freaked them out so they shot up the place. And that's fair. Those rabbits freak everybody out, Clio," Terpsi looked at her sister severely. She was, of the family, the most realistic. The other sisters secretly called her 'the grouchy one.'

"So then. Who would want it? Who would do this?" Terpsi really wanted to resolve this and get back to bed. Her kids were going to wake her up again in five hours.

Harmony and Clio looked glum. "Rival companies, foreign governments, our government," Clio answered.

"We have no idea," Harmony concluded. "But at least we should be able to find who our turncoat is."

"If it happened once, we should expect more." Kalliope chimed in decisively. "I'll start looking into better security systems. We'll have to hire out for most of that. I never could get into the digital stuff. If they are after information, then it's a tech company that we'll need."

Harmony cleared her throat significantly and paused. "Just so I understand clearly. There wasn't anything they might have noticed in the lab that they shouldn't? There wasn't anything they took or anything about those monkeys that might indicate that you have certain hobbies, shall we say, that the government would frown upon?"

The girls looked at each other. They knew what their mother was talking about, but didn't want to break their mother's continued policy of ignorance.

"They didn't take anything or see anything that would indicate that Floracopia engages in illegal activities," Clio replied carefully. "But if they had spent a little more time, they might have gotten the impression that some of our projects were not strictly legitimate."

Harmony tapped her fingers against a table and frowned. She looked for a minute like she might embark on one of her epic lectures, but then she just sighed and rubbed her temples.

"We are definitely going to need better security. And maybe move some of your less justifiable work to a different lab," she gave her daughters a steely look.

"Oh, this is all so stupid." Clio cried in exasperation. "If they could afford to break in and they wanted it that badly, why didn't they just try to buy it from us? Or if it was the government, why not just demand we give it to them? Both of those would have probably worked."

"And that's the big question," Harmony sighed and ran her hand through her straight brown hair. "Well, we won't solve the problems of the world tonight, girls. Let's wrap this up and try to get some sleep."

They gently ushered all the excited police and worried friends out into the dark, but none of them got any real sleep that night.

Clio was completely exhausted once she got back home. She owned a snug cabin on fifty acres of untouched Edwards Plateau woodlands just behind the lab. She didn't think anything could keep her awake. Just before she drifted off, she remembered something she forgot to tell her family. Four of her rabbits were missing. Since they couldn't possibly have been carried off, they must have gotten loose.

As anyone who has ever thought too hard about the Fibonacci sequence will tell you, four rabbits can do a lot of damage in a short amount of time. Clio didn't sleep for a week after that.

CHAPTER THREE

Two men sat in the sleek hovercar, mesmerized by the sight of a shabby diner in the middle of nowhere. The hovercar was a shiny black teardrop, quietly bobbing above the dirt parking lot as the men peered through the darkly polarized windows. They took in the dented pick-up trucks in the parking lot with their obviously secondhand biomass retrofits. They observed the peeling paint on the dingy sign that optimistically proclaimed: “Best cow you can git in yer mouth!” They were utterly depressed.

“We’ve found hell, Seth,” said the older man. The younger man said nothing, but in the way that you do if you don’t want to agree but secretly believe the other person is right. He looked at the diner as if hoping it would suddenly turn into a five-star sushi restaurant.

The two men were both tall, thin and very pale. They both had dark hair and dark eyes and could have been any age from twenty to fifty. Even if they weren’t in a hovercar, they were very obviously not from around here.

“No,” the older man corrected himself, “We are in Texas. I think I’d rather be in hell.”

Seth Boucher smiled as he began rummaging behind his seat, “Don’t be so melodramatic, Max. You just need to eat.”

Max rolled his eyes and began brushing dust off his comfortable, but obviously expensive, outfit. “What I need is a glass of champagne, a four-course meal cooked by an actual French person, and a five-star spa where beautiful women rub my feet until I forget Texas even exists. Why on earth did I let you talk me into this trip? We are programmers. We sit in dark rooms. Dark, cool rooms with comfortable chairs and pleasant people who bring us food. We don’t do the scouting trips. You told me this would be a vacation."

This was delivered in a glum monotone. Seth could tell Max was working hard not to whine.

"I told you this would be an adventure," Seth corrected him. "You cannot deny it has been very different and very interesting."

Max sniffed elaborately. "I had no idea you hated me this much."

Seth just smiled, found his handheld, and touched it on. Max smiled slightly as Seth carefully lined up his handheld and took a picture of the diner. He wanted proof that the overly refined Max had actually eaten in such a place.

"Look over there. I think that is a real, live tumbleweed," Max pointed for Seth's benefit.

"Are tumbleweeds alive?" Seth wondered aloud as he obligingly took a picture.

Max pulled his own handheld out of the slot in the dashboard and tapped away at it. "No, apparently not. Well, on the bright side, this is the last horrific little town to check out before we may shake the dust of Texas from our feet and never return. Are you sure you don't want to just give up and go home now?" Max eyed Seth hopefully.

"My dear uncle, we came here to investigate new sites for a server farm. You know why Texas is a desirable location for us. Even though it does seem as though everyone here hates us on sight. Even though they made it clear that they find the idea of our business moving here repulsive, we must try to find a way for this to work. We must at least look at this last town, Ambrosia Springs."

Max snorted. "We were obviously wrong. Even the weather here hates us. I swear the sun is actually brighter here than at home, not to mention broiling hot and baking the life out of everything. Seriously, it's nine in the evening and the sun only just went down. How can we live with that?"

"I admit that I am not optimistic," Seth replied.

Max sighed, but his hungry stomach caused him to rally bitterly. "I suppose must eat. Let us venture forth and let the angry and rude owners of this restaurant do their best to poison us."

Seth attempted a cheery smile. "You want to give up? Just

because everyone else in this state seems to believe it's his or her personal duty to make us very sorry that we were so stupid as to come here? This could be where they hide all the nice people who like foreigners. After all, this diner was specifically recommended to us by the woman I've arranged to guide us around Ambrosia Springs."

They noticed a few old men had gathered at the dusty windows of the diner to stare out at them. Seth's smile faded under the suspicious squints of the locals.

Max rolled his eyes again and opened the door of the car, slipping his handheld into a pocket. "In that case, it's sure to kill us. Or keep us up all night wishing we were dead."

"Well, if that's the case, then we will know that this town doesn't want us here either and we can leave tomorrow," Seth replied equably.

This cheered Max up quite a bit. He entertained a brief fantasy of leaving Texas and getting home in time for a long weekend filled with fine wines and sophisticated company.

"Come on, boy, let's do this thing," Max replied as he stepped out into the new night.

Seth nonchalantly ignored the glares of the men inside. He promptly slammed the car door on his shirt. Why did this sort of thing always happen to him?

Max chuckled as Seth wrestled himself free. "That's why I don't let you borrow my clothes." Seth glowered at him as he tried to smooth out his torn shirt. He sucked on the thumb he'd jammed trying to free the shirt.

"I don't borrow your clothes because I don't want to look like a stuck up nancy boy," Seth muttered.

"You don't borrow my clothes because they look like rags on that scrawny scarecrow body of yours," Max replied with a grin. "Come on."

As they walked through the rusty door, the locals made no attempt to disperse from the windows. Seth half expected one wrinkled old man in overalls and a battered baseball cap to pull out a shotgun and start blasting away at them. A large, swarthy man in a cowboy hat wiped a froth of beer from his lips and asked with a thick Texas twang, "You boys get lost in that there fancy hovercar of yours? Because we'd be happy to give you directions back to Austin."

Seth could see Max was about to take the man up on that offer when a plump middle-aged woman erupted from the kitchen with a business-like smile on her face. She had the most improbable bouffant they'd ever seen. Max stared at it as she came bustling up.

"Y'all ain't from around here, that's for sure. Never seen skin that white in my life. Oh my goodness, I didn't mean to say that out loud. Anyway, what brings you out our way?" she asked breathlessly as she wiped off a menu.

"We are on our way to Ambrosia Springs, to see what we can see of this beautiful state," Seth smiled at her pleasantly.

Max seemed to be struck dumb by the storm cloud of hair bobbing above her as she walked. The waitress stared at him for a minute and then something must have clicked in her mind as her eyes went round.

"Oh!" she cried. "Oh my word! Y'all is those boys Miss Joanna said to look out for and here you are! Lordy, that woman knows everything. She runs the Chamber of Commerce and the Junior League and lord knows what else, you know. Well, here you are! My gracious, my heavens, well come sit down! My name's Bessy." She beamed at them as though they had performed a very impressive trick and then ushered them over to a table. Seth and Max shared a bewildered look as they followed in the wake of hurricane Bessy.

"Well, now, Miss Joanna said she'd recommended us to you and of course she would. I don't like to brag, but we do a fine dinner here," she said loudly over her shoulder as she conjured up a checkered tablecloth and sparkling clean silverware. "She said you were foreigners and we wanted to be extra-special nice to you."

This last part she seemed to direct more to the other patrons than to the two men themselves. Seth noticed the suspicious glares of the locals seemed to fade and the harsh silence was replaced by the gentle buzz of gossip.

Bessy burbled on as she produced glasses filled with some sort of drink, a cloth wrapped bundle of cornbread and a little tub of honey-sweetened butter. "My sister works for Miss Harmony at the Co-op. You know, the Floracopia Co-op? Those girls are mighty smart. Anyway, she said y'all was thinking about building some sort of computer factory or something right here in Ambrosia Springs? Wouldn't that be interesting! Well now, even if we are a little rural, we got the Co-op so we already got experience in living with you high-tech smart people and all."

Betsy could talk all day without stopping for breath. "Now I bet you are thinking you got nothing in common with them just because you all work with computers and they mess around with genes and plants and that DNA whatever. But what I'm saying is, we're used to all that crazy stuff here in Ambrosia Springs. Well of course, our little restaurant isn't quite in Ambrosia Springs, but we almost are, what with it being only five miles down the road and of course, nothing else for just miles and miles. And you know, I don't like to brag but even though people just don't get out too much these days, we do see a lot of folks here in our diner." She paused her monologue and patted her hair in a self-satisfied way.

Seth was content to wolf down cornbread and honey butter while she talked, but Max squinted at the menu. When Bessy noticed this, she snatched it out of his hands.

"Oh, sugar, don't you bother your little foreign head about ordering. I promise your mouth will think it died and went to heaven." Max made as if to protest, but stopped when she fixed him with a suspicious glare.

"Do not tell me y'all are vegetarians."

Max and Seth both smiled and shook their heads. "Most definitely not."

"Good, because you two sure do look like you could use some feeding up." And she was off to the kitchen with her bouffant threatening to crash down like a tidal wave at any second. Soon she was back with plates piled high that she kept bringing until there was no more room on the table. She still managed to find room for two ice-cold beers. Seth looked at the unfamiliar Mexican label.

"Tecate?" he asked.

"Never heard of it," Max replied.

Seth took a swig and smiled. "If you don't like it, I'm drinking yours."

Max looked uncertainly at the spread in front of him, but

within a few bites he progressed to emitting little sounds of full blown rapture. In the week they had been in Texas, they had eaten bland, tasteless food served to them by hostile waitresses who they strongly suspected of spitting in their food. Max was starving and applied himself with enthusiasm.

"Bessy, you angel," he declared the next time she stopped by their table. "What is this divine thing I am eating?"

"Well, my gracious, you poor boys never had chicken-fried steak with cream gravy? Lord a mercy, who would have thought of such a thing? This here is cheddar-jalapeno grits. That right there is potato salad and this over here is creamed spinach with chipotles. Oh my! I just now thought of it. Y'all must be Yankees!" Seth could hear several nearby patrons gasp.

"I understand up north y'all don't have any real peppers. I hope the food is not too spicy for you?" Bessy asked anxiously.

Max beamed at her between mouthfuls, "This food is making me so happy, I could just cry." His cheeks were pink.

Seth, for his part, looked upon the diner with newfound appreciation for the fine art of decorating displayed. Actually, the decorations were primarily an assortment of old kitchen gadgets and lawn equipment tacked to the wall, from back when they used electricity like it was going to be around forever. He saw a pasta maker and one of those crazy old Foreman grills.

"We are from Queen Charlotte Islands. It's near Canada," Seth interjected. He had been eating so fast, that he dropped his chicken-fried steak into his lap and was now trying to wipe gravy off his pants without Max noticing. Seth was cursed with chronic clumsiness and Max made fun of him every time. Every single time.

"I knew it! Yankees!" Bessy was clearly storing any information about the two strangers up for future gossip. "Well, save room for pie. We got pecan, apple, chocolate cream, and peach tonight and I made them all myself. Oh sugar, you got something on your face." She leaned over and briskly scrubbed Seth's cheek with a napkin. The diner was starting to fill up so she was off again.

"Apparently this is, in fact, the place where Texas hides all the friendly people who like foreigners. I don't know how we got to be Yankees, but I'm not going to disabuse her of the notion," Seth observed cheerfully around a mouthful of potatoes.

"What do you think this drink is here?" Max asked, pointing to a glass of something.

After an experimental sip, Seth knew. "I think it's sweet iced tea. I read about it before we left." Max was disappointed by its obvious lack of alcohol.

After a few slices of pie, and a minor spasm of joy after getting the bill, they were sipping coffee and amiably watching the locals. "It's a fifth of the price we'd have spent in a restaurant in Vancouver," Max gloated. He called to Bessie when she came to collect the bill, "Bessy, you marvelous woman, marry me!"

"Oh, sugar, that pie has gone straight to your head." She giggled and blushed like a teenager. "Don't let my man Bubba hear you talking like that. He's the cook here and he's got one of them temperamental attitudes, if you know what I mean."

"I shall have to content myself with eating here every chance I get," Max said, fixing her with a devilish grin. For a brief moment, Bessy forgot she was a middle-aged woman with bunions and two kids in high school as she waved them out the door with a smile.

CHAPTER FOUR

Bessy's smile was still in place the next afternoon when a battered old motorcycle spewing steam careened into the parking lot. The short but curvy young woman riding it whipped off her goggles and helmet and charged up to the door as the steamcycle sputtered to a stop.

"Bessy, where are they? Did Bubba chop them up for steak? Did they give up and go home? We told everybody to be nice to them. Real Nice. Extra-special nice. So where are they?" she cried. Bessy put a cup of coffee and plate of smoked chicken in front of the girl as though she hadn't spoken.

"Now, Miss Kalliope, you need to not get so fussed. Those boys seemed real happy with life when they left here, so I imagine they are still poking around somewheres." The blond woman shot Bessy a look as she took a bite of broccoli casserole. "Oh now I'm sorry, Miss Clio, I forgot you gone and cut your hair. What are you doing, tearing across the countryside on your sister's contraption like that?"

"My scooter sprang a leak," Clio grumbled, pulling out her handheld, "Kalliope's fixing it."

"Well that girl can fix anything and if she doesn't add any of her little inventions to it, you should have it back right quick," Bessy replied sympathetically, "And how's your Momma?"

"She's fine. She and Joanna are stuck talking to those damn Malsanto people this afternoon, so I'm supposed to roll out the red carpet for these visiting computer geeks. What were they like, anyway?" Clio seemed to relax under the soothing spell of smoked chicken and coffee.

"Well, they was real nice for poor, uncultured Yankees. Imagine not knowing what chicken-fried steak was! A little standoffish but they had some real pretty manners. Not too bad looking, but they were peaky like they needed feeding up." Bessy beamed, happy to give her opinion.

She leaned closer to Clio conspiratorially, "So why are we being so nice to these boys?"

Clio smiled mysteriously and mock-whispered, "These boys are looking to set up a satellite office for Omerta Corp. They specialize in computer security. They are very good at helping people keep secrets. And between worrying about the government and the terrorists, we sure do need some security. I'd explain more, but I've got a zillion things to do today and now I've got to figure out where these guys went."

"Well, sugar," Bessy said, producing a slice of apple pie like a rabbit out of a hat, "You could have just called, you know."

"If I'd called, I would have missed out on your apple pie," she laughed. Clio's handheld chirped and she answered it. After listening for a few minutes, she flicked it off and paid Bessy.

"Mom says Dan Martinez called to tell her that aliens are camped out in his south pasture, scaring his goats. So I think I found my missing geeks." Clio cranked up the steamcycle and roared off.

An hour later, she was hiking through the tall brush to get to a large black tent in the middle of a field with a hovercar parked next to it. The tent looked like it could comfortably hold a maharaja and most of his harem. She noticed a collapsible satellite dish and two large fans built into one side.

"Hello in there," she called. "I'm Clio. My friend Joanna was supposed to meet with you gentlemen today, but she's stuck doing something very boring so here I am to help you out. You all need a local guide?"

After a minute, a man called back, "Of course, please come in." When she did, she found the entryway had two sets of zippered doors, like an airlock.

"Man, you guys really love the black, don't you? A dark tent like this ought to be scorching hot." It was actually quite cool with the fans, however. She looked around with interest at the dimly lit interior. It was packed with various screens and sensors. Clio wondered how all this equipment came out of the tiny hovercar. Then the two men captured her attention.

"Hello, I am Seth and this is my uncle, Max," Seth shook her hand formally.

She smiled, delighted with his manners and his strange accent. "Well I'm sure glad I found you. We thought y'all had given up and gone home. Looks like you are prepared to camp out on the moon in this thing."

"Your chamber of commerce group graciously offered to arrange for us to stay at your local inn. I am sure it is charming, but we really wanted to get started with our survey of the area. We also wanted to test out the tent. It's made out of solar fabric. It generates enough electricity to run the fans and some of the equipment," he smiled like a kid with a new toy. She couldn't be sure in the dim light of the tent, but he looked kind of cute.

"You know old Farmer Dan thought you were aliens come to scare his goats?" she said, taking in Seth's longish dark hair and generous smile. He seemed just as interested in her flyaway curls and generous curves.

"Imagine what a fright we will give them if we buy this land and install our server farm," Seth replied. "We have plans for simply huge solar installations. The goats will think we've taken away the sun." He pulled up a map of the property on one of the screens and overlaid it with building plans to show her what they had in mind. She whistled low in appreciation. As she stepped forward to study the plans, he studied her backside with appreciation.

Clio turned and caught his look. She arched an eyebrow. Seth blushed and turned to fumble with some equipment.

"Is there anything I can help you with?" she asked, turning towards his uncle. Her attention was captured by the images and data streaming across the large screens while Max's hands flew over the touchpad.

"Yes actually, there is," replied Max. "We wanted to get started with our survey as soon as possible. However, while we are getting excellent transmissions through the globenet, we can't seem to get the local satellites to do a deep scan of the area. Everything else seems to work fine, but the satellites aren't able to take a picture of the ground here. It's very strange. And the maps we were able to pull from the globenet were rather old and not particularly high quality."

It was Clio's turn to blush and stammer. "Ah well, it's Texas, you know. Since The Troubles, we don't have the most reliable equipment here, especially out in the sticks like we are. Most of our satellites are maintained by a company out of Houston and they have been known to have a few problems." Seth looked at her. She seemed nervous just now. He decided she was probably just embarrassed to admit that they were technologically behind.

Some people referred to The Troubles as "The Global Crap Out" or "The Big Screw Up" but the government frowned on that sort of negativity. Frowning meant they'd lock you in a torture prison until you saw the error of your ways. Or you died. They weren't picky.

The effects of dumping tons of chemicals into the soil to produce vast swaths of monoculture corn and cows finally combined with the effects of dumping garbage in the water, air and everywhere else. The result made the old hype about Global Warming seem like worrying about getting gray hair and then finding out you've got lung cancer. The environment couldn't have gotten more messed up if God himself grabbed the earth and gave it a good hard shake. But people muddled through like people always do.

It probably would have been fine if the governments of the world hadn't started viciously fighting over the last of the world's natural resources like oil. The U.S. had been at war for so long that most people couldn't remember who we were fighting now and which war this was anymore.

The environment couldn't take all the side effects of a world at war on top of everything else. The sea levels went up. The Sahara desert became a swamp and Europe hadn't seen rain in years. Most places couldn't support large cities anymore, so everyone spread out over the land, hunkered down and hoped the weather would stop acting so crazy. It made for interesting times.

"I'm sure you've heard all about our little terrorist problem?" asked Clio. "I think the Texas government is trying to make it more difficult for them to target places by keeping things like satellite images off the globenet. Not that we've ever had a problem with terrorists out here! I really think the media is just over-hyping what must be a few crazies with too many matches. Anyway, we have detailed geological maps in town that I'll be happy to supply you with. Is there anything in particular you were looking for?"

"Caves," Max abruptly joined the conversation from behind a large screen. "One of the attractions of this area is the limestone bedrock and it's high propensity to form caves. If we could find caves large enough, they would be ideal for storing the servers. Also we have some ideas for using caves to store compressed air from the wind farm we'd like to install."

"Well peachy keen. That's something I can help you with," said Clio. "I know the county agriculture department did deep scans of this area when they were planning out local reservoirs sixty years ago, but probably nobody ever cared enough to put them on globenet. They'll be pretty old, but caves system aren't exactly a highly changeable thing. I'll call Beth." She'd already tapped it out on her handheld and was chatting away as she walked outside.

*****

Seth listened with amusement to about fifteen minutes of "How's your mama doing?" and "Well, have you tried giving him some hot peppers?" Eventually she wandered back in to tell them that Beth had located the needed maps and would upload and send them over as soon as she could.

"Which could be a while. She says her computer seemed plumb tuckered out and she was giving it a rest," Clio cautioned.

Max looked horrified. Clio shrugged, "The Ag Office isn't exactly high on the list for new equipment and you know the government, always ten years behind at least. I can tell you that there is an extensive cave system over to the north if you just want to take a look."

"That is very kind, but I know that you are a very busy woman. You are the lead scientist of one of the foremost genetic engineering companies in the world. I must say your work is very impressive." Seth privately thought that her work was one of the many impressive things about this woman and wished he'd looked up her age when he'd researched Floracopia. Surely someone with such an extensive list of achievements must be older. Clio didn't look a day over twenty-five.

"Besides these caves will probably be dirty," muttered Max. "If we have maps there is no need to actually go crawling through them."

"Ah, well, Texas is a tricky place. The locals say that the land here laughs at maps. I've been elected to roll out Ambrosia Springs's welcome mat for you, so I'd be more than happy to feed you and take you to look at some caves," Clio offered amiably. "Besides, I'm stumped on a project at work and need a distraction."

"Thank you, that would be lovely," Seth stammered. He liked the idea of distracting this woman. "We have much to do today so I think we will decline to look at these caves. But we'd love to join you for dinner this evening. Perhaps after dark?"

She shot him a slow smile that sent shivers up his spine. "Hope you like it hot," she drawled as she swept out the door. She didn't see the handheld clatter to the floor, ignored in the wake of her exit.

Seth stared after her for a full minute before his uncle laughed. "You are lucky the food is so good here. Even though the heat here is repulsive, I will visit you often," Max smirked.

"We haven't confirmed this site, even if it is promising. It was not part of the plan for me to move here for the satellite office," Seth replied absently, bending to pick up his handheld. He tried to remember what he had been doing before she walked in.

"Oh, I think we will have our energy farm here and you will stay," Max said firmly. Seth thought of several retorts, but didn't bother. Seth knew his uncle too well to think he'd ever get the last word. Besides, moving to Texas really wasn't such a bad idea.

Although he wrote cutting edge software that catered to the rich and powerful, he was getting bored with his life. As glamorous as it might sound to guard the secrets of every major organization in the world, the reality was long lonely days with his computer. Part of the reason he came on this trip was the thirst for new experiences and this little town definitely seemed to have plenty of those.

CHAPTER FIVE

"Just so I'm clear, why exactly are we having a meeting with our evil arch nemeses?" Thalia asked the other members of the Floracopia Cooperative Board of Directors.

Her mother, Harmony, sighed. "They asked for a meeting. We want to know what they want. So here we are." Harmony stirred her coffee casually, but her eyes had a pinched, worried look.

For a moment, Thalia realized that her beautiful mother was getting older. She'd have known her mother was stressed out without looking at her, though. Her Texas twang always got worse when she was worried. Thalia was happy to have inherited her mother's green eyes and curvy body, but wished she could have gotten her height and shiny bronze hair as well. *Well, you can't have everything,* Thalia sighed inwardly and smoothed the skirt on her Chinese-style suit. She'd made sure it exactly matched her green eyes. She wasn't going to let one little meeting ruin one of the rare weeks she had at home.

Her position as site evaluator and sample collector for their gene mod projects meant she was one of the few people on the planet who traveled extensively. Since The Troubles, only a very few could afford the luxury of travel. It was nice to be back home in Texas though, at least for a little while. She checked to make sure her long blond curls were still carefully arranged and sipped her coffee.

"But why did I have to come? And why are we wearing these stupid suits?" asked Kalliope plaintively. She felt more at home in overalls and a baseball cap. She'd much rather be knee-deep in tractor engines or hammering on the water recapture system from their mini-nuke generator.

She tugged on her tie mournfully as she thought of the

temperature system in Greenhouse Five that needed work. They were testing a tobacco-like plant for use in the Alaskan desert and the refrigerators were running overtime to simulate that environment. Of course, it was hot everywhere now, but the trick with Alaska was the extreme highs in the summers and the lows in the winters.

Kalliope meditated on the problem of reproducing an icy sandstorm in Greenhouse Five while the others worried about their impending meeting with the largest gene warfare company on the planet.

Harmony straightened Kalliope's tie for her and smiled soothingly. "Honey, you are a Board Member for the Co-op and although we try to keep you from too many official duties, we thought we'd like to see you today."

"Is that the suit we made you buy for Terpsi's wedding, Kalli?" Thalia asked with an encouraging smile.

"Yep. That was a real fine shindig," Kalliope replied. She rubbed the laser tattoo on her forearm thoughtfully and seemed to unwind a bit.

Thalia helped herself to a breakfast taco left over from the morning, trying not to get any on her new dress. Privately she hoped she looked as competent and professional as Joanna and her mother did, but she rather doubted it. Then she remembered to freak out about this meeting again.

"So, are we thinking the new wallscreen is going to impress them? It's big enough to drive a truck through." Thalia asked the room, in awe of the huge screen that could be rolled up and moved almost anywhere. She briefly wondered if their tech guys would watch porn or action flicks on this monstrosity at night after they all went home. She winced at that mental image and tried to think of something else.

This time, Joanna Guerrero looking every inch the power broker, answered without looking up. "Yes. And I know they won't see it because we'll be looking at them through it. But we've been needing to upgrade our connectivity for a while." She never paused tapping away at her handheld. She'd had its view screen enlarged so she could run more applications simultaneously.

Thalia was in awe of Joanna. She managed the business aspects of the Co-op, a task they were all thankful to give to the dynamic woman. Not content to manage a cutting edge genetech company, Joanna also ruled the local Junior League with an iron fist and was practically the local Chamber of Commerce all by herself. Really, they took this meeting with Malsanto today because Joanna said they had to and she further threatened them with dire consequences if they failed to show up in anything less than their finest business wear.

Joanna's suit was obviously tailored to hug her well-toned curves and highlight her lovely Mexican coloring. It did a remarkable job. It was all the more amazing since they were located in a very small town in the middle of Texas, and there really wasn't anywhere to go that required a suit. People here were mostly concerned with fashion choices that would keep them cool and protect them from the sun and bugs.

The bugs had gotten to be a huge problem since The Troubles, but Harmony was working on a few solutions of her own. It was the sort of side project she liked.

Kalliope finally asked the question Thalia was dying to. "Seriously, what's the deal here? We hate these guys. Right? They stand for everything that's wrong with the world. They crank out cheap, crappy gene mods that strip the local flora and make the buyers forever dependent on Malsanto for upgrades and resplices. And that's not even considering all the gene warfare products they churn out for any government that asks nicely. If any of their junky splices actually worked, the whole world would have been an empty rock years ago. Why are we suddenly having a cozy little chat with them in our most uncomfortable shoes?"

Bob Breun, AKA Bob the Money Guy, finally breezed into the room and replied, "They wanted to chat. That means they either want to buy us out or they want to buy some of our cool stuff or they want to do something evil and nefarious to us. Aren't you curious which it is? Personally I'm rooting for buy some of our cool stuff, but I could go for evil and nefarious too. It's been a slow week."

He grinned confidently at Kalliope and winked lecherously at Thalia, even though he was closer to their mother's age than theirs. Thalia had always wondered what a smart frat boy from Texas Tech would grow up to be and in Bob they had the answer. She couldn't help but return his smile.

She noticed that his short brown hair had gotten thicker and more stylish since his latest divorce. The rest of him was looking more toned and buff too. It was wonderful what you could do with your looks these days. Fruit from India was a thing of the past, but if you wanted lush hair and shiny teeth no matter your age, you could have it, for a price. She didn't realize that the Co-op paid him that well. Thalia hoped that when Bob went trolling for a new lady friend, he would do it outside the office. But this was not a high hope.

"Alright boys and girls, let's get this party started," said Joanna, pointing her handheld at the wallscreen like an old TV remote. Immediately it flicked on to reveal another conference room crowded with people in suits. The room had no windows so it could have been anywhere, but Thalia seemed to remember the Malsanto headquarters were in Missouri. She'd never been to Missouri.

The man at the head of the conference table was obviously in charge. He stood up and smiled at them warmly. Thalia thought he looked like that James Bond character in Uncle Eugene's old movie. He wore his suit with easy grace and the touch of gray at his temples would have been sexy if Thalia wasn't sure that every inch of his appearance was designed to be appealing by an expensive image consultant.

"I am delighted to meet the leaders of Floracopia at last. I've followed your little company with great interest. I am Gordon Hellerman, CEO. Let me introduce my team."

As he went through the introductions, Thalia noticed an unfamiliar man staring at her with an intense, black expression on his face. She stared back, trying to figure out who he was and what his problem was. *Was he disgusted? Did he hate her? What?* He kept darting looks at her sister, as if he wasn't sure which of them to loathe. He was in his late twenties or early thirties. He looked Hindi and spoke with a New York accent.

"And this is our lead gene developer, Shiva Perun." Gordon was saying. Oh. Thalia did know this guy. She couldn't believe how much he'd changed. He'd studied advanced genetech with Clio. Since it was all at virtual university, Clio had spent late nights studying with this guy, but had never actually been in the same room with him. He lived in New York then and Thalia had been in the area for a Floracopia project. So Clio recommended she go meet this guy. He must have put on at least fifty pounds and cut off the ponytail he'd cherished then.

Thalia was willing to bet even his own mother wouldn't have recognized him under the thick mustache he was now sporting. Judging from the death glare Shiva was giving her right now, he remembered her very well.

After introducing the Floracopia team, Harmony asked casually, "Well Gordon, what can we do for you this morning?"

Gordon's smile reminded Clio of a shark. "Well, there are so many possibilities available with your excellent team and our connections and resources, aren't there? We'd like to explore working more closely with you. Currently, we have a US defense contract that requires some techniques that your team has used successfully before. Medea, would you mind presenting the details?"

Medea was a suited stick insect that appeared to be all elbows and teeth. She pulled up several graphics silently and efficiently. Clio was glad they were not actually in the same room, as she would worry that this painfully thin woman might kill and eat the first person to attract her attention.

"As you know, the nation's war effort demands that we do all we can to beat our enemies," Medea was saying as she worked her way through a slick presentation.

After thirty minutes, Thalia was bored. It had been mildly interesting to let Shiva glower at her for a while. He'd been attractive enough to fool around with in New York until it became obvious that he was having some sort of transferred dominance issue with her sister. She couldn't be bothered with some egomaniac's mind games and she hated it when guys got all wrapped up in the 'You look just like your sister' thing.

Getting away from that was one of the reasons she liked traveling so much. Being one of a set of identical quadruplets could be such a drag. When the job in New York wrapped up, she'd left and not thought of him since. Apparently, he had not appreciated that.

Thalia fiddled with the hem of her dress. She wondered how she could get them to wrap it up, because she was pretty sure they'd have to sit around and talk about what jerks the Malsanto guys were after they were done. She wanted to have lunch out at Bessie & Bubba's Diner and hopefully get in a little flirting with some cute farmer from the next small town up the highway.

Then she noticed how stressed out her mother was looking. She must have shot a note to Kalliope by handheld because Kalliope suddenly sat up and began paying close attention to the presentation. Thalia clued in enough to realize that Malsanto was proposing Floracopia work on a project to create super soldiers for the military.

Harmony's forehead wrinkled with concern. "I'm surprised a DARPA contract got you clearance to do human gene modding at all, even if it is for the war. The UN has strict bans on that. I understand you can't share all the details unless we take on the project, but I'm a little confused on the approach you are taking. What are some techniques that you have considered using on this project?"

"Oh various techniques, the gene gun, for example. But you know how unreliable that technique can be. Forced mutation, p-modding. We haven't really settled on an approach yet," Medea replied with a glance at Shiva that clearly implied the reason they hadn't settled on an approach was because Shiva couldn't find one that worked and that's why they needed to hire outside help. He pretended to ignore her.

Everyone at Floracopia did ignore the look since they were stunned into silence by the p-modding comment. Thalia vaguely remembered that p-modding had something to do with the break-in they'd had in the labs a few weeks ago. It had really shaken the rest of the family up. Clio was now inexplicably spending her nights hunting in her woods and Kalliope had installed a million new security measures in all the Floracopia buildings.

Thalia interrupted Medea. "Just so I'm clear, the projects seems to involve feeding something to a person that would cause their DNA to alter in such a way as to cause them to rapidly turn into huge super-soldiers with hyper-twitchy reflexes, right?"

"Well, there are many applications for this kind of technology," Gordon interjected with his toothy smile and a velvety chuckle. "I'm sure the government knows best the uses for these things. We just do what they ask. These contracts pay well and they bring a measure of other kinds of power. After all, the government isn't going to look too hard into a trusted supplier. It gives you a certain security that other companies just don't have."

"Once the rockets are up, who cares where they come down? 'That's not my department,' says Wernher von Braun." Harmony sang under her breath. Thalia arched an eyebrow but Harmony just shook her head.

"Thank you Gordon, but I believe that, as interesting as this project is, we will have to decline," Harmony declared. "We simply have too many other projects right now. I don't think we will be available any time in the foreseeable future."

Gordon produced his shark smile. "This is such a vital project for us that we would be willing to compensate Floracopia for any inconvenience." He proceeded to name a sum so staggeringly large that several people at the Floracopia table audibly gasped.

Bob the Money Guy grabbed Harmony's arm and began whispering rapidly in her ear. She gave him a dirty look.

"No, Gordon. I understand your urgent need to help our government, but we really cannot put off these projects. They are for critical areas that desperately need these splices," she said firmly. Bob sat back and sulked.

Thalia knew her mother was right. Half the projects they had were for malnourished or starving populations. She knew that no matter how much money was involved, they should work on saving lives before they worked on making America's soldiers better at taking lives away. But she did daydream about what she could do with a huge paycheck.

But now that the Co-op had refused to help the Malsanto suits as politely as possible, Malsanto was doing the veiled threats bit and taking just forever. Eventually, they wrapped up the meeting. The Floracopia team promised to think over the Malsanto proposal and get back to them if they changed their minds.

"Those are some scary people," Joanna said as she collapsed into a chair after graciously saying goodbye to the Malsanto team for fifteen minutes.

"You know they dropped that hint about p-modding just to taunt us. 'A measure of security' he says. Ha!" Kalliope muttered darkly.

"It doesn't mean they were behind the break in," Harmony replied, thinking it over. "But it does seem probable that they knew about it and mentioned it as a threat."

"I don't know. I heard rumors on the globenet that Malsanto was behind that lab in India burning down after they were cloning and selling Malsanto products at a discount," Thalia interjected, shaking her head. She didn't know what to think. The whole meeting had been horribly depressing.

"If we give them this technique, the government could use it for all sorts of horrors and they could do it to anyone. If they can change a person's genes through the food that they eat, they can change you without your knowledge or consent," Kalliope said.

"But if we don't they'll just come up with another way to do it. That's the way it always works out," Bob spoke up. "My goodness you ladies are gloomy today. You may not like him, but that man talked a lot of sense. If we do what they want, we don't have to worry about what threats they made or what they might do. All we'd have to do is start counting all the money we'll have and stop worrying about the government rolling in and shutting us down. Sounds pretty good to me."

Joanna rolled her eyes. "I don't really think that's an option, Bob. We don't need the money, for starters. We have a backlog of work for the next two years. And even if we suddenly took leave of our senses and wanted to give the government yet another way to make people miserable, an action like this would require a full vote of the Co-op. Remember? That's why we call it a cooperative. And I sincerely doubt that it will pass in this town."

Bob left the room in a sulk.

"Well, at least we know what they want," Harmony said as they got up to leave.

"What is that exactly?" Thalia asked.

"They want to threaten us. They want the p-mod technique and they want us under their thumb, doing all the stuff they can't do," Joanna summarized. "But they can't buy us out and we won't play ball. So they are going to make trouble for us."

"Why is it so difficult to run a genetech business?" asked Thalia with a sigh. "I mean it's hard enough coming up with a product that works while keeping the cost down to something our clients can afford."

"It could be worse, daughter dearest," replied Harmony. "I started this business the year after they legalized splicing again.

It had been outlawed for forty years before that. You want to talk about difficult? It was practically a full-time job just convincing those farmers that they wouldn't wake up to attacking killer tomatoes if they bought my splices."

"That was a crazy time," laughed Joanna. "I just wish they would end the ban on human splicing. We could really make some money if medical genetics weren't so heavily regulated."

Harmony cast her a look. "There were some very good reasons they banned gene modification for so long and it all had to do with human splicing." She gave a quick shudder.

"We are going to need airtight security," Kalliope said with a grim smile.

"This is really not a good time for anyone to be taking too close a look at us and anything we might be involved in. The government does not have the best sense of humor these days," Harmony sighed, looking at her daughters pointedly. Thalia and Kalliope looked embarrassed. Thalia made a mental note to have a talk with Clio about some of their extracurricular projects.

CHAPTER SIX

It was just after dark when Seth and Max headed towards the location Clio had sent to their handhelds. It was another visually disheartening diner called *'The Tequila Shack.'* As they opened the doors, a wave of mariachi music rolled out into the night. Despite their initial urge to run for it, the smell of mouth-watering Mexican food sucked them inside.

"God, it's like a clown car," Max laughed. "How do they fit so many people in here?"

"I'll go check the bathroom and see if they've got Narnia in there too," replied Seth.

Through a sea of people packed into tiny tables, Seth spotted Clio waving from a large booth in the corner. Pints of Mexican beer were pushed into their hands as they sat down. Sitting next to Clio was a girl who looked exactly like Clio, but with a grease-stained shirt over plaid golf pants and combat boots.

Max stared openly at the two purple-streaked pigtails exploding out of her head. The not-Clio girl gave him a grin and shoved a basket of warm tortilla chips towards them. Max couldn't think of how he wanted to form his question, so he dipped a chip into the bowl of fresh salsa sitting on the table and took a tentative bite. After a minute, he rolled his eyes back with bliss and rapidly began making the chips and salsa disappear.

Seth took a bite and hot peppers punched him right in the taste buds. His mouth was on fire and his eyes watered. He wondered if he was going blind. He fumbled for a glass of water.

"Oh, sorry. I forgot to warn you that the salsa is a little spicy tonight," shouted Clio over the band. "But don't stop eating or it will only get worse. Here, have a beer."

Seth thankfully drowned his screaming tongue in beer.

"Delicious," said Max around a mouthful.

"This is my sister, Kalliope," Clio shouted back.

"Twins?" asked Max.

"Quadruplets," Kalliope answered. Seth's mouth formed a silent "Oh." Kalliope continued to grin while swigging her beer, as if daring them to ask how her mother, a splicer, came to have quadruplets if human gene modification had been banned for over forty years. They didn't.

Then an older woman arrived who looked so much like the two girls, they must be related. Harmony was taller than her daughters and had straight, should-length hair like spun bronze. She usually kept it up in Chinese hairsticks, but tonight she wore it down with a thin summer dress.

"I see you men have met my daughters. I'm Harmony," she said with an easy smile as the mariachi band finished their last ode to lost love. She'd had a long day full of worries, but decided to leave them at work for the evening. Harmony hoped the men would provide interesting conversation.

Max leapt to his feet and hastily wiped his mouth. He almost tripped over a waitress as he pulled Harmony's chair out for her.

"You cannot possibly be old enough to be their mother," he declared, kissing her hand outrageously. "No, I will not believe it. This must be the famous Texas twit I have heard so much about."

Harmony could help but laugh. "I believe you mean Texas twang, darlin'," she said, laying the twang as thick as she could.

"Ah yes," Max laughed. "And no doubt y'all is fixin' ta ride you a cow?" He said, enthusiastically mangling the accent.

They fell into easy conversation as plates of warm handmade tortillas, enchiladas, and fajitas competed for table space with pitchers of margaritas and beer. Since The Troubles, it was prohibitively expensive to import or export food. Which had an unexpected upside. People tended to focus more on their local cuisine. So while there wasn't a sushi restaurant for a hundred miles, the Tex-Mex and other local favorites were even better than before.

For all the advances in technology, most people found that the cheapest, tastiest and healthiest food was grown locally, eaten in season, and prepared using recipes from your area. And since most people didn't travel much, they had time to do things like keep a kitchen garden and cook their own dinner.

"So, I'm sorry, but what does your company do exactly?" Harmony asked.

"Omerta provides complete security solutions for a wide variety of businesses and organizations," Seth recited from the company brochure. He failed to notice as Harmony's eyebrows rose. She shot an inquiring look at Clio who nodded without taking her eyes off Seth.

Since The Troubles, more and more happened in the virtual world. All education from kindergarten to college was now done via globenet from the home. Most people worked at home or very close to home since travel was, for the most part, expensive and slow. Most businesses and governments did their work on the globenet. Omerta made sure that they could do this without worrying about their privacy.

"We protect people's secrets. Most governments and businesses use it. The most interesting are the mafias or other groups who mainly engage in illegal activities," Max informed them.

"But how do you do that?" asked Clio. "I mean, say someone stores all their information on your system. How do you keep a spy or hacker from impersonating the rightful owner and gaining access to their information?"

"Well, in order to access the data, your handheld takes several biometric readings. Everyone knows about the thumb print scanner these days, right?" replied Seth. The women nodded. "It also takes your pulse and temperature to make sure you are alive. One of the security features raises a red flag if your pulse is racing while you are trying to access secure data. It alerts the administrator of your network that there may be a problem."

Max cut in. "Your handheld also scans your retina and your face and compares it to what is on file. Another red flag goes up if your pupils are constricted or your face shows signs of stress or injury. So we know it's you accessing the data and we can tell if you are being forced or are otherwise under duress."

"So that's how your handheld knows to call emergency services or the police if you turn it on while you are having a heart attack?" asked Harmony. Seth nodded.

"I read about that," Clio said excitedly. "All those people that have been saved after an accident because the handheld knows to call for help. Amazing. Your code does that, but also protects a person's private data? How?"

"Abstract cryptography." Max answered. "I don't know how well you are acquainted with the mathematics of codes, but we are way beyond public-key encryption methods. We could discuss it further, but I would need to drink some coffee first. I believe this excellent beer has gotten the better of me." The women graciously declined a lecture on mathematics for the evening but Max called for coffee anyway.

Seth had finally noticed the salsa he dribbled down his arm thirty minutes ago and was trying to save his last stain-free shirt. It didn't look like he was having much luck.

"But why would the mafia put all their information in your care? What if the police demanded that you give them access to it?" Kalliope wanted to know.

Seth smiled as he continued to wipe ineffectively at his sleeve. "Ah, there is the secret to our success. We can't. We cannot access the data. It is mathematically impossible for anyone but the owners of the data to do that. And we use cloud computing so even if they came to one of our offices and took a server or even a hundred servers, they could not access the data. They could destroy a hundred servers and it would result in only a minimal loss of anyone's data. It's stored all over the world and all jumbled up. The encryption program reassembles it only for the owner. They could hit Queen Charlotte's Island with a bomb and it would only disrupt our clients minimally. Worst case scenario, they might lose a few memos or a few pages out of a book."

The women looked impressed. Seth was feeling very good about his job as he saw the admiration in Clio's eyes.

"And besides, no policeman could demand such things of us," Max added. "Omerta bought Queen Charlotte Islands from Canada and declared it a separate country. The UN recognizes us as an independent corporate nation. Since the company is the country, our police are actually employees who work to help keep the data secure. It's one of the reasons so many countries entrust us with their secrets. We are a neutral country, like Switzerland. So you see, we are safe as safe can be." He finished grandly. He accidentally spilled some beer on his shirt as he raised his arm.

"I suspect the rest of us would be safer if I gave you a ride home tonight," Harmony laughed. "The beer sneaks up on you sometimes."

*****

Clio excused herself to have a word with a friend she saw in the corner and left them deep in a discussion over them merits of sod warehouses.

After chatting with her friend, she turned around and bumped into the table behind her. There was Bob the Money Guy having dinner with Nancy Kolstad, their head office assistant. Nancy was a solid middle-aged woman. She worked hard, stayed late and had the office running like clockwork. She was also a twice-divorced single mom. Clio liked her, even though Nancy delivered daily lectures on the importance of orderly paperwork and meticulous planning. Although she knew Nancy hated her haphazard notes, Clio always found her lab well stocked and running smoothly. Nancy was a big believer in regular maintenance on all of the equipment.

Clio was not sure she liked seeing Nancy sitting so close to Bob. She thought Nancy was way too good for Bob. Bob had obviously had a few drinks. He happily flirted with Clio and Nancy by turns, his face getting redder and redder. Clio kept looking between them to try to figure out what the story was. Nancy leaned over and patted her hand.

"It's alright, honey. I know how deep the water is. I'm just looking for a weekend swim is all," Nancy said, sipping on an excessively fruity drink. Clio laughed out loud and left them with a clear conscience. Friday nights were no time for sober thinking, but she didn't want to see a nice lady upset by a playboy like Bob.

She waved to Joanna, still every inch the power broker, sitting in one corner with her husband, Eric. Eric was a lawyer who occasionally did some work for the Co-op. Clio had always wondered why he stayed in Ambrosia Springs. He always seemed vaguely dissatisfied. Right now he was toying with his dinner, looking bored while Joanna talked away on her handheld. He halfheartedly waved back at Clio as he slumped in his chair. She always forgot how large the man actually was. He slouched all the time.

As she made her way to the bathroom, she heard a few grumbles about foreigners. Looking around, she saw a table of people casting hard glances towards Max and Seth.

She knew that Floracopia would have to make very sure that everyone in town knew these foreigners were an exception. It was too good an opportunity for this town to have Omerta in their own backyards. She was tapping a note to herself on her handheld when she sat back down.

"Tell me something, pretty lady," asked Max with a courtly air although he was dead serious. "Why is everyone being so nice to us? I mean, Seth and I have never been on the scouting tours before, but in general most places are eager to have us. When we came to Texas it was the opposite. Everyone was rude and went out of their way to let us now we weren't wanted. When we persisted, the local officials came up with all manner of rules and fees and really made it sound like it would be completely impossible for us to open a business anywhere in Texas. Yet when we got here to Ambrosia Springs, it has been nothing but charming ladies and fantastic food. That Joanna woman from your City Council assures me that all obstacles will be cleared away for us. What's the deal with that?"

Kalliope leaned back and arched an eyebrow at her sister and mother. Harmony cleared her throat while she tried to collect her thoughts.

Clio leaned forward and tried to answer as best she could. "Well, like I said, we've got our little terrorist problem that tends to discourage non-Texas companies from coming here in the first place. Since they aren't targeting oil or military targets, the US government gave up trying to find them. Texas is trying to fix that on its own, but the state has limited resources. Also, we know that Texas is famous for our high crime rates and poverty. I mean, we are basically a third world country these days. Many cities really can't support more people so they try to discourage you."

Max nodded. This was actually one of the reasons Texas had been chosen as the site of their new server farm. Obviously they had much more important reasons, like the plentiful sun and wind they would need to power their warehouses of equipment. Putting a security firm in the middle of one of the poorest and most-crime-ridden spots in America was like hiding your favorite dessert at the back of the refrigerator behind a bunch of health food. Just as camouflaging chocolate brownies keeps them from your greedy siblings, hiding server farms full of secrets in the least likely place worked too.

Harmony cut in, "One of the things we have tried to downplay is that outside organizations are heavily targeted by the terrorists. Many cities don't want to have to protect a new company from terrorists or deal with the fallout if you do get hit by the terrorists."

"Is it really that bad?" Max asked.

"Not here." Clio replied quickly. "We've never had a terrorist attack in this area and we don't have any worries about water or power in Ambrosia Springs."

"That's true," Harmony agreed. "But one of the reasons we are so anxious to have Omerta here is that we could really use your expertise on security issues, both for Floracopia and the city. We do what we can, but..." She shrugged.

"If the terrorists target outsiders, what would you guys have to worry about here? Wouldn't you be in more danger if we moved here?" asked Seth.

What they said sounded plausible, yet he was having a hard time envisioning these women anxious for anyone to rescue them from anything. If they hadn't been worried about the terrorist problem for the last ten years of attacks, why would they be worried now?

Clio and Kalliope shot a glance at their mother who shook her head slightly before answering Seth.

"Sometimes the terrorists kidnap locals and hold them hostage in exchange for weapons or money," admitted Harmony. "Again, it hasn't happened anywhere near here, but it pays to be safe. And for all our poor statistics, is there really anywhere in the world that's safe these days?"

"Is there any food that's safe from your Uncle?" Kalliope asked Seth. She watched in fascination as he polished off another bowl of guacamole and stack of tortillas. Max smiled and shrugged, but didn't stop eating.

"We do feed him at home. Sometimes." Seth laughed.

"The presence of attractive women stimulates my appetite," Max declared, wiggling his eyebrows theatrically. Max made a habit of flirting obviously with every woman he met.

"It's nice to see a young man like yourself with such good

manners," Harmony laughed as he helpfully poured another round of beer.

"Ah, the ability to recognize beauty is ageless, madam," Max replied. "And I'm not so young as all that."

The conversation wandered to local cuisine, current events, and how to tell whether a mariachi band is any good or not. As the evening wore on, Kalliope eventually left with the mariachi band after belting out a few Spanish serenades in her husky voice. After repeatedly swearing to Harmony and Clio that his head was clear, Seth drove his half-asleep uncle back to their tent.

"You talked me into it," mumbled Max blearily.

Seth had not sworn to the Somata women that his uncle's head was clear. Seth was hoping that the smooth ride of the hovercar would keep Max from throwing up all over the seat.

"What?"

"I said you have convinced me. I will stay with you in this adorable heathen country. Obviously Omerta needs both of us at the new server farm," Max said without opening his eyes.

"Uncle," Seth sighed, "I don't know. There's something weird going on here. There's something about these Texas terrorists that they are not telling us, for starters."

"I know. Isn't it nice? It's settled then." And with that, Max began to snore so loudly that Seth left him in the car to sleep it off.

CHAPTER SEVEN

"So are you boys settling in alright?" Clio asked as she put a steadying hand on Seth's shoulder. They were trying to pick their way through a muddy field in as civilized a fashion as possible and meeting with little success.

"Sure," Seth replied. "The new office is going up very quickly. I can't believe we've already been here three weeks." He turned to look at her as he said this and stopped paying attention to where he was going.

Seth slid across a mud patch like a surfer, only to trip over a shoelace and scrape his elbow on the one patch of grass as far as the eye could see.

"I begin to see the point of those uncomfortable looking cowboy boots everyone wears," he said as he slipped again. This time he planted both knees in the mud. Clio had to help him up.

"Watch out for that rock," she replied.

He turned to look and promptly tripped over the rock, anyway. He did a wobbling little dance to keep from falling and then blushed with embarrassment. "The past few weeks have gone much smoother than this," said Seth with a self-conscious laugh, looking down. "I just put this shirt on."

Seth turned to look at the lights strung up just ahead like a mirage in a mud desert. The parking lot was just a field and after hard rains and heavy trucks, the field had gotten fed up and struck back with a resentful tide of sticky muck.

"Whose birthday party is this again?" Seth asked her. "I felt I should bring a gift, but what do you get for someone you've never met?"

"Oh, sugar," laughed Clio. "Nobody here ever met the birthday boy. Bigfoot Wallace has been dead for over two hundred years. He's not even buried here." Seth turned to face her. He could see by the amused glint in her eye that she was serious. He raised an eyebrow.

Clio answered his unasked question. "He's a local folk hero. He fought in the war against Mexico for Texas independence. He was one of the first Texas Rangers. They say he kept the peace by being the scariest man south of Dallas. We celebrate his birthday because, well, I don't really know why. Mostly I guess we like having a reason to have a big barbeque and a band. We all get together to drink beer, eat ourselves sick and dance until dawn."

"Ah." Seth said. That sounded reasonable to him. "Sure. So, is the rest of your family here?"

"Oh yes, they all took the day off and got here when the party started this afternoon. I had some work to do so I'm late. I always have some work to do so I'm always late," Clio said with a sigh. "What about you? Didn't anyone else from your new office come? I can't imagine your uncle missing a party."

Seth laughed. "No, Max would never miss a party, especially one with food at it. I too was working late so Max came with some of the others around eight. No doubt he is lying in a food coma in some corner of this field now. We've had to install some of those treadmill generators at the new office. We have to walk far enough to generate the electricity if we want to play globenet games. And we all love our games. Otherwise we'd have to build a bigger office because we'd all be enormously fat from eating all the delicious food."

"It's a problem that's hard to complain about, what with so many parts of the world having problems getting enough nutrition. But yeah. Those treadmill generators are very popular around here. I have one at home for gaming too," Clio replied as they walked into the laughing crowd of townspeople.

Clio put a hand on Bob the Money Guy's shiny new convertible to steady herself as she cleared the last mud puddle. Where did he get the money for things like this? She knew Floracopia paid him well, but she thought he'd need a lot more money to support his expensive habits. Maybe he got money out of his many lady friends? She didn't like to think about that. She turned to survey the scene. At one end of the big field a band was playing swinging honky-tonk to an enthusiastic crowd of dancers. A line of large black barbecue pits filled the field with delicious-smelling smoke. An enthusiastic crowd milled around in meaty bliss.

"What games do you play?" asked Seth. His eyes had wandered away from the scene to the blue jeans that hugged Clio's curves. Clio caught his gaze.

She batted her eyelashes at him and struck a sultry pose. "Why, honey. I don't play games, I win them." Then she laughed at his expression. "No, I'm just kidding. It just sounded like a bad pick-up line the way you said it."

"I'll be sure to think of better pick-up lines," he replied awkwardly.

She watched him blush in confusion and hurried to answer, "I spend way too much time playing Revolution World actually. It's the re-enactment of the Texas Revolution, you know? There are other versions for a bunch of other revolutions or rebellions too. I hear the American Revolution and the Taiping Rebellion worlds are very popular. It's kind of dorky, but I'm hooked on it and all my friends here play too."

"Oh yes, I know that one. I actually designed some in-game security elements for the Texas Revolution World," Seth replied, clearly more comfortable with virtual reality games than with flirting.

They spotted Max and a tall, pale woman talking to Kalliope. They were sitting at one of the long picnic tables set up next to large fans to cut the heat. Seth and Clio were both starving so they grabbed plates and hit the food tent.

"You worked on Revolution World? Really? Wow," Clio said as she loaded up on potato salad, coleslaw, smoked chicken and peach cobbler. She set down two large bowls of guacamole and salsa she brought as her offering for the party.

"Yeah, just the security elements. It was an application of our privacy networks. The original programmers wanted a way to have secret meetings that couldn't be infiltrated. Personally, I would think spies and secret agents would be part of that kind of game, but that's what they wanted. It was fun to design," Seth replied. He had piled his plate so high with sausage that there was no room for peach cobbler. He looked at it mournfully until Clio passed him another plate with a wink. They walked to meet the others while dodging a group of kids racing through the crowd.

"I use that security system for my gaming team," said Clio. "So it really keeps people from impersonating someone with access to the secret meetings? I always wondered about that." She spotted Eric and Joanna Guerrero sitting next to Kalliope and gestured that shc wanted to join them. The group began rearranging itself to make room for them.

Seth dropped a link of sausage as he sat down. A dog snatched it up almost before it hit the dirt. "With so many people working remotely, there are companies that hire people they've never seen," he answered. "So it's much harder these days to make sure the person logging into the network is who they say they are. That's what Omerta originally designed it for. I just adapted that software to the game. In the case of the game, it makes it impossible for someone to log in and play another person's in-game avatar. I actually used Revolution World to test out a network system that keeps people who are supposed to have access from sharing any of the secure information. So your Revolution doesn't have to worry about turncoats who sell secrets to the other side."

"Really? I'm friends with the designers of Revolution World and that's what they said, but I just don't understand how you could do that." Clio replied.

Seth shrugged. "Actually, that feature is only in the Texas part of Revolution World. I made it a while ago, but it's still in test phase. I used a combination of cloud computing to distribute the information and encryption algorithms to make it secure. Basically, it involves a lot of ring theory and other abstract algebras. But the idea is that the only way to share the information in these encrypted meeting rooms is to be in the room. You can't take it out with you. To get in the room, you have to agree to a downloaded program on your handheld that won't let you even describe what you heard in the room. It wipes any mention to that information out of spoken or written communication. The only way you could do it is face to face or written down on an actual piece of paper."

Kalliope had stopped her conversation with Max and Eric to listen to this last part.

"So it's like you are a witch and you put a spell on the secret. So if anyone tries to tell the secret, they can't speak. I didn't know math could be that groovy, Seth," Kalliope grinned and passed him a beer.

"Something like that," Seth said modestly, but grinned with pleasure. Then he discovered mud in his hair and began trying to pick it out while still eating.

"We are all witches at Omerta," Max said cackling like a crone, "I'll get you my pretty! And your little dog Toto too!" He took an enthusiastic bite out of a turkey leg he'd been waving around for effect. Joanna laughed, but soon turned back to command the legion of little old ladies who kept the festivities running smoothly. Eric looked bored and wandered off towards the dancing.

Kalliope leaned forward and gave her sister a wicked grin. "Revolution World? Did Clio tell you she used to be hot and heavy with the guy that invented it? He still comes around, doesn't he?"

"No, he does not," replied Clio, kicking her sister under the table. "You know perfectly well I've been single for a while. Jason is just a friend."

This last part was more for Seth's benefit and her words did not fall on deaf ears. He grinned and moved closer to her. "Jason Schmidt? I worked with him. He's a good guy," he said.

Clio turned to find the tall, pale young woman sitting with Max giving her the evil eye. She wondered how she had failed to notice her until now. The girl would have fried Clio's head off if she had laser vision. She scowled at Seth, too. Clio smiled. This woman was obviously interested in Seth and just as obviously hating Clio for sitting so close to him. How fascinating. It was rarely apparent to her what was going on socially. She almost wanted to brag to someone for having picked up on body language for once.

Clio stuck out her hand. "I don't believe we've met. My name is Clio," she said cheerfully.

It almost looked as though the woman would refuse to take her hand before Seth jumped in. "Clio, can I introduce my cousin, Gloria? She's in charge of the satellite office here," Seth said as he gestured to the young woman. Gloria shook Clio's hand and inclined her head coldly. Clio gave her a big smile and wave. Kalliope shot Clio a look that plainly said she hadn't been impressed with Gloria so far.

"Another relative?" Clio said as she eyed Gloria. "It sounds like Omerta is just as rife with nepotism as Floracopia is. Can't throw a rock in our labs without hitting a family member."

The woman looked to be in her early twenties. She was strikingly beautiful with long black hair, dark eyes, and a haughty expression on her pale face. Clio couldn't understand how someone so young was put in charge of an office, especially with older and more experienced people like Seth and Max in it.

Gloria leaned forward gracefully as a cold smile curled her lips. "So it is with Omerta. Everyone is very close. Although we are not so closely related, Seth and I." She gave him a smoldering look. "We are what you might call kissing cousins."

Seth gave her an odd look. "I never find jokes about incest very funny. And it's been a long time since I kissed anyone, being single like I am." He looked at Clio significantly. She smiled and took a quick bite of pie. Seth did too. Except he was so busy looking at Clio that he missed his mouth and nearly jabbed himself in the eye with a fork.

"I'm afraid the ladies do not appreciate a man who spends more time with his computer than with them," Max observed, handing Seth a napkin to wipe the pie off his face.

Gloria tossed her curtain of hair in a snit. "Seth here is actually the heir apparent to our little throne, you know. His parents are both on the Board of Directors. He and Max are our lead programmers. The rest of the family cannot understand their sudden insane desire to move out to this… well, this little place. So I was sent to keep an eye on them until they return to their senses and go home."

She turned a disapproving eye on Seth who was now so close to Clio their shoulders were gently touching. Gloria reached over to smooth a flyaway strand of Seth's hair. The contact startled Seth into moving away from Clio.

Clio took an instant dislike to this exotic woman. She reacted like a true Southern girl. Her smile got wider and she became even more charming. "Well I hope our little town will grow on you since you'll be here for quite some time, won't you?" she said sweetly, scooting closer to Seth just to make Gloria angry.

"Come. We must dance," declared Max, spilling beer as he stood up. "I have been watching those young men near the stage twitch about like epileptic zombies and I am convinced I can look more foolish than they do." He grabbed Gloria and dragged her across the field. Kalliope cheerfully joined them. Following in Kalliope's wake was the gaggle of adoring farmers that always seemed to surround her.

*****

Seth and Clio remained seated and continued to eat as they watched the dancing. They talked enthusiastically about nothing much at all.

Some large, beefy men came over to talk to Clio about their next session of Revolution World gaming. It seems she was part of a group that met every Wednesday night. Seth listened and idly wondered if every man in this town was six feet tall and built like a refrigerator.

"You hear that Mr. Dennard was taken?" one of the men said to Clio.

"And his wife is sick," the other man interjected with outrage.

She glanced at Seth, but he couldn't read her face. "Government or terrorists?" she asked in a low voice.

"Government of course," the man replied, his mouth set in a hard line. Clio cursed fluidly and pulled the two away for a quick conversation.

Seth looked around and it was large beefy men as far as the eye could see. He was six feet tall himself. He knew he was skinny, but he'd never felt so scrawny before. He could easily pick out Max's lithe form in the crowd, dancing like a possessed hillbilly with Clio's mother just now. Near him, Gloria looked bored as a large farmer whirled her about in an expert manner. Seth was really impressed by the dancing skills these rough men possessed.

"Hey, I'd like to play Revolution World like the locals. Can I join you on Wednesday night, maybe?" Seth asked after the men had gone and Clio sat back down.

Clio flushed and looked flustered. "Oh no. I mean I'm sure it wouldn't really interest you," she stammered. "The game is really only fun for Texas nuts like us."

Seth was taken aback. He'd really just wanted some way to

spend more time with her.

"I'm sorry. That came out rude," she said quickly, putting a hand on his arm. "I just meant that those Wednesday meetings are for a bunch of us who are pretty hardcore into the game. Maybe we could play together on a different night until you decide whether or not you like it enough to keep playing?"

The feeling that she was trying to blow him off evaporated under the heat of her hand. "That would be great," he said quietly. She took her hand back and they finished eating, occasionally looking up to smile at each other.

"This corn is good," said Seth, just to have something to say after conversation petered out.

"I'm glad you like it. One of my early projects actually," Clio laughed. "Mom let me start splicing as soon as I was old enough to pull things off her lab bench. This one is adapted to the high heat and low rainfall, but see?" She cupped her hands over the corn. He could see that it glowed a repulsive green color in the dark.

"I spliced in a fluorescence tag so I could tell if the graft took, but then couldn't get it out without messing up the new genes." She shrugged. "We sold it cheap to the local farmers."

They got up and began strolling around the field when Seth heard gunfire. He was about to hit the deck when he thought the better of it and jumped to cover Clio with his body.

"No, it's alright," she said, pushing him back. "Look, it's alright." She giggled and pointed to a cleared area away from the main group. It was filled with people facing away from the party.

Seth watched as a line composed of everything from teens to graying ladies took aim with a variety of weapons and suddenly fired off a volley into the trees. As they walked up, he could see two holographic birds suddenly dart out and fly around in front of the line of gunners. They took aim again and fired. One of the birds flickered out of existence.

"Bubba wins!" called out the woman operating the holograms. The crowd cheered for an older man who accepted the praise with a nod.

"Sweet! So I guess they are using bullets with RFID tags in them to tell who hits the targets?" he asked Clio.

"You got it. We have a guy who makes plastic bullets with the tags in them. He can make all sorts of bullets."

Seth laughed appreciatively. "I guess you couldn't use laser guns?"

She shook her head. "Nope. They aren't popular around here anyway. They gobble too much energy and most gun enthusiasts here take pride in the old-style shooters."

"Do they do this regularly? Because I really want to play." Seth rubbed his hands together gleefully.

"Oh sure. The Lions Club holds practice every other Tuesday. Nancy is the woman running it. Here, I'll give you her contact information." Clio tapped away on her handheld and it was done. Seth smiled at her with satisfaction. Every day he spent here, he was more convinced he'd made a wise choice in moving.

Seth watched a group of children lead around a small pony with a headless straw man tied to its back. Clio explained that one of Bigfoot Wallace's escapades had been to tie the headless body of a horse thief to a wild mustang and turn it loose.

"He thought it might get the word out that horse stealing was frowned upon," she said. "That horse ran around with a headless corpse on its back for a couple of years before someone caught it. Scared the bejeezus out of everyone for miles."

"Charming," he said, looking at the straw man.

Clio shrugged apologetically. "Not many of his stories are child friendly so we altered a few. In the kid version, he puts a headless straw man on a horse to scare everyone."

The smile on his face disappeared and he stood up abruptly. Before she could ask what was the matter, he strode off without a word. Her mouth hung slightly open as she followed his path. Then she looked beyond him and understood his alarm.

*****

In the distance, she could see a group of men surrounding Max and Gloria. They were too far away to hear, but their gestures and posture were obviously hostile. She darted after Seth. Her pulse raced as Max backed away from the men with his hands up in an entreating gesture. He was clearly trying to diffuse whatever the situation was, even as they pushed him roughly. Max backed up and the group disappeared from view into the brush.

Seth plunged into the woods. As Clio hurried after him, she caught the eyes of Kalliope and Harmony and gestured to indicate that trouble was brewing. They quickly followed her.

Harmony made her way through the crowd, but her path attracted notice. She heard some of the workers from the next town over grumbling that these foreigners were asking for trouble and deserved what they got.

Clio knew she was just behind Seth, yet it seemed like hours before she caught up to him in the woods and stopped in amazement at what she saw.

There were five large, red-faced men wheezing on the ground in various poses of pain. Gloria was gently dabbing blood off Seth's lip while unleashing a tidal wave of curses. Max was leaning against a tree, breathing hard and probing his jaw tenderly.

"What happened?" Clio cried. Max gestured to the men but didn't elaborate. Clio had trouble believing that Seth and his uncle could have taken out five corn-fed rednecks even if they had some weapons. And to do it so quickly was simply impossible. Seth pushed Gloria away and gave Clio a broken smile as she rushed up. Gloria clenched her fists as she watched him stumble away from her towards Clio.

"These two fools decided to show off," Gloria spat out heatedly. She stalked off towards the parking lot, flinging her shiny black hair over her shoulder.

Harmony arrived and, after a moment spent sizing up the situation, wordlessly began helping Max. Clio sputtered incoherently as she examined Seth and tried to form her question delicately.

"How on earth did two skinny nerd boys like you take on those huge rednecks?" she asked. She winced, knowing that had not been as diplomatic as it could be. Seth looked offended, which is to say he looked like a stuffed frog.

"We've been practicing Wing Tsun martial arts for decades," he said indignantly. He flung the empty beer bottle in his hand down for emphasis.

"Really?" she asked, quirking an eyebrow with a hint of a smile on her lips. "Decades?"

"Years." Max wheezed. Harmony began herding the men towards the cars. Kalliope bent down and spoke to the men on the ground in a low, growling tone. As Seth limped off with Clio in his wake, Kalliope waved them on and stayed where she was.

Seth got halfway to the parking lot before he turned and opened his mouth to lecture Clio on the benefits of not leaping to conclusions about people based on their physical appearance. Before he could start, Max spoke up.

"We also hit them with beer bottles the second they started throwing punches. All that time spent playing virtual games gives a man mighty quick reflexes," said Max quickly, shaking his head at Seth.

Max whispered so only his nephew could hear him, "Sometimes it's best to lay low, nerd boy." Then he clapped the younger man on the shoulder and began walking briskly towards the cars.

"Well ladies," he announced with gusto, wincing just a little. "It appears we foreigners have derived all the fun allotted to us at this party. However, the night is cool, the stars are twinkling and it's the weekend. We should continue this party elsewhere. Also that magnificent cow, Gloria, took my car. Can I tempt any of you ladies to give me a ride back to our site? I can offer quite an elaborate array of alcoholic delights in exchange." He beamed at them optimistically.

"Uncle, I have my car," Seth began.

"You shut up." Max said to him with a poke in his ribs. "I think your car may be broken. Yes, it definitely looks broken. And who would not take pity on two marooned men?" His winning smile encompassed Kalliope as she walked up, shaking her head.

"My car is a nuclear-powered hover car," laughed Seth. "It never breaks."

"Really?" Kalliope asked with interest. "Nuclear?" She eyed the car with the piercing gaze of one who enjoys taking apart new things.

Clio knew that look well, since she currently possessed a compressed-air scooter that still made strange pinging noises after her sister had tinkered with it. She leapt into the conversation.

"Seth, you've been hit in the head and before that you had quite a lot of beer after a long day at work. You really shouldn't drive. Why don't we give you guys a lift over to our house for a while? Mom always has margarita fixings and an awesome collection of classic kung fu movies."

The plan was enthusiastically endorsed. Seth insisted on driving his car and asked Clio to go with him. He claimed that he needed someone with him in case his head wound made him woozy. She agreed and the rest of them smirked openly. As they drove, Clio warned him not to leave Kalliope alone unattended near his car, especially with tools in her hand.

"And she always has tools in her hand," Clio said as they followed Harmony's battered old truck, retrofit with an algae fuel-cell battery. They could see Max's animated form as he sat between Harmony and Kalliope.

"So those guys picked a fight with Max for being a foreigner," Seth said with a frown. "But I don't think they even realized that we aren't from the US. They kept calling us Yankees."

"I think Texans have always been a little house-proud," Clio said sadly. "It's pretty common to refer to all non-Texans as Yankees. Some folks around here think even Dallas is too far north to be considered safe from Yankee-ness. Since The Troubles, anti-foreigner sentiment has been pretty high. But I didn't think you'd have that kind of problem," She hoped this wouldn't spook him into leaving, but she could understand if it did.

"Me neither," he replied, lost in thought.

"Heck, most everybody in town is just tickled to have you here," Clio continued. "Even the anti-foreigner guys were impressed after they heard how Omerta negotiated those islands away from Canada and set themselves up as an independent country. They all want to hear that story from y'all firsthand. Those boys that bothered you aren't from our town, so they must not have heard when we put the word out."

"And we do look like foreigners," agreed Seth. "I think I must thank you again for helping to welcome us here. We can hardly expect everyone to be so receptive."

Clio had to agree that the Omerta people all seemed to be exceptionally pale. She decided it was because she was used to darker skin. After all, she lived in a sun-drenched state where Caucasians were a minority. Even she and her sisters were all deeply tanned. She supposed the Omerta transplants would get darker if they would ever leave their compound during the day.

"It could be worse. You could be from the government. Everybody hates those guys," she replied.

"Everyone outside of the US certainly hates your government," he said. "They are not popular inside their own country either?"

"They do to us what they do to everybody else," she said with disgust. "They accuse anyone who has what they want of being a terrorist and use it as an excuse to attack. At least other countries can fight back. Here, people just disappear in the night and their families find all their assets disappeared into the Homeland Security's grubby little hands. It's been pretty bad in Texas. We have lots of oil here and other things they want. On top of all the other problems, we have to worry about the government coming in to bulldoze our houses to get the oil underneath them."

"No wonder you people drink so much," Seth laughed as he pulled into the yard of a large rambling country house. The lights flickered on to reveal a long covered porch facing a large garden. Fireflies and the smell of honeysuckle floated through the night.

"Too true," she said as she got out of the car. More cars pulled in behind them. Kalliope and Harmony had apparently called a few friends.

The group headed into the house, but Kalliope caught Clio and pulled her aside.

"He has a nuclear-powered hovercar," Kalliope said significantly.

"I forbid you to take apart that man's car," Clio replied with feeling.

"No. I mean, yes, I would if given half a chance. But I was thinking the intruders in the lab a few months ago had a nuclear-powered hovercar."

Clio dismissed the idea with a laugh. "You can't be serious. Why on earth would Seth break into our lab? What could a bunch of computer guys want with gene techniques?"

Kalliope shrugged. "I don't know. Why is a high-powered country-owning company like Omerta moving into a backwater nowhere town like this? And why would they send their top guys to run it? Look, the whole thing is strange. Maybe they needed the money and they couldn't just hack in with their computers. I'm just saying they beat the snot out of those guys at the party in five seconds. That's weird. You need to be careful, my dear sibling."

"Oh come on, Kalli. We might as well suspect Bigfoot Wallace. We still have no idea who at Floracopia helped them out, do we?" Clio cried and threw up her hands.

Kalliope winced. "We are narrowing it down, anyway. And with all the new security features, it's much harder for someone sneak stuff out," she said defensively.

"Who is on the short list?"

"Bob the Money Guy, Joanna our Management Goddess, and Nancy the Super-Secretary," Kalliope replied.

Clio winced. "Dang! Not a good list. I would have said any of them were one hundred percent on our team. If any of them are passing company secrets out the back door, it hits us pretty hard."

"My bet is Bob. You know how he is," whispered Kalliope dramatically. "He gets all choked up at the idea of a pile of money. He'd sell his Grandma for the right price. And where does he get the money for all those suits and trips to the big city?"

Kalliope shook her head. It was not good to wonder if your lifelong friends and neighbors were selling you out to make a quick buck. "Well, look into him and the other two, but do it quietly. We can't really afford to lose any of them."

Kalliope raised a hand. "What am I? An idiot? I'll be the soul of stealth. We don't want the guilty party to leave before we figure out what they sold and to whom they sold it."

Clio shook her head again and changed the subject. "What did you say to those guys who attacked Max anyway?" Clio asked.

"I just explained a few things to them. We can't have too much attention drawn to this town right now. It's a sensitive time for us, as you well know." Kalliope was referring to certain little side projects the sisters were involved in.

Clio nodded heavily and turned to enter the house with a sigh. Kalliope stopped her again.

"You like him," Kalliope stated, giving her sister her total attention.

Clio just shrugged and blushed a little. "I'm single. He's single. There are possibilities there."

"Seriously. You need to be careful here. We have a lot going on right now and he is a foreigner. This really isn't a good time for a romance with some mysterious stranger."

"I know, alright?" Clio said and pushed past her sister to enter the house. "I know. But I can't help liking him."

"I suppose you can't. On the bright side, you will inevitably say the exact wrong thing at the perfectly worst time. You have a gift for that, sis," Kalliope called after her. Clio just scowled by way of a reply. She knew it was true.

They both joined the cheerful group as they made themselves drinks, turned on low gentle music, and collected on the back porch to watch the fireflies.

"Hey Clio, did you hear? The news is reporting that Jack Townsend over in Austin was snatched by the terrorists," called one of the faces in the crowd. "His sister lives here. I bet she's pretty upset."

"Now is not the time to talk about tragedies," Harmony interrupted with a sad smile. "Let's drink tonight and worry about the problems of the world tomorrow."

*****

Seth maneuvered himself into a seat next to Clio. She found herself unconsciously moving closer to him or brushing against him when she talked.

Seth, on the other hand, was acutely conscious of every movement she made. He watched the moonlight play over her face and felt that no man could resist the siren song of romance in such a setting and with such a woman, even if he had been smacked on the head that day.

As Max launched into a colorful and highly improbable story that involved fleeing platoons of Canadian Mounties, Seth leaned close to Clio and asked, "So Floracopia. I understand that with the collapse of the environment, there is a great need for modified crops, but how exactly does it all work?" He really was interested, but he also liked to hear her talk.

"Oh well, before The Troubles, most crops were grown in monocultures," she started. "They'd have huge fields of just one type of potato or corn or whatever. Sometimes practically whole countries would be growing one kind of non-native crop. To do that, they had to use huge amounts of chemical fertilizers and pesticides. Not only did it destroy the local plants and wildlife that could have been cultivated, it killed the soil. There are still huge swaths of South America where nothing grows."

She went on to explain how The Troubles practically stopped the import and export of all but the most extraordinary, and thus most expensive, crops. With everything grown locally in a rapidly changing environment, gene modding became necessary to survive.

"Imagine farmers in those parts of California that used to be lush farmland but are now deserts. They contract us to provide fruit or other crops for their new conditions. We send out Thalia to take samples of their water, soil, bugs, and any crops they currently have growing. I try to use natives as a base because they are best adapted to the area, but sometimes it's not possible. Once a crop has done well in an area, we are usually called in to make complimentary species, either other crops or farm animals."

Seth nodded and murmured encouragement. He also admired the way her eyes lit up when she spoke about a topic she loved.

She explained that they usually tested several potential splices in their greenhouses before sending out the most likely candidates. She told him about a project that required highly productive pollinators that could survive extreme cold.

"Those bees could make a hive on an icicle after I got through with them," she finished.

"It seems strange that with gene modding so commonplace, the UN and the US would be so vehemently against human splicing," he commented after he'd gone to get them more drinks. The group was winding down. Seth could see Harmony yawning and knew the evening was drawing to a close.

"It is silly that humans should be trickier than other animals, but they are. Mostly because no one cares if a gene mod in a cow makes it die younger of a heart attack. If it produces enough calves and milk, that is. And if a spliced strain of corn gets cancer, no one notices after they've eaten it. People, on the other hand…"

"People are complicated," Seth concluded. He gestured to Max who was stretched out on a bench and openly snoring.

Although he wanted to wrap his arms around her and smother her with kisses, he settled for a lingering hug as he collected his uncle and made the journey back to their site.

CHAPTER EIGHT

"Oh sweet mother of vacuum tubes," cried Max the next morning in response to the vile bleating of the alarm. Max staggered up the stairway from his rooms and beheld a group of uniformed men standing in the newly finished lobby of Omerta's new Texas headquarters.

When a large colonel advanced towards him, Max shied like a colt presented with a bit and saddle. His head throbbed. His eyelids were crusty. He'd had three hours of sleep. Max couldn't deal with an invasion of American armed forces today. He wheeled around, staggered back to the stairwell and slammed the door shut.

The colonel stopped, chewed his cigar and scowled. He looked askance at the group of uniformed men. After a minute, Seth popped out of another corridor holding his beeping handheld over his head like a sword.

"Uncle! Show yourself! I'm going to kick you into next week. Never again will you wake me up for your stupid jokes," he was yelling when he saw the colonel. He stopped. His jaw dropped to his chest. He hesitantly ran a hand over his wild hair and stubbly chin. The colonel looked spectacularly unimpressed with him.

"Ah. Do you know it's Sunday?" Seth asked feebly.

"I do, son. But Sunday is no excuse for sloth and licentious behavior," the colonel sniffed.

Seth stopped himself from rolling his eyes, but it was difficult. He extended a hand. "Well sir, you have caught me at a disadvantage. Is there some reason your group is here today?" Seth tried to sound business-like instead of irritated.

The colonel grabbed his hand and shook it like a terrier might shake a rat.

"Son, you people put a warehouse full of terrorist plots and enemy sins in our great country. You must have been expecting a visit from America's protectors eventually," the colonel declared belligerently. Seth squinted at him. Surely the man was joking. Who talked like that?

Gloria breezed into the room on a cloud of delicately scented perfume, looking like an advertisement for clean living. Seth wondered if he'd ever actually seen Gloria with a hair out of place. It just wasn't natural.

"What a pleasure to have such a fine-looking group visit our insignificantly little shop," she purred as she oozed up to the colonel and allowed him to take her hand. Seth sighed with relief and began edging out of the room. Gloria was having none of that. She snaked a shapely arm around him and gracefully shoved him over for introductions.

The colonel was thoroughly charmed by Gloria. He introduced himself as Colonel Roger Bucksmith and explained that the group in the lobby represented DARPA, the agency responsible for providing new technology to the military. Gloria graciously invited them to breakfast.

"Had breakfast hours ago," the colonel said brusquely.

"We have gotten an unusually late start today," Gloria replied. "All Omerta employees were at a social function last night honoring Bigfoot Wallace, a local hero." Then she allowed a hint of coldness to creep into her voice. "Had we known you would be gracing us with your presence this morning, we would have explained that we cannot allow you access to our facility. As a security firm, Omerta is not in the habit of giving tours. We can't exactly throw open the doors to anyone who drops by for a chat. I'm sure you understand."

There was one man there dressed in a cheap business suit instead of a uniform. He stepped forward now and flashed Gloria a broad smile. "Naturally, we appreciate your security concerns. In fact, concerns over security brought us out today," he said easily. "I'm Bill Baker. We would love to join you for breakfast."

Seth hoped that the move to the dining area would give him a chance to escape back to his room, but Gloria kept her iron grip upon him. With her other hand, she tapped away at her handheld, calling other Omerta workers to get breakfast together.

Max eventually made an appearance, a much cleaner and more

coherent appearance. Gloria was always threatening to deliver electric shocks to them via handheld if they failed to do her bidding. Seth wondered if she'd actually done it this time. Max was rubbing his hand and wincing.

Gloria gave a quick tour and explained that the satellite office was to find a more reliable energy source for their equipment than Omerta's island, as well as increase the dispersal of their data.

"There are only about a dozen of us here during the construction phase. But even when we are fully functional, there won't be more than twenty people in residence at any given time," she told them.

While the colonel loudly delivered an unwelcome monologue to everyone in the room on the joys of sacrificing for America, Bill told them why DARPA was here.

"DARPA has been interested in working with your company for a long time," he began. "We have approached your company in the past about helping us further our research into encryption methods." He then droned on about DARPA's efforts to win wars through technology.

A couple years ago, Max and Seth had created a program for their handhelds that allowed them to silently enter text and send it to others unobserved. They both also made a habit out of wearing a microbud in one ear to receive messages like this. The microbud transmitted sound directly into the wearer's auditory nerve. Silent to everyone else, it was very popular with teenagers who wanted to tune out their parents and bliss out to their favorite song. Seth's was barely distinguishably from his ear, while Max's microbud was a sparkly jewel.

Max and Seth did this primarily so they could trade snarky comments in meetings. Omerta Board of Director meetings were deadly dull. They placed their handhelds on one knee under the table and began the series of taps and gestures that made up their sign language.

Max sent, "A couple years ago, DARPA asked us to give them our encryption algorithms. Just give them the basic component of our success. For free! And we both know that the minute DARPA gets hold of anything, the American government would classify it and then declare war on us for using 'their proprietary research.' That's the excuse they used to invade Bolivia last year. Can you believe these jerks? We laughed them out of the building."

Seth smiled to himself. He privately thought that none of the DARPA guys would be smart enough to understand the algorithms even if he explained them.

"We have got someone setting up a defensive perimeter right now, don't we? How on earth did these guys just waltz in here?" he sent to Max.

"Of course, it's already set up. " Max sent back. "We just forgot to turn it on yesterday. We overestimated the intelligence of our opponent apparently. We thought they'd try to spy on us or rifle through anything we sent home. Who knew they'd just wander in? Bad news, though. There are more troops outside. They appear to be prepared to storm the place. Also some of them are roaming around, trying to poke their noses into everything. Like we don't lock our doors."

"Obviously we don't. We left the front door wide open," Seth replied. "When we get them out of here, the defense perimeter goes up and doesn't come down for anything."

Max grimaced. This wasn't his best morning ever. He heard Gloria telling Bill, "Oh yes, all Omerta employees live here in the complex. We are hiring some local contractors, but since this facility is also a UN sanctioned embassy, we really cannot have American citizens doing the work."

She paused. "You do realize you have violated UN protocols by coming in here, right? A host country may not enter the representing country's embassy. We have received no formal declaration of war. What did you hope to accomplish?"

The colonel leaned forward and answered her question. "Just because you Omerta people bought off the UN doesn't mean all that legal hocus-pocus is going to impress us here. You are in the Unites States of America now. If you are harboring enemy secrets, then you are terrorists. And we know what to do with terrorists here." He smiled like a cat looking into a goldfish bowl. Seth entertained uncomfortable visions of the prisons that America was so famous for.

Bob the Bureaucrat interrupted, "Now, we aren't looking to start a fight. We just want some help with this terrible war we are in right now and we think you people could provide that help."

"Look, seriously, enough with all the witty banter. What do you want?" Max interrupted, holding a pale hand to his throbbing head.

Bill gave a small smile. "We want access to the data in your computers concerning certain institutions and governments. Not that many. We know you advertise that your encryption methods are mathematically impossible to break, but Lineman here says they aren't." He nodded at one of the uniformed men in the back, a somewhat shabby little man who smirked at Seth. Seth looked up to make sure the cameras recorded this man. He wanted to find out exactly who this hateful little creep was.

The little creep cleared his throat. "The mathematics involved might be difficult and time consuming to solve, but not impossible." The man had a very nasal voice.

Seth tried to look shocked. "Oh? I really thought those codes were unbreakable. How shocking. Perhaps we could discuss this further sometime? How did you arrive at this conclusion, without knowing our encryption method or the equations involved?"

Seth knew perfectly well the codes were breakable. But he also knew that Omerta had the only system in the world capable of breaking them. He designed it that way. But there was no way this little worm would know that. The whole encryption method had multiple layers of code and several different security measures. The kernel of the system involved a method of randomly generating the encryption equations. Even if he explained the method, they'd never be able to crack the encryption since it always changed.

"Well, I'm afraid that's classified," Lineman sniffed.

"He knows nothing," Max sent him via handheld. Max also included many colorful expletives to more vividly convey his disappointment in how the day was shaping up.

Seth sent an urgent message to both Gloria and Max. "More bad news. The team tells me our outbound communications are blocked. We can't call for help." He could tell when they got that because they both paled considerably.

"Look, we would love to help you, but we are just a satellite office. We have no authority to let you access data, even if we could do it," Max said, trying to sound reasonable. "If your government works with our government and negotiates something, we'll be happy to help. Until then, I'm afraid we must show you gentlemen the door. If you go now without a fuss, we will not have to file a complaint with the UN over the violation of our embassy."

"Actually, this is technically not an embassy yet. Not until the ambassador is present," Bill said, adjusting his tie.

"God bless bureaucrats," laughed the colonel. "So right now you are just a handful of foreigners giving me a serious headache. Now let us look around. If you play nice, we'll just borrow a few files to make sure they don't contain any nasty secrets. We may not even need to take a any of you for questioning, if you cooperate."

Seth felt his stomach sink into his shoes. So that was it. DARPA wanted to poke around their facility and have a look at their servers. They took advantage of a legal loophole to come out here, thinking they'd be pushing around flunkies. With so few Omerta people here, they could all be carted off and tossed in a cell somewhere and no one would ever know what happened to them. He wasn't worried that they would hack the servers, but there were plenty of rooms in this facility that the military should not see. And the American military was not known for returning people once it had them in its clutches.

The colonel raised his hand. The soldiers pulled out their weapons and pointed them at the bewildered Omerta group. Some of the soldiers started herding them towards the door while others set off down the halls, breaking in doors and rounding up the rest of the Omerta people.

"I think we're screwed," said Gloria, suddenly looking like a lost little girl as a soldier slapped magnetic cuffs on her slim wrists.

Things were looking bleak when three blond heads bounced around the corner, looking with wide-eyed wonder at the uniforms.

"Hey, Max," Kalliope called cheerfully. "You know you got some kind of SWAT team on your front lawn? What are you boys doing in here? Making moonshine and stocking up on guns or something?"

Seth groaned as Kalliope, Clio and what had to be yet another quadruplet sister inspected the soldiers like they were an exhibit at the zoo.

"Seth, honey, you boys really shouldn't leave your front door open like that. All sorts of nasty varmints can crawl in." Clio shot a look at the colonel that clearly showed her estimation of him.

"What are you doing here?" Seth asked desperately. He really hoped he was not going to get carted off to some secret torture camp in front of Clio today. He had a horrible thought. What if the colonel took Clio and her sisters too? He couldn't bear that.

"These DARPA boys made a whole lot of noise rolling through town this morning," Clio drawled, nodding at the colonel. "We thought we'd come see what all the fuss was about."

"So your trucks out front say DARPA on them and they spew smog I can see from a mile off," Kalliope said with ill-concealed disgust. She had no use for those who stooped to gasoline. "I'm starting to understand why we are having so much trouble winning all these wars we're in, if y'all are in charge of our stealth technology."

"Hi, I'm Thalia," the other sister grabbed the colonel's hand and shook it enthusiastically. "We don't get too much excitement in this town, so pretty much God and everybody is out there," she said loudly. "Including the news. There must be about twenty people out there filming all this. It's just so exciting! But you know what? We called the Defense Department to ask what was cooking and they had no idea. Imagine that! A plan so secret your boss doesn't even know about it."

She looked about her as though admiring their ingenuity. "Why we got concerned you were really the terrorists so we called just about everybody we could think of."

Bob the Bureaucrat looked anxious and rushed outside, flipping out his handheld and tapping away frantically.

Clio looked steadily at Seth and raised an eyebrow. He knew she was silently asking him what to do next. He had never seen a more beautiful woman than the one he stared at now.

"They are jamming our communications," he told her in a low voice. "We need to call out."

She nodded and strode out the door. The soldiers, unsure what to do with these women, kept their weapons trained on the Omerta people and let her go.

"Oooh, Kalli. Look, this one is cute," called Thalia, batting her eyes at a soldier holding a huge gun. "You married, honey? Gonna be in town long?"

She giggled coyly while Kalliope inspected a gun in the hands of another soldier like she was actually trying to figure out how to get this soldier to let her take it apart. Kalliope gave the nervous soldier a toothsome grin. He refused to meet her eyes and kept edging away from her.

The girls continued their chatter in a desultory fashion. The colonel shook his head as though gnats were attacking him. He looked about with a frown.

One of the soldiers that had gone down the hallways came rushing in. "Colonel, we found a few hardened doors with locks that are resisting our cracking gear. We'll need to get one of them to do it, if we want to get into those areas today."

"Fine," the colonel said savagely. He pulled out a pistol and aimed it at Seth. "Someone open that door or all the clever secrets in this boy's head get splattered across a wall."

"No," Gloria said with terrible clarity. "We have humored you enough. You may not harm him." In an instant, she kicked the nearest soldier and grabbed his gun, her hands still in the handcuffs. She pointed the gun at the colonel.

Everyone in the room sucked in their breath. A shoot-out seemed inevitable. Bob the Bureaucrat walked back into the room and immediately dove to the floor, momentarily distracting everyone.

Simultaneously, the Omerta handhelds began twittering loudly. Also, several large cylinders of what appeared to be old-fashioned television static appeared in the room. The soldiers swung their weapons, startled. Fortunately nobody fired. The colonel lowered his gun, much to everyone's relief.

"Holograms, gentlemen," Gloria announced, recovering her poise and retaining the gun. "Our communications are back up and our bosses are checking on us."

"Cool," said Thalia. "Why don't we have hologram projectors?" she asked her sister. Kalliope rubbed her fingers together to indicate that they cost a prettier penny than Floracopia had for fancy tech right now.

Thalia shrugged. "Just as well. They'd probably make me look fat."

One of the holograms resolved into the image of an older, stouter version of Seth in a very fine suit. "What on earth is going on down there?" he bellowed.

"Spot of trouble with the army, brother," replied Max. "Seems our paperwork is not in order and these nice men were coming to make sure we were all right." The man in the hologram could obviously see the guns. His face burned purple with rage.

"When Max and I decided to join the Texas office, we upset the plan a little," Seth explained to Clio, who had just walked back in. "The guys who were supposed to be the ambassadors got bumped and I guess there was some hold up getting us declared the official ambassadors?" He looked questionably at the bureaucrat. The man ducked back out of the room again. Max just shrugged.

"We'll fix this right now," roared the man in the hologram.

"Is that really your brother?" Kalliope whispered to Max.

Max beamed with pride. "My older brother, yes. He is also Seth's dad and CEO of Omerta and President of Queen Charlotte Islands. I am the family slacker, but I got all the looks, don't you think?"

Another of hologram appeared of a somewhat rumpled older gentleman with gray hair that had not been combed recently. He grumbled in a thick Russian accent, "As the head of the UN Security Council, you would think I could get some sleep once in a while." He looked around and realized people could see him. Bob walked back into the room, talking on his handheld. He paled when he saw the hologram of the Russian UN diplomat.

"What are you doing?" the UN diplomat barked at the colonel, smoothing his suit with a tired hand. The colonel began to sputter about America's need for security, but he was having none of it. "You Americans running around messing up everything you see. You make me tired. I don't care what idiotic reason you have trumped up. You cannot mess with Omerta. Got that?"

The colonel turned beet red while Bob the Bureaucrat started calling up data on his handheld that, he explained, clearly showed that Omerta was maintaining records for the mafia and the terrorists.

"Who cares?" the head of the Un Security Council snapped, mumbling Russian curses under his breath. "Who do you think maintains information security for the UN's computer network and most of the countries in the UN? Omerta. Do you think we want you or anyone else to have access to that? If I hear that you have bothered them again, I swear I will call for a total world war against the United States and I think it will receive whole-hearted approval. Most countries think we should do that anyway, with you arrogant bastards traipsing all over the world, snatching up oil like pastries at a buffet."

"Bah," the colonel shot back, "I don't answer to you. I answer to the United States government. What we do in our own country is our own business." This scenario was clearly not playing out the way he had intended, but he was still trying to bluff his way through it.

"Funny you should say that," grunted Seth's father.

A third hologram flickered into view. This one was a plump bald man wearing the same uniform the colonel had on, but with several more stars on it. He was chomping an even bigger cigar that he spat out to say, "My god, Bucksmith. I was having dinner with my wife and you had to go and create an international incident."

The colonel said nothing and turned purple. The soldiers let their sights dip slightly, but didn't drop their guard.

"Let's clear this up right now," the Russian UN diplomat said. He pointed at Max and Seth. "I hereby confirm these two men here as Omerta's official diplomats to the USA. That means the US has troops in a UN sanctioned embassy. If your troops are not out of there in ten minutes, the UN will consider the US a rogue country showing overt hostility to the UN and its member countries. From there, we will proceed to commence military activities on behalf of Omerta." He squinted at the assembled group grimly while downing two pills with a glass of water.

"No need to be hasty," the hologram general said. "Our troops became confused during a training exercise, didn't they, Bucksmith? They are going to leave peacefully, now." He looked at the troops beadily. "They are leaving right now," he emphasized.

The colonel continued to stare about him in disbelief. Under the glare of the general, the soldiers lowered their weapons and began slowly shuffling towards the door.

"Move out!" cried the colonel, attempting salvage his dignity. Once he was sure they were actually leaving, the Russian UN diplomat briskly said goodbye and his hologram winked out. The US general awkwardly welcomed Omerta's embassy to America and hastily left as well. Seth's father stayed to make sure all was well.

"Excuse me, but I do believe you men are attempting to carry off important equipment," Gloria called loudly. The colonel looked like he would refuse, but Bill the Bureaucrat swiftly intervened. After a whispered argument, the soldiers left the equipment scattered about the hall as they filed out.

As they came to the doors of the lobby, the colonel swiftly turned. He stepped towards Max menacingly. "You'd have done better to help us, boy," he hissed. "You'll be sorry yet. These little girls won't always be here to hold your hand. In fact, something tells me these girls won't be wandering around loose too much longer if they don't start doing their part for the war."

He cast a contemptuous glance at the Somata Sisters. "You are those Floracopia girls, aren't you? We know all about you and that mother of yours. We've got our eye on you too. The US has no use for those that don't help their country." The girls rolled their eyes, although Clio looked worried.

Gloria sashayed over to the colonel with a small box full of electronic equipment. "I believe you men forgot a few things," she said, handing it to him. He looked inside and realized that the box was full of bugs and cameras the soldiers had attempted to hide throughout the building. He cursed loudly and stormed out.

"God, what a drama queen." Thalia remarked as they watched the trucks roar away. Then she went outside to disperse the crowd of locals gathered out there.

Max heaved a huge sigh. "We are the foremost security company in the world and they just waltzed in here and would have carted all of us away if it hadn't been for you. I am so embarrassed. I am seriously considering seppuku."

Kalliope laughed. "We drop by for a visit and you decide to commit ritual suicide? That's hard on a girl's ego, mister. You do that and I might give up and become an alcoholic bag lady."

"Well, I must go and clean up this mess," Gloria sniffed. Her face soured as she watched Seth turn to Clio. "The mess that would not have happened if you two had not decided to put a facility in this nasty little hellhole." She turned and stalked down the hall, the click of her stiletto heels tapping out her disdain for all.

"Ah, Gloria," Max murmured. "She's really quite wonderful

with people when she wants to be. And such a colossal pain in the ass when she doesn't." Seth's dad barked with laughter, then drew Max aside for a private conversation.

"She sure can open up a can of the smack down when she wants to," said Kalliope with a whistle. "Did you see the way she grabbed that gun? I've only seen stuff that smooth in movies."

"She practices Wing Tsun martial arts with us," Max replied. "Three mornings a week."

"Oh man, that's awesome," Kalliope replied, doing air karate kicks. "You have to teach me."

Max and Kalliope made plans for a group martial arts class while everyone else started cleaning up.

"Welcome to the neighborhood," Clio sighed as she helped pick up some of the mess.

"Thanks for coming," Seth said with shining eyes. Only the presence of so many others kept him from twirling her in the air like a princess and promising her the moon.

Clio shrugged and smiled, "It was nothing."

"Got us out of Sunday brunch with the family," Kalliope interjected, picking up bits of broken door. "Mother is a terrible cook."

"I've been eating those repulsive waffles every Sunday for over a quarter of a century," said Clio with a shudder.

"I think she actually puts cement in them," muttered Kalliope. She was sad that she had missed her chance to take apart one of the weapons. She brightened as she inspected the construction of the Omerta facility.

"Wow, you guys are really tossing this place up. Is that bacterial concrete you are using?" she asked. Seth broke out of the trance he'd been in, watching Clio.

"What? Oh yes. And of course layered solar panels and wind turbines on the roof. We have a small nuclear generator, but we need every scrap of energy we can get for those servers," he replied.

Thalia walked back in. "Did you hear the government snatched Ed Martinez over in Driftwood? Happened just last night!" she cried.

Kalliope swore fiercely and stalked out the door with Thalia close behind her.

"Too bad you couldn't allow a little more natural light," Clio said as she followed her sisters out. The complex was completely enclosed under a large roof that extended twenty feet past the building in every direction. "Even with these fluorescents, it's like a cave in here."

"We use special light bulbs here to improve the efficiency of the cooling system, but we programmers are used to the dark." Seth replied.

"You'll have to give us a tour sometime," Clio said with a smile.

"Not today, though," Max declared rejoining them as Seth's dad waved goodbye and his hologram winked out. "Or Gloria will use my skull for a soup bowl."

"Oh, sure." Clio said. "We had a break-in a few months ago ourselves, so I know how paranoid you are afterwards. I was ready to hook ants up to lie detectors for weeks."

"Did you ever find out who did it?" Seth asked.

"No, but we're pretty sure they had inside help. You guys should think about that too. Maybe the DARPA guys were working with an informer," she replied as the girls made their goodbyes and headed for the door.

"Oh, we are going to think about a lot of things," Seth muttered as he watched them go.

CHAPTER NINE

Seth violently threw down his VR gloves. He almost picked them up and threw them down again, just for emphasis. He felt like throwing things right now.

"I can't believe she stood me up," he cried in frustration.

Max smirked. "The path to love is never smooth."

"You shut up," Seth replied. He fidgeted for a minute in a frustrated way. Then he pulled up some work on a screen. He tried to tell himself he could just get some work done since Clio had totally forgotten that she was supposed to meet him online to play Revolution World tonight. Max watched him from the couch with a bemused smile.

Of course women forgot him. He was just a boring nerd. Seth wondered if there was a vat or two of liquor around he could drown himself in. He should probably do something more socially correct, like spend a few hours down in the exercise room, practicing his martial arts.

He wondered if Clio was off with Jason Schmidt, the designer of Revolution World. He'd met Jason once and remembered thinking at the time how handsome and charismatic the man was. Now Seth realized that the world could do with fewer handsome, charismatic single men.

"A rose without thorns would not smell as sweet," offered Max. He had been hanging around for the last half hour, snacking on nuts and offering bad dating advice.

Seth ignored him and proceeded to write horrible code for the next ten minutes. Max watched him for a while before losing patience.

"Why don't you just call her?" he asked.

"Why should I? It's no big deal. She is obviously too busy to play with me tonight," Seth shrugged a bit too hard.

"Right. So there's no reason not to call her up and make sure she's alright," Max replied.

Seth thought on this. The more he thought, the more sense it made. Perhaps she just got overwhelmed at work. Or maybe there was something wrong with her home equipment. That could certainly happen. Maybe he'd call and she'd need help.

He saw himself going over to her house bearing food and tools, rescuing her from the horrors of a bad satellite connection. She'd fall into his arms with gratitude. Seth recalled the many nights that Max escorted lovely ladies around town while Seth had stayed home alone, playing computer games and eating junk food. Max clearly knew more about women.

"Maybe I should check on her," Seth said cautiously. He wondered if the Omerta on-site chef was still awake. Their chef did not suffer after-hours requests gladly. He tended to require elaborate bribes. But Seth knew his limitations and food preparation was one of them. Maybe instead of having to promise his first-born child to their chef, he could just stop at one of the local cafes. He was already reaching for his keys when Max responded.

"Have you seen Harmony lately?"

Seth paused. "No. Why?"

"Oh, no reason. Interesting family," Max replied, turning to a screen to call up a few mathematical constructs. Seth eyed his uncle. They were over twenty years apart in age, but Seth had always felt as though Max were the older brother he would never have. And right now, he was acting suspiciously.

"Have *you* seen Harmony lately?" Seth asked Max deliberately.

"Oh you know. Here and there. Now and then. She's a very busy woman." This last part he said wistfully. Max had been gently tweaking a rotating representation of a fourth dimensional differential equation, but now he paused to stare off into nothing like a lovesick teenager.

"I thought you were interested in the engineer one. Kalliope?" Seth replied.

"What?" Max replied shortly. "God, no. Cute for a girl her age, but no." He toyed with a set of nonlinear variables like a cat might toy with a bit of string after it had eaten a bucket of fish. More because he felt he should than because he really wanted to.

Did Max have a crush on Clio's mother? Seth decided that while torturing his favorite uncle would be very entertaining in a revolting sort of way, he had much more important business at hand.

Less than an hour later, he was on Clio's doorstep with a bag full of steaming Indian food, feeling like a fool. The house was pitch black. She was obviously not here, even if her scooter was parked right out front.

He called her for the hundredth time.

"I'm on your doorstep with curry," he sent. He waited for a bit, listening to cicadas buzz eerily and swatting as mosquitoes circled him like buzzards at a hit-and-run. He sighed and gave up.

She had really forgotten him. She didn't care. She was probably out having a fabulous time with her friends. Her muscular and attractive man friends. He was an idiot to believe a woman might care for him. He left the containers of food on her doorstep and trudged back to his car. Halfway there, he heard a rustling in the bushes. He turned to look as something burst out of the underbrush and headed toward him.

Reflexively, he delivered a perfect open-handed strike to the head area. He was pretty pleased about that since he hadn't been practicing much lately. Then he realized the head was covered in blond curls and emitting a very feminine shriek.

"Damn it! That was cool. I mean, it hurts like hell, but how are you so fast?" Clio said. Her voice was muffled because she had fallen backwards into a bush and was fumbling back to her feet.

"Oh holy Christ on a stick!" Seth cried. It was no wonder women didn't like him, he thought despondently. His natural impulse was to smack them around. He was born a monster and should not be allowed in polite society.

"Can you teach me to do that?" she wanted to know, rubbing her forehead.

"Uh. Well. Actually, we've arranged weekly sessions with our martial arts instructor for the Junior League at the Omerta campus," Seth babbled. "Remotely, of course. Max has been going to their guns class and wanted to reciprocate. You could join us."

He looked at her. Clio was filthy. She had dirt smeared on her face and twigs in her hair. She was wearing some sort of military camouflage with night-vision goggles pushed up on her forehead and combat boots. She was so beautiful.

"That will probably bruise," he said miserably. Clio wiped her nose and shrugged, fiddling with some sensors on her wrist.

"Whatever. Look, sweetheart, this isn't this best time. Maybe we could get together for dinner or a gaming session sometime? I'd love that," she looked at him with that heart-melting smile of hers.

"We were supposed to do that tonight," he blurted out before he realized it. There was something about her that made him tell the truth, despite his better judgment.

She looked at him for a long minute before she remembered.

"Oh no."

She saw the little cartons of food on the porch and her face fell.

"Oh crap."

"It's OK," he rushed to say. "Really. You are busy doing, uh, something. I understand."

He tried to soothe her even as he backed towards his car, his heart breaking a little with every step.

"No. Wait," she said. "Wait."

There was another rustling movement in the bushes. Clio turned to focus on it. And then the biggest, scariest bunny Seth could imagine popped out of the bushes. Seth thought he'd seen everything on the globenet, but nothing prepared him for the total horror that was a rabbit the size of a bicycle with fangs like fence-posts.

"Ah, crap," said Clio.

She raised her arm and fired off a series of little popping projectiles. The rabbit monster shrieked and flailed. Seth found himself in his car with the doors locked. He was pretty sure he'd screeched like a small child on his way to the car. Not his best day ever. Clio bent over the still form of the animal, then straightened up and plunged into the scrubby Hill Country undergrowth. Seth was reminded of every action-movie hero honey he'd ever watched.

Seth waited for a long minute before deciding he was acting like a sissy boy. He got out and looked at the beast on the ground. After a moment, he rolled it over, cringing at the enormous claws and fangs. It was asleep, not dead. So he followed Clio. He'd wondered whether or not these were test subjects escaped from her labs or some new horror. He'd heard the wildlife was bigger here, but this was ridiculous.

*****

Clio couldn't believe Seth was here to see her dressed like G.I. Jane. It was so horribly embarrassing. As soon as she rounded up the last of these rabbits, she would find a nice hole to crawl in and die.

"Look, this really isn't a good time," she whispered to him as her wrist sensors pulsed gently. They were watching several hulking rabbit shadows sedately munch on bushes. Seth didn't reply. She just knew that he was so repulsed by her appearance right now, he didn't even want to look at her.

"They aren't mean," she began. "Well, alright, they are a wee bit mean and vicious. And they breed like, well, rabbits. Our local ecosystem can't deal with an incursion of this, uh, magnitude," Clio whispered again, her eyes on the beasts. She really couldn't imagine a scenario that was worse than this one. "If this wasn't a problem that I created, do you think I would be out here in the mud and the bugs when I could be at home flirting with the most interesting guy I've ever met?" she rambled.

Clio straightened up suddenly, realizing what she just said. She looked at Seth. He gave her a goofy grin. Why, oh why, did she always say the dumbest things?

That's when she realized that the rabbits in the field were a diversion. A second group of rabbits attacked.

It was like Clio flipped to automatic pilot. She began aiming and firing rapidly. In the back of her mind, she sobbed helplessly as she watched three huge beasts leap towards Seth. She had put down four. She quickly reloaded her sedation gun and looked for Seth. Seth was fighting and he was fighting well. What a man.

All her life, she realized she had been thinking of her romantic partners as boys. Seth was a man, a man worth fighting for. But how would he ever make it through this? She tried not to think as she systematically took down more of the attacking animals. After what seemed like hours but could only have been a few minutes, she stopped. No more rabbits attacked. Clio realized she was kneeling on the ground surrounded by bunny bodies, gasping for breath.

Where was Seth? She stumbled towards where she'd seen him last, quietly letting sobs shake her to the core. There he was, lying on his back under a pile of twitching rabbit corpses. She collapsed next to him and drew him into her lap as gently as she could. He was as still as death. Oh no.

Clio wiped the blood off his face as she cradled him in her lap. She held him to her gently, quietly sobbing.

CHAPTER TEN

"Why the hell did you make mutant huge rabbits?" Seth asked into her chest. He quite liked where he was, but Seth had begun to feel like a pervert, letting her hold him like this.

Clio shrieked and flung herself away from him.

"Seriously. Didn't you ever watch *Night of the Lepus*? Huge bunnies are always bad news," he continued, slowly getting to his feet and wiping blood off his face.

There was an awkward silence.

"Well," Clio said briskly, "I think that's all of them." She grabbed a rabbit by its ears and started dragging it back to the house.

Later, after they'd rounded up the bodies and had showers, they warmed up the Indian food and had a very late dinner.

"Sorry about the lack of warm water in the shower," Clio apologized, "My generator has been out. Kalliope was supposed to come by and replenish the bacteria on the chlorophyll battery, but I guess she forgot."

"Don't worry about it," Seth replied, munching on *naan* bread and *saag paneer*. He had taken at least three showers to get the bunny gore out and didn't care how cold the water was.

"It's interesting that Indian food translates so well to the locally grown Texas vegetables and spices," Clio said. "You would think that halfway across the planet the cuisine would be totally different, but I guess latitude is more important than longitude. All their vegetables and spices either grow easily here or the flavors adapt well to our local produce. We haven't had to tinker with any of them. Actually we keep getting requests to create a super-pepper with so much capsaicin it'll make your eyes bleed, but I just feel no good can come of something like that. Other than planting it in your yard to keep the deer out." Seth got the impression she was talking just to be talking.

Seth cleared his throat. "So what are you going to do with them?" He jerked his head towards the shed in which they had stored the rabbits.

Clio ate quietly for a minute, looking intently at her food. Then she looked up, gave him a broad grin and said in her thickest Texas twang, "Shoot boy, I'm makin' me some jerky. Rabbits is good eatin'."

He just stared at her. Maybe he had made a huge mistake in moving to Texas. The locals were obviously a lot crazier than he thought.

Clio cracked up laughing. "Oh my God, you should see your face," she giggled, wiping a laughter tear from her eye. Seth stuck his tongue out at her.

"Oh come on, the whole situation is nothing if not ridiculous," she said, by way of reply. "Anyway, we definitely got all of them and they will be incinerated in the lab. The mega-bunny menace is contained. From now on, I'm implanting GPS devices in everything that moves. I really can't thank you enough. I haven't had a full night's sleep in weeks trying to track them down. It's a huge embarrassment that they got out. I would have asked Kalliope to help, but she tends to have a 'Scorched Earth' philosophy when it comes to hunting and I wanted to have some trees left when we were done." She heaved a huge sigh of relief and gave him a grateful look.

Seth wondered if she really was crazy and he just couldn't tell because she was just so darn cute when she smiled like that. He decided he didn't care and grinned back.

"Oh well, after you swooped in and saved us from that serious confrontation with Colonel Crazypants, it was the very least I could do," Seth said modestly. "You should have called me sooner. I could have come prepared. All those years playing first-person shooter video games made me a pretty good shot."

"A gun? And miss you drop-kicking bunnies across my field?" she laughed.

He paused for a minute and then carefully asked, "Does this sort of thing happen often?"

"No, I'm not really big on hunting," she said.

He gave her a look.

She sighed. "And no, I don't have many escapees from my labs. And a further no, I don't normally make huge mutant herbivores."

He didn't say anything, but she could see his shoulders relax just a bit.

"There's not really a point to changing the size of animals. They adapt to the size their environment can support normally anyway," she chattered away as she cleared away their dishes. "But those guys were failed tests subjects for growing transplant organs. The vat organs we use now tend to be more fragile, you know? They have to be replaced more often and they fail more easily. Finding a better organ growing method that doesn't involve headless human clones is like winning the lottery in the genetech world. We'd be on easy street. Unfortunately, no luck with these guys." She said as she meditatively washed dishes. Seth helpfully dried and put them away.

"What really has me up at night is trying to figure out what I did that boosted their intelligence like that. They had some pretty advanced group defense methods and a rudimentary language they'd come up with and they were only a few months old. How cool would it be to be able to boost intelligence on command? Let's see the UN try to keep people from getting that one for their kids."

"Well, if you figure it out, sign me up. I could use a boost to my brains," Seth replied.

"Don't be silly, you are the smartest guy I know. And let me tell you I know a whole lot of nerds," Clio replied, putting a gentle hand on his shoulder. He winced hard and she realized his sleeve was sticky with blood.

"Oh my God, why didn't you tell me about this?" she cried as she pulled up his sleeve and found a set of long gashes oozing blood.

"It's fine," he muttered, but she wasn't listening. He was interested to discover that Clio had enough first aid supplies in her house to stock a minor emergency room. He followed her into a supply cabinet stocked with enough food and supplies to let a family of four live comfortably after an apocalypse or two.

"What do you have all this for?" he asked.

Clio just shrugged as she rummaged around. "It never hurts

to be prepared, I guess. After the Cow Plague, Texas was hurting pretty bad for food and you remember how slow the government was distributing emergency supplies? Well, maybe you don't. Anyhow, everybody around here does this."

Seth had the thought '*Crazy Texans*' so clearly written on his face that she said, "Oh please. I've heard how deep the foundation on that compound of yours is dug. Don't tell me you don't have some serious storage space of your own over there."

"That's different,' he said primly, but she just smirked.

*****

Clio cleaned out the gashes and sealed them up with wound glue. Then she spent a few minutes poking and prodding him to make sure he wasn't hiding any other injuries. After a little bickering, he agreed to take a painkiller and a small bottle of antibiotics. Finally satisfied that he was fine, she poured them both a cold beer and herded him into her small living room.

"This is nice, having company like this," she remarked.

"Maybe for our next date, I can just come over for dinner. You don't have to release dangerous monsters into the wild just to lure me over, you know," he said.

She punched him lightly on his good shoulder, "You wish. No, other than a few plants species that snuck some seeds out of the greenhouse, I've never had anything get loose before. Even the bunnies wouldn't have gotten out if we hadn't had that break-in."

"Really? Someone broke into your lab? Oh, that's right, I heard about that. Weren't you actually in the lab at the time?" he asked with a worried frown.

"Yep, all by myself," she said. Then Clio launched into an enthusiastic retelling of her little adventure. She was pretty sure that she hadn't delivered any karate kicks or thrown anything at them that actually hit, but she saw no need to ruin a good story with reality. Clio noticed that the longer she talked, the deeper his frown got.

She wrapped up the story with what she thought was a pretty good joke, but Seth didn't laugh. He just frowned and fiddled with the label on his beer.

Finally he spoke. "Well, I have talked to your sister about providing some security measures for Floracopia. We haven't really set anything up, but I'm thinking we really need to start on this immediately," he said. "From what it sounds like, the only reason that break-in wasn't a total disaster is that you have bad handwriting. And you don't scan your notes in and back them up like you should. If they try to break in again, I don't think sloppy documentation is going to stop them."

Clio bristled. Sloppy? Did he think she couldn't take care of herself? This guy had some nerve. She could have rounded up those rabbits by herself. Eventually. If not, she could always gas the forest. She sat back and glared at him.

"No, please don't take offense. I am terrible at talking in person," he said quickly. "You should meet me on the globenet. I'm really quite suave."

That was so stupid that she couldn't help but smile. Clio remembered how much Floracopia needed digital security, so she took a breath. She stood up, turned towards him and said, "You are right. We do need better security. I know you are trying to help and I appreciate it. Thank you for offering." There. *That sounded like a mature response,* she thought with satisfaction.

Seth jumped up and gave her an exuberant hug. Clio allowed herself to snuggle into his shoulders a bit. Just when she decided that his shoulders were at just the perfect height to rest her chin on, she realized he had been holding her for too long to be considered a friendly, meaningless squeeze. Her pulse raced. She felt his breath catch. She tilted her chin back and looked into his eyes.

"Clio," Seth whispered hoarsely.

"Yes?" she whispered, her mouth going dry.

As luck would have it, the wound glue was only barely able to hold the deep cuts on his shoulder closed. Hugging her caused them to break open again and ooze blood into her fingers. Oozing blood is always an instant mood killer.

Clio hastily put Seth into her car and drove him to her sister, Terpsi, to let the doctor fix him up. Six stitches and a shot of horse tranquilizer later, Seth was lightheaded from pain and queasy from the medicine. Terpsi apologized to Seth for not having any human painkillers in the house and sent them off into the night.

Much as he would have liked to sweep Clio off her feet and into a bedroom, he could do nothing more than let her drag him home, covered in bandages.

CHAPTER ELEVEN

The first time Seth told Clio that he was a vampire, she laughed so hard that she shot beer out of her nose and almost drowned. So hard, in fact, that she fell out of the old inner tube in which she had been gently floating.

"It's true," he said.

"Don't be stupid," she said.

"I'm totally serious," he slurred a bit, realizing he'd had a beer too many and perhaps this ruined his credibility.

They were night tubing down the Comal River. Because it is primarily spring-fed, it was one of the few rivers still running after The Troubles. Normally, people grab some old inner tubes and a cooler full of beer and tube during the day. The combination of cold river, hot sun and cool beer is something everyone should experience before they die. To go at night was a little dangerous, but Clio liked to think she lived dangerously and Seth claimed he sunburned easily.

It was to be their first date. It had been a few weeks since the rabbit escapade, but they had both been extremely busy at work. Seth hadn't been on very many first dates and he was nervous. He'd had a few beers to try and steady his nerves. They had done too good a job and now he was just blurting out whatever popped into his head.

"It's true," he said again. Leaning towards her, he accidentally poured beer in his lap. As he cursed, Clio started hiccupping and giggling at the same time. Seth sensed she was not taking him seriously.

He tried to compensate by lowering his voice seductively. "I really am a vampire. I can't go out in the sun or else I fry. I have a condition that requires fresh blood. Don't worry though, I confine myself to willing donors." He attempted to lean forward and give her a smoldering look, but fell out of his tube instead. Clio laughed even harder. He splashed and flailed down the river to prevent his tube from floating off without him while trying to keep his beer in its can. Clio sat in the cold water giggling and snorting, because beer really hurts when it shoots out of your nose.

"So I would assume that's why you lock yourself in with your computer all day and are the whitest man in Texas? Because you're a vampire?" Clio said eventually with a thoughtful nod. "I can see that. So do you have any special vampire powers? Turn into a bat? Read my mind? Influence my thoughts?" More snorting little giggles accompanied this last part. Seth knew he wasn't the best at social interaction, but was he really so bad at understanding her?

Seth sighed. This was not how he imagined his first official date with the girl of his dreams would go. In his mind, right now she should gasp and quiver and eventually there would be some hot and heavy make-out action like in all those old vampire movies he'd watched. That didn't seem too likely right now.

He had read scientific studies that indicated symmetry played a large role of attractiveness. He had scanned in his face and after many calculations comparing the evenness of his features, come to the conclusion that he must be reasonably attractive. He had made sure his dark straight hair was cut in a style that was currently socially acceptable, if a little on the long side. Gloria told him he was cute in a tall, skinny nerd-boy sort of way. Yet he worried that Clio would want someone more like the large, beefy men her sisters seemed to prefer.

"I have really good night vision," he countered.

"No you don't. You tripped twice getting into the water. And don't try to bring up the fact that your eyeballs and teeth glow the way they do. What? Did you think I hadn't noticed that? I'm a splicer, sugar, I mod out genes for a living. And even though our idiotic, narrow-minded government won't let us work on humans, I do know a porphyriatic episode when I see one. You should get that checked out. Hell, you should stop drinking beer and cut out all that crap you eat."

Clio realized she was about to start lecturing him and closed her mouth. It was insensitive to lecture someone about a medical condition. She'd get Terpsi to do it later. She thought about asking him for more details, but this didn't seem like the time. What if his symptoms included irritable bowels or chronic flatulence? *No, that would not be good first date conversation*, she decided.

For his part, Seth began to think that this would not be the magical night Clio fell into his arms and declared her undying love for him. He also began to think that he should start doing some exercise. How does one become beefy?

"It's a genetic disease," he sighed, ruminating on the mysteries of exercise. "The glowy eyes thing, I mean, not the clumsiness. I have an excellent specialist that I see for it."

"Oh good." She said quickly, "I just worry about you is all."

They found they could not look at each other for a while after that.

Clio was exhausted. She had been working long hours lately on a strain of hyper-intelligent guard dogs as a kind of surprise present for Seth. Strictly speaking, this was totally illegal. But with the DARPA people hanging around giving Seth a hard time, she figured it was better safe than sorry. She assumed they were trying to get him to work on another one of their evil warmonger projects. She felt that while all his high-tech security gadgets were neat, there's really nothing like a frothing mad dog chewing on your leg to deter someone. Clio was old fashioned like that.

Seth was exhausted too. He'd been working long hours lately on some software to camouflage Clio's genetech lab from DARPA's satellites. He knew she had a few questionable little side projects and he worried that she'd attract the wrong kind of attention. The wrong kind of attention could get her thrown in jail or snatched by terrorists. He'd already come up with some software variants to hide her information trail on the globenet, but he wanted to make sure that no one would accidentally see something weird if they took a closer look at her labs.

By the time they floated down the river and back to Seth's hovercar, they were both fighting to keep their eyes open. Clio had been hoping this would be the evening he finally kissed her. All this time they had spent together and he still hadn't made a move. She could tell he was interested and this tubing trip should have been a prime time for romance. Everything was going so well until he start that stupid joke about being a vampire. Was he just trying to talk to her about his medical condition? That seemed like an odd way to go about it. Was it supposed to be some sort of pick up line? Maybe it was the sort of joke you had to be a tech geek to understand. These computer guys were frustrating.

As they were loading the car, Clio stumbled over some tree roots. Seth had her in his arms before she could scrape a knee. He gulped audibly as he gazed into her deep green eyes.

Clio caught her breath and tried to tell herself calmly that her pounding pulse was just a natural response to the hormones flooding her system right now. Hormones were temporary and didn't mean anything. But then she felt the strength in his arms around her and forgot pretty much everything.

Seth just decided to go for it. The worst that could happen is that he slobber all over her and she'd be totally repulsed. Then she'd slap his face and he'd never see her again. Actually, since they both lived in the same tiny town, he'd probably just see her everywhere and it would all be tragically awkward. Unless he put in for a transfer back to Canada. Which wouldn't be too bad except it was so cold there and he'd be ridiculed by everyone he knew. He really needed to stop thinking and do something now. Oh brother, he better make this good.

Beneath the wide and starry sky, Seth gently pulled Clio to him and kissed her for the very first time.

They rode home in a cloud of bliss. They were giving each other sly smiles and giggling for no reason at all. Seth wondered what would happen when they got back to her house. His mind filled with overheated fantasies until red lights and little alarms started going off on the dashboard of his hovercar.

"Oh you have to be kidding me," he practically screamed when he realized what the readings were telling him.

"What? What's going on?" Clio asked anxiously. Lights and alarms couldn't be good.

"There's a van following us. I have infrared sensors extending a mile in each direction. I thought it was weird that this van has been behind us for the last thirty minutes but now they've just tried to scan us. What a bunch of amateurs," he scoffed and tapped commands into his handheld angrily, letting the autopilot drive for a while. Of all the ways to kill the mood, getting pinged by DARPA was one of them.

he stood up. "Well, see you gameside!"

The governor watched the man leave. The senator sliding into the booth opposite him obstructed his view. The senator gave him a brief nod as he pulled off his suit coat and ordered a beer. Without a word, the governor pulled a small device out of his pocket and turned it on to ensure they could talk comfortably without being monitored, overheard or recorded.

The governor once again blessed those boys at Omerta for coming up with such easy-to-use privacy scramblers. He wordlessly cursed the current government policies that made such devices necessary.

"Shouldn't you be in Washington doing your job?" he greeted the senator with a scowl. It was a good-humored scowl. They were from opposite political parties, but after thirty years working the same rooms, they had come to a truce. Their truce was primarily based upon meeting up in dive bars, drinking heavily, and arguing about the state of the world.

"Nothing to do there but have the military tell me my job and expect me to shut up and like it," the senator said with a sigh. "Might as well come home where the food is good and the beer is better." He took a hefty swig and sighed, his mood easing.

"Let me guess. In your day, America was the land of the free, the home of the brave and dinosaurs still roamed the earth?" The governor teased the senator about his age although, in truth, he was only a few years older than the governor himself. The governor did not like to see his friend looking so utterly despondent. Dark hollows around the senator's eyes made him look even older.

"In my day, young whippersnappers did not make jokes at the expense of their better educated, more handsome elders," the senator replied with mock severity.

"Not only were we the land of the free, we practically invented the idea of the right to privacy. And you can see how that's gotten all screwed up," the senator replied, warming to the topic. "I know this will shock you, but we used to have the right to due process. Everyone got a trial with a judge and jury of their peers. They had to let you call your family. That was before military tribunals and secret courts and torture prisons." He knew it didn't change anything, but it was cathartic to be able to say these things out loud once in a while.

"Did we now? And I even hear we used to be considered innocent until proven guilty. Not terrorists until proven otherwise. But you can't countenance such wild talk," countered the governor with only a little sarcasm.

"It's true. Then we had that terrorist attack at the beginning of the century. A real one. Not the fake ones the military reports every other day now," said the senator as he emptied his first beer. The bartender brought him another unasked. They'd been through this routine before.

"So, in a way, if those original terrorists were trying to disrupt the American way of life, they accomplished more than they ever dreamed possible, didn't they?" the governor said, thinking out loud. "That's got to really chafe the hide of all the good patriots out there. What we did to ourselves was worse than what our enemies could ever have dreamed up." He had meant this statement to be funny, but somehow it wasn't. He rubbed the back of his neck.

"Ah well, we'll keep working at it," the he continued bracingly. "We'll keep fighting the good fight. Things will turn around, you'll see."

The senator squinted at his friend. "I can never understand how an educated and intelligent man like you could be so blindly, stupidly optimistic. It rankles."

The governor made a rude gesture. "Did you hear about that military raid on the Texas Omerta Embassy a few weeks ago?" The senator winced and nodded. He wondered if the stress of his job would finally turn him senile.

"They even have DARPA out pawing through people's dirty laundry now," the senator cried with outrage. "DARPA is supposed to be a lab full of R&D geeks. Instead of hanging around the lab, building us bigger guns, they go tearing across the countryside, ruffling the feathers of the few remaining people in the UN that tolerate our military's antics."

The governor nodded wearily. The events of the last few weeks had dented his armor-plated optimism. "Look, can't we just talk about football for once?"

The senator didn't even bother to reply. He was busy tossing beer down his throat. As soon as he came up for air, he bellowed,

"And apparently that insane commander they have running DARPA was five seconds away from hauling the entire embassy off to prison. If they hadn't recalled him in time, the only living thing left in Texas would be radioactive pigweed. I tell you this mania for torturing people is going to get us all killed."

The senator was like an excitable terrier with a fat rat. The governor realized the only way his friend would turn loose of this topic was if he had thoroughly shaken it to death. Resigning himself to a lecture, he leaned back in the booth. He let his mind wander as his friend ranted.

"This craze for electrocuting people's eyelids started just after all the Patriot Act and Homeland Security stuff did. They passed a law that legalized torture for what they called 'unlawful enemy combatants.' They decided it was all right to torture people whether they were in or out of the United States. And we've been at it ever since," the senator finished triumphantly.

"But that was almost eighty years ago," the governor protested mildly. "Maybe 9-11 hysteria caused this or maybe it was emo music or all the hormones in the drinking water. If it was really as bad as you make it out, surely we'd have stopped by now."

The senator shrugged. "I don't know. We have been awful busy with The Troubles and all the wars over the last couple of decades. Maybe people are just too scared to protest."

"God, if I weren't drinking, you'd depress the hell out of me," sighed the governor.

"Just looking at your face depresses the hell out of me, Bubba," the senator shot back with a grin. "We need another round."

The governor often noticed that when the political outlook got dismal, the senator got positively chipper. He was willing to bet the man walked around during the height of The Troubles with a song in his heart and a skip in his step.

He got up to go to the bathroom, winding his way through the eight-piece string quartet inexplicably but enthusiastically plucking out the blues. On the way back, he stopped at the bar to grab more drinks.

Sitting at a table near the bar were three people. They were so obviously trying to avoid attracting attention that they drew every eye in the room. There was a tall, thin woman who was talking in a low, urgent voice to an aggressively handsome man in a beautiful suit.

The governor watched them out of the corner of his eye, purely because they looked so uncomfortable. He noted the untouched drinks sitting in front of the first two. The third man had finished his drink and was playing with the ice in his glass. This man was shorter, darker and a little chubby.

The musician had taken a break or else the governor would never have been able to overhear their conversation.

"Our project is vital to national defense and we are prepared to pay quite handsomely for your time and effort," the woman was saying. If the governor had to guess, he'd say she was trying to charm the man, but her smiled just looked menacing. He expected her to start growling and snapping at any moment.

The man in the suit said nothing, so she continued, "I'm sure if you are concerned with the legality of the arrangement, we can get our military contacts to ensure you some sort of pardon for any, shall we say, ambiguous interpretations of your actions." The smaller man shot her a startled look.

She's just trying to con that guy, the governor thought. He dawdled at the bar to satisfy his curiosity.

"Medea, I don't think…" the smaller man started to say.

She cut him off. "Shiva let me handle this."

The large man in the suit studied them both for a minute and then said slowly, "So, what I'm wondering is, if Malsanto is so rich, why not just buy whatever it is you want from Floracopia all above board and legal? Or if Malsanto is so powerful, why not just get your big impressive military friends to seize it and declare it classified?"

"We tried to get the bosses at Malsanto to buy it, but you guys won't sell," Shiva said, petulance heavy in his voice. "This military contract is in a holding pattern until we get it."

"Shiva, will you shut up?" Medea hissed. "If you were half as good at splicing as you are at running your mouth, we wouldn't have this problem."

"It's not my fault Malsanto doesn't give me the resources to do the job," Shiva replied sulkily.

"What? And those women at Floracopia have so much more money and equipment than you? Please. Their splicer has always been better than you. You can't even reproduce her inventions. I don't even want to think about those monsters you created from the notes we got out of that break-in," she sneered. Shiva gave her a black look and got up for another drink.

Medea seemed to realize that she was not making the best impression on her mark. "So do we have a deal?" she asked smoothly, turning back to the man.

Unfortunately, a large, loud group trooped through the bar door at that moment. The noise was just distracting enough that the governor lost track of their conversation for a bit.

He tuned back in when the large man in the suit got up and began to leave.

"Wait," Medea cried. "We have a deal, right?" Shiva shot out of his chair. The man in the suit said something the governor didn't catch. And with that he walked out of the bar. The other two fumed and stormed after him.

The governor walked back to his table, deep in thought with a beer in each hand.

"What did you do, get lost?" asked the senator blearily. He had kept himself busy watching the flickering wallscreen above the bar. It was showing a football game. He fell upon the beer the governor passed him like a starving man on a steak dinner.

"Where is Floracopia located? You've done some work with them, right?" the governor asked.

"What? Oh those splicer women? I worked with them to fix the honeybee problem in my hometown. Charming women. Kind of strange. They're out in Ambrosia Springs," the senator replied.

"Isn't that where that Omerta embassy is?" the governor asked.

"Why you are right, now that I come to think on it. And that is a tiny little town. Imagine that," the senator said, his mind on the football game.

"I think we better keep an eye on Ambrosia Springs," the governor replied.

"Should we get some food before proceeding with our beverages?" asked the governor, with a mild slur in his voice.

"Oh well, I suppose. Has that restaurant across the street gotten any better?" he replied.

"Not a bit," said the governor cheerfully. "But the chicken-fried steak is plentiful and they will give us a discount on drinks."

"Let's do it," said the senator. He could tell they were in for a long night of serious drinking and a man needs to have something in his stomach on these occasions.

CHAPTER THIRTEEN

The second time Seth told Clio he was a vampire, it slipped out by accident and she almost missed it. They were bouncing down a dirt road in the middle of nowhere through the pitch-black night in a pick-up truck with a biomass retrofit. The truck stank like rotting fruit, but neither Seth's hovercar nor Clio's scooter would have survived the muddy road.

They were following half a dozen little red blips on the GPS. Clio made a mental note to ask Seth how he'd managed to get such detailed and obviously recent maps to this area. Since The Troubles, satellites had been notoriously unreliable over Texas, especially satellite imaging.

"Tell me again what we are chasing out here," Seth barked sternly, gripping the wheel.

Clio was kicking herself for letting him overhear the conversation she'd had with her hysterical lab assistant. It's just that she'd never had a test group escape before. The rabbits had been let out by accident. Two test groups escaping within a matter of months reflected poorly on her ability to maintain order, she felt. Luckily, they all had GPS tags imbedded so she could track them down. Unluckily, Seth had insisted on coming with her.

"It appears that a group of my gene mod dogs have gotten loose." She said this calmly as her eyes stayed glued to the map.

"I don't understand. You normally work on plant mods for farmers, right? Why did you have a dog strain in the lab? Some old lady decide she wants Mr. Tumtums back with some special new tricks?" Seth was trying to crack a joke since Clio was wound up tight.

"Oh well, you know, research," she said vaguely, hunching her shoulders. She rummaged around in her bag, found a package of cookies and tore into it.

"I'm sorry we had to skip dinner," she said as she offered him the cookies. After their tubing date a few weeks ago, things had seemed so promising but then she hadn't seen much of him. She had been hoping their date tonight would get things back on track towards some kind of a relationship or at least some more making out. There seemed to be little chance of that now. Instead of sitting in a nice restaurant flirting, they were out here.

He shook his head, too focused for food. "So, what happened? Did someone screw up? Did your security system break? You didn't have a break-in, did you?" Already he was mentally improving her security system. His uncle was going to kill him for spending all this time on her lab, but he'd already come up with some great algorithms for keeping her out of trouble.

"No, that's actually the part that concerns me," she admitted. "Either these dogs just got really lucky and knew exactly which wire to chew and which set of doors to duck out of or my intelligence booster experiment worked a lot better than I planned."

Seth was reflecting on what Max and Gloria would to say to him about tapping into DARPA's spy satellite network so that he could make sure his security measures were working. Wait, what did she just say?

"You boosted the intelligence of a carnivore? An already fairly intelligent carnivore?" Oh man, that was illegal in every country in the world.

"Oh come on. Dogs? The ability to learn silly tricks is not an indication of intelligence. And how can one really measure intelligence? You and I know tons of very bright, very useless people. Have you met my Uncle Chuck? He can splice genes like a timeshare salesman can fleece old people, but he still gets lost in the grocery store. You can't tell me that's intelligence." she scoffed.

"Clio!"

"All right, fine. I got the idea from those rabbits. They were so much smarter than they should have been. I wanted to isolate the splice so I could recreate it. I was working on some guard dogs for you since those DARPA guys keep showing up. But I wanted to make them kind of like ninjas, you know? Around but not looking like security. So they needed to be smarter. So I could teach them to talk," she blurted this out in a rush and looked at him guiltily.

Seth stopped the car and stared at her for a full minute. Then he laughed. He laughed harder than he had in a long, long time.

He turned to her with a grin and said slowly, "Just so I'm clear. You were worried about me, so you genetically engineered a pack of talking ninja guard dogs for me?"

She nodded, feeling silly.

"Wow. You are so perfect for me."

Clio had a sudden revelation. Seth was a great guy but he got a little weird about social interactions. Maybe if she wanted to have a relationship with him, she needed to be direct and clear so that there would be no misunderstandings.

"I really like you," she said slowly. Seth turned to give her his full attention. He felt she was trying to tell him something. But the moonlight shone through her hair and she was so beautiful. Seth forgot every thought that had ever passed through his head.

"Fantastic," he whispered, his eyes going soft and luminous as he leaned towards her. The cab of the truck became quite steamy before they remembered the whole 'escaped genetic monsters' issue. Luckily, the dogs appeared to have stopped.

"Would you like to come over for dinner with my family on Sunday?" she asked him as they rounded the final curve. She felt sure he understood what she was trying to say earlier. "I have to warn you that my mom is a terrible cook."

"Who cares?" he laughed light-heartedly. Kissing Clio was like downing six shots of vodka. Seth always felt a little tipsy afterwards. At least, he had both times he tried it. He planned to continue that experiment as much as possible. He was a good scientist and felt it was his duty to verify if the effects were reproducible. He chuckled to himself over that idea.

"What are you laughing about?" she asked.

"Wait until I tell all my vampire friends that I have my very own pack of hell hounds. They'll be so jealous," he replied, not wanting to seem overeager.

This was when the dogs finally came into view. They were sitting calmly in a half circle as if waiting for the truck.

Seth stopped the car and just stared at them. Then he turned to Clio and asked in a slightly strangled voice, "My pack of hell hounds is a bunch of Pomeranians?"

"You see why I had to boost their intelligence?" she said as she eyed the tiny, fluffy little dogs. "Normal ones snort when they breathe. I couldn't take it."

"But. Seriously? Pomeranians?"

"Hey, I have limited space in my lab and these guys grow much faster than larger, more imposing breeds. And no one will ever suspect these are vicious guard dogs."

"People will suspect quite a lot of other things about me with these ridiculous creatures following me around," Seth said sadly. He would tell no one about these dogs.

The dogs did not move as they got out of the car.

"So how exactly are we going to recapture them?" It finally occurred to Seth to ask this.

"Oh no problems. Actually, it's good you are here. I've been using a modification of the Ludovico conditioning technique to make them pathologically love you." Clio unwrapped a large bag of drippy, strange-smelling cheeseburgers and walked towards the dogs.

This did not make Seth feel safe. After all, dogs pathologically love bacon, too.

Within thirty minutes the truck was bouncing down dirt roads towards the dim lights of town with eight vicious Pomeranians yapping away joyfully in the back.

"So, they don't want to go back to the lab and that's fine. It's time for them to start protecting you anyway." Clio was telling him. "They just love these liver burgers I've been feeding them. They understand that no one but you will ever give them liver burgers and if anything happens to you, they'll never see another liver burger again. Neat, huh? So just be sure to toss liver burgers on your back porch every few days and you'll be set. They like a lot of cheese. I'll teach you the word commands and hand signals they know later."

Seth had been eyeing the dogs in the rearview mirror. They did not look smart at all, but they really could talk if you knew to listen for it. He tapped a reminder to himself on his handheld to reprogram the security scans around the compound. If the little guys got fried in the defense perimeter, there would be awkward questions.

"So you have vampire friends?" Clio asked after a few minutes.

"What? Oh." He'd forgotten about that. His uncle was going to kill him. Gloria would vivisect him. All those lectures about never revealing his true identity on the first date and he blurts it out to his girlfriend the first chance he gets.

"Well, yes," he cleared his throat. "Remember, I told you about that?"

Clio shot him a look. "I thought you were kidding."

Seth just shrugged.

"Seriously?"

He nodded.

She thought about that for a while. Was he crazy? She'd been around him a while now and he seemed strange and aloof, but not crazy. Was it some sort of kinky thing? Code for that medical condition he had? It was true she never saw him during the day, but nobody from Omerta came out during the day. They all worked crazy long hours.

Then she remembered she had some friends in college that talked about playing a game on the weekends where they dressed up like Robin Hood and hit each other with foam 'swords.' They called it Live Action Role Playing or LARPing, for short. They had talked about a vampire version. She remembered they said it was like acting and most of the people who played were tech geeks. Maybe that was it?

The more she thought about it, the likelier this seemed. Last week they didn't go out because he wanted to meet with his gaming group and she got the impression it wasn't an online game.

Well, fine. So he had a nerdy hobby. That wasn't a big deal. Though she could see how he might be embarrassed about that. She was president of the local bridge club. That was kind of embarrassing. But no big deal.

So Clio nodded, playing it cool. "Oh yeah, you did mention that. I guess you've got to be yourself. That's all right with me. Does it take up much time, meeting with other vampires and all?"

"Oh. Well. Not too much time." He looked at her in disbelief. "Are you really fine with this?"

"Sure," she shrugged. "It's Texas. We've got all sorts of weirdoes out here. I'm fine with having a weirdo boyfriend." She grinned at him, teasing. She decided not to inquire further, fearing that she'd have to confess to being queen of the bridge club if she did.

He couldn't believe she was accepting this so calmly. His heart swelled. He'd been right to tell her. This really was the girl of his dreams. As they pulled into his yard, he pulled her close.

They discovered that the dogs howled whenever he tried to kiss her. This became a real problem for them in the following weeks.

CHAPTER FOURTEEN

"I don't care how perky her curves are, you cannot trust that girl," Gloria snapped. The slight Eastern European cadence of her speech became more pronounced when she was angry.

"Which one?" Max asked, idly peeling a lime.

"Any of them. All of them," she threw up a hand dismissively. In the wall screen, Seth's father and Gloria's mother smiled indulgently while they lounged in armchairs. Through the wallscreen, you could see a few other people in the room. Most of them had glasses of wine and were dressed for a much colder place than Texas.

"Darling, I think it is good for you to be out among normal people, at least for a while. Omerta is a wonderful place, a safe place for us, but you need variety," her mother said. She was beautiful and exotic like Gloria, but her expression was more tranquil.

"They cannot trust us," Seth pointed out as he finished his dinner. "Why should we expect to trust them?"

He tried to time it so that he could eat during these Omerta Board meetings. That way the two hours would not be completely wasted.

"That's different," Gloria replied. "We keep quiet for noble and true reasons. They are just sneaky. They are probably working with their foul government. They probably have the same fanatical need to imprison strangers. Americans." She spat the word as though it were a curse, looking at Seth.

"Yes my dear," Seth's father said, looking tired, "We obviously agree that the current US policy of aggression is wrong and must be stopped. However, your reports indicate that the US is engaging in the same acts of belligerence towards its own citizens.

We did not realize this."

"Yes, it's quite depressing," said Max, wiping some crumbs off his shirt. "I was statistically mapping people taken by the Texas terrorist groups and it soon became evident that the number of people taken by the so-called terrorists was small compared to the number of people taken by the military. They seem to arrest people as rebels simply so they can take their money or land and call it terrorist support funds."

"Really? How barbaric," muttered Seth's father, toying with his wine glass.

"It's true," said Seth. "Others are arrested as dissidents for political reasons. They criticized the American war efforts or questioned US policy and found themselves locked in a jail cell. Half the time, they just disappear and no one can find what happened to them. We don't know if that's the terrorists or the government."

"Actually, it looks as though the Texas terrorists are snatching people just before the government gets to them. That might make them allies," Max chimed in.

"That's supposing they aren't just shooting these people and leaving them in a ditch somewhere," Gloria pointed out.

Several people nodded thoughtfully. Seth thought it was a bit rich that they were all discussing the problem like they planned to do anything about it.

A few months ago, Seth had written a program that periodically hacked into the US defense databases to find people the US government had taken. It pulled out lists of any foreign nationals held in detention or killed. It then anonymously forwarded that information to the appropriate government.

So every time US soldiers snatched a German businessman off the streets, the German government received a message from "A Friend" that detailed when and where the German citizen had been taken. It had really cut down on the number of foreign kidnappings. He occasionally had to go in and tweak the program when the military changed up their encryption package, but otherwise he felt it worked quite well.

When he let Omerta and his parents know what he had done, the resulting tidal wave of commotion was not at all what he had been expecting. It was practically forty days and forty nights of discussion and debate. Many felt that Omerta had enough problems without becoming a target for the US and their fanatical crusade against terrorists. However, they were all convinced that it was only a matter of time before they became a target anyway.

He was very glad he had not brought it up before he had released the program or they'd never have let him do it. Especially since the program was doing exactly what was needed. The governments now knew when their people were taken and could respond appropriately. The result was that the US dramatically reduced the number of foreign nationals they kidnapped.

But he still couldn't believe the furor over one little act of perfectly justified rebellion. It was one of the reasons he jumped at the chance to come to Texas and get away from the insular community on Omerta's island.

Seth decided now would not be a good time to mention all the extracurricular work he had been doing on Floracopia's security. He had hacked into several US government systems to install software that would track any interest in Floracopia or Omerta. He had set up other programs to erase their signatures on satellites and tracking software. He didn't think his family was ready for that kind of thing just now.

"All the more reason that I think we should make contact with these terrorist people and find out what they are up to. Texas has been particularly hard hit by this rising tide of US attacks in the name of their national defense. Maybe it is because Texas has so many natural resources to begin with. Also, Texas was a hotbed of new technology before The Troubles. It makes sense that they would have some sort of underground resistance group." Max continued.

"Now that it appears this DARPA group may cause us trouble, we must seek allies. This is true. But we must not make ourselves a target for the US and their war machine. So, if you must ask questions, ask them quietly," Gloria's mother spoke with easy authority. "You must be subtle, Max. It would not do to give DARPA or anyone else something they could use against us."

"And you must stop becoming involved with those Floracopia women," Gloria said severely.

"Oh come now," Seth protested. "You must admit that having them work on the ZFD problem could be a huge success for us."

This made everyone in the room intensely uncomfortable. One of the traits the Omerta family shared was a distinct loathing for all things medical.

"Telling an outsider about the Z-Factor Deficiency is not an option right now," Seth's father replied, his voice heavy with disapproval. "We have been over this."

"We wouldn't have to tell them everything, just enough to work on a cure. Or even figure out what the problem is," Seth objected. "Even if it is illegal, I am sure they would help us."

"How do you know that they won't roll over and give every word you say to their government?" Gloria snapped.

"The fact that they have things they need to hide from the government like escaped mutant lab animals." Max replied. "It means they won't ask too many awkward questions about our family's health problems."

"Bah. You would risk us all for practically nothing," Gloria said scathingly.

"We give up a few secrets and we can gain an understanding of the problem," Seth shot back. "We cannot hoard information like a dragon sitting on a pile of gold. That is stagnation. If we want to increase our wealth, we invest it and watch it grow. We don't bury it under a rock. If we want to solve our problems, we must give some information away to people who can help us."

"Information is power, Seth," his father reminded him. This was Omerta's motto.

"Information is nothing if you do not use it," Seth countered.

"If you do not use it *correctly*," Max amended. He smiled gently at Seth, wondering how someone so close to him in age could still seem so very young. He was beginning to doubt that anyone ever really grew up. But he also did not think that was a bad thing.

"Well, this has been fun, boys and girls," Max said briskly as he stood up. "But now we must go. We have an engagement to go view the local blood sport."

Gloria's mother raised an eyebrow. "What?"

Gloria rolled her eyes. "Football," she explained. "We are to watch their celebrated Friday night football games. I believe afterwards they slaughter a fatted calf for the victors."

"Only if we're lucky," said Max cheerfully as he ushered Seth and Gloria out the door.

"Max, keep our babies safe," called Gloria's mother.

Gloria and Seth were still bickering when they arrived at the football stadium.

Gloria sighed. "Seth, I'm tired of fighting. I just worry, you know? You grew up so sheltered on Queen Charlotte's. I don't want to see you trust the wrong person and get hurt."

She took his arm. "Come on, let's get this over with. I assume there is a beer stand? Texas seems to have one every fifty feet. I will buy you some of that pathetic excuse for alcohol that you boys like so much."

"Would you hurry up?" Seth asked Max. Max seemed to be laboring even longer than usual over his appearance.

"Like it or not, people make assumptions based on your appearance and then act upon them. So why not use that to your advantage? For a change." Max said dryly, running a critical eye over Seth's worn jeans and faded shirt.

Seth didn't care. He was sure he would meet up with Clio tonight and she was too wonderful and intelligent to care how he looked. He craned his neck to search for her, almost dragging Gloria along. Gloria was dressed in all black, but would not fail to attract attention in her skintight cat suit and dramatic make-up. She towered over him in high-heeled boots.

The roar of the crowd and the pounding drumbeat from the band made the small arena seem vast. Seth searched the crowd but couldn't find her. Max tugged him into an open seat while Gloria went in search of drinks.

Seth tried to follow the game, but found he couldn't make sense of the action. It did not help to have Max enthusiastically explaining every move to him and getting it all wrong. Seth began to wonder if his uncle had read up on rugby or something by accident. Not that it seemed to matter.

Max cheered happily when everyone else cheered and had a fantastic time. Fortunately, the people sitting next to them explained that the game was won by whoever had the most points. After that, all they had to do was watch the scoreboard.

Gloria brought drinks and introduced herself to the people sitting next to him. They turned out to be Joanna and Eric Guerrero. Max had met Joanna at the Junior League Target Practice so they amicably discussed range finders and the many deficits of heat-seeking missiles and rail guns. Seth was interested to meet these people. He had been discussing the Co-op's break-in with Clio on the handheld a few nights ago and Joanna was on the short list of people who may have been passing information to outsiders.

She certainly seemed capable of anything, unlike her husband. At first glance, he would have ruled out Eric as lacking the energy to do anything so sneaky. The man slumped into the bleachers with his eyes roaming the field. His answers to Seth's questions were virtually monosyllabic.

"So what is there to do around here?"

"Not much." Eric shrugged and watched the game.

"I hear there is quite good fishing up at the Pedernales River?" Seth tried again.

"If you like fish," Eric answered his shoes.

Joanna had too much energy for one person. As she chatted to Max, she watched the game and tapped away on her handheld. The first quarter ended and Seth stood up.

"Well I think I'll stretch my legs," he said, thinking he'd go look for Clio.

Gloria quickly stood up too and gave him a flirty smile. "I'll go with you," she said.

Seth frowned at her a minute. She'd been acting so weird lately. Her family moved to Europe when they were both still young. He lost touch with her until they moved back to Omerta's island last year. Gloria had been quite happy to taunt him and hide his toys as a child. He mistrusted how nice she was being to him now.

She followed him out of the stands. Almost immediately, he bumped into Harmony carrying a large bag of popcorn and a drink.

"Seth, how nice of you to make it out tonight. We missed you at the Chamber of Commerce lunch," she said, not missing his glances over her shoulder as if she might be hiding Clio in her back pocket. She gave Gloria a pitying look.

Gloria did not miss the look or its meaning. "Our distance from town and heavy work load make daytime appointments very difficult," she said stiffly. She looked as if she were fighting the urge to toss her hair in contempt. Max had been making fun of her for that unconscious mannerism. Then her face lit up with malicious joy.

"Oh Seth," she cooed in a suspiciously honeyed voice. "You seem to have got a little something on your collar." He looked at her with confusion. She leaned in close to him, managing to snuggle her ample and impressive bosom up against his chest as she snaked an arm around his neck to fiddle with his collar on the opposite side. Harmony raised her eyebrows as Gloria stumbled a bit too perfectly into Seth's arms.

Seth tried to pull away from her. He thought she was trying to slip ice down his shirt. Then he spotted Clio walking towards him with a cold look in her eyes. He grinned at her but she just scowled at him. Then he looked down and realized Gloria was plastered all over his chest. This can't look good.

"Oh my," Gloria said breathily, "I got some lipstick on your neck. Let me fix that." She tickled light fingers under his jaw and wiped away a smudge of her screaming red lipstick. He shoved her away like a man who picked up a puppy and realized it was covered in fleas. He wiped his hands down his shirt trying to get any remaining Gloria off him, keeping his eyes on Clio.

Gloria righted herself and gave a smirking grin to Clio while managing to cling to Seth's shoulder. Clio wore cowboy boots, dark jeans and a long tunic that flowed down her curvy body. As Seth gazed at Clio, he realized there was a distinct flaw in the picture of perfection before him. That flaw was the huge blond man draping his arm around Clio in a possessive manner. Clio looked uncomfortable.

"Ah, my darling daughter. I see you have Jason with you," Harmony said flatly, leaning to kiss her daughter's cheek. Then she turned to Seth. "Is your uncle here?"

Seth nodded, scowling at Jason Schmidt. He pointed in the direction of their seats. Seth had spent quite a bit of time working with Jason when Seth had that consulting project for Revolution World. At the time, Seth got along very well with Jason and enjoyed working with him.

When Clio said she had a previous relationship with Jason at the barbeque, Seth had only found her more attractive for choosing to date someone he liked. He watched Jason treat Clio with easy intimacy. Seth realized now that the hearty blond ex-football player was richer and more handsome than he was. He didn't understand how he had failed to notice these flaws in the man's character before.

"Excellent. I will just go see him," Harmony said briskly and marched off. Seth was glad to see that Clio's mother was distinctly unenthusiastic about Jason and his huge arms all over the place. Seth thought that Harmony was a very wise woman. You can't trust people named Jason, he felt.

As she walked away, Harmony paused. She leaned in to Gloria. "Well played," she whispered. Gloria allowed a sulky look to cross her face before she went back to simpering at Seth.

"Schmidt, it's been a long time. Aren't you a long way from home?" Seth said, extending a hand to get thoroughly shook by Jason.

Jason laughed with ease, showing his gleaming smile. "Great to see you! Aren't you even farther from home? I heard you'd moved to our neck of the woods. Welcome!" Jason squeezed Clio in a possessive way. "I hate to miss one of these football nights even if it is a heck of a drive for me."

As Seth tried to formulate a response that did not involve snarling and gnashing his teeth at the man, Kalliope wandered up sporting mismatched knee socks, combat boots and a polka dot cocktail dress.

She popped her gum as she studied the group. Then she turned to Seth. "Jason here drives a bio-diesel truck." She managed to put more contempt into that statement than Seth would have thought possible. He wondered what she had against bio-diesel, but decided he would rather help her sneer at Jason than find out.

"Jason, I'd like you to meet Gloria," Clio said loudly. "She lives with Seth in his compound in the woods." She cut her eyes to Seth. Seth could tell Clio was mad at him about something, but how could she expect him to control Gloria?

"Well, with something like this at home, it's hard to see why you ever leave the house," Jason said, amiably leering at Gloria. Gloria smoldered back at him.

Seth laughed nervously and edged away from Gloria. "We both live at the Omerta office site, but not together like a couple. That would be gross. We are cousins." His eyes appealed to Clio.

Kalliope rolled her eyes and wandered off as the band started playing.

"Oh, do come sit with us," cried Gloria, grabbing both Clio and Jason by the arm. The game started up again and Seth found himself seated next to Max with Gloria, Clio, and Jason several rows away.

Harmony was sitting on the other side of Max. They ignored Seth as they briefly discussed the game and an article Harmony had just read about using forests as bioelectrical generators. Then Seth leaned across Max to ask Harmony, "So what's the deal with that Jason character?"

Harmony chewed on her lip thoughtfully. "Jason grew up here in Ambrosia Springs so they've known each other since they were children. They dated for many years. When his game really started to take off, he wanted to move to Austin. Clio wanted to stay here. So he moved, she stayed and they broke up."

Seth thought about that. "But I guess she really couldn't move away with her labs here and the Co-op and all?"

Harmony gave him an appraising look. "I offered to set her up with a satellite lab anywhere in the world she wanted to go. She refused."

"Oh," said Seth, feeling better. He turned to look at Clio as their team scored another touchdown. When they all jumped up to cheer, Jason hugged Clio. Then he leaned to hold his lips close to her ear. Seth couldn't tell if Jason just leaned over to whisper something to Clio or if he just kissed her. It was awful.

Seth could only stare at Clio despondently. He was considering whether it would be too terribly pathetic to try sending Clio a handheld message when a woman tapped him on the shoulder to ask if he happen to have any napkins. He turned to find Terpsi sitting behind to him. Terpsi smiled at him and introduced her husband. They looked tired but cheerful.

"How is everything?" he asked, handing them his handkerchief. Once again he marveled at how the girls could be the same genetic model and still look and act so differently. Perhaps he could work the conversation around to Clio and what she thought about Seth and, most importantly, how to get rid of Jason.

"Oh fine," Terpsi said. "Well, not fine but as good as can be expected." Seth looked at her enquiringly.

"You know we've got two little kids? They both caught a stomach virus this week. We were up three days straight with puking children." She sighed and rubbed her husband's back.

"I think everything we own is covered in vomit," her husband said hollowly. "I may burn the rugs."

"We love them. We love our kids with every fiber of our being, but raising kids is hard," Terpsi said with a crooked smile.

"But it's totally worth it," Terpsi's husband added, looking frazzled.

"Although if they ever stop making liquor, we are totally screwed," she laughed as she took a swallow of beer.

"Yeah, we used to drink before we had kids," her husband laughed as he pulled out a flask to 'freshen up' his coffee "Now we drink a whole lot."

Terpsi pushed him playfully. Her husband took her hand and they looked at each other. Seth watched their genuine affection for each other with fascination.

"I want what they have," he thought.

"Me too," said a voice in his ear that had to be Clio. Seth jumped. He didn't mean to say that out loud. Especially where Clio could hear. He turned to find her standing beside him with a gentle smile on her face.

"Care to take a walk?" she asked, her eyes sparkling.

Seth looked over to see Jason sitting next to Gloria. Jason was caught up in the game, but Gloria was watching them. She gave Seth a withering look and pointedly turned away from him.

"Won't you need to get back to Jason?" he asked somewhat sheepishly.

Clio hesitated and looked over her shoulder. "Not for a while," she said.

Seth stiffened. So she had plans with Jason for later tonight. Well. She was free to do what she liked. So was he. He wished he knew someone he could flirt with right in front of her so that she'd know he had options too. He turned towards the field.

"I am watching the game right now," he said, concocting elaborate scenarios in which whole groups of attractive women sang his praises in front of her. She'd be sorry then. He saw Gloria waving at him, but ignored her.

Clio looked at him for a minute then elbowed a seat for herself between Terpsi and Seth. "Budge over, Terpsi." Seth edged away from her. His breath caught when her hand brushed his shoulder. That made him angry with himself and the whole world. He jerked away from her.

"That reminds me. I want to have a look at that shoulder and see how it's healing," Terpsi said, misinterpreting his movement as protecting an injury. She leaned over and drew up the sleeve of his shirt before he could stop her. Then she stared open-mouthed at the smooth red scar.

"Honey, look at this," she said, tapping her husband on the arm. "This was a deep cut that needed stitches not a week ago. This scar looks you were wounded months ago. No way it could heal that fast." Clio and Terpsi's husband both leaned over to look at the scar.

"Jesus, I had no idea medicine was that advanced in Canada. How did you treat it?" Terpsi asked in wonder, tracing the scar with her finger. "Please tell me."

Seth pulled away and yanked his sleeve down. "Wasn't that bad after all," he muttered. Both women insisted that it was, in fact, a very bad cut. Seth didn't want to talk about it. He stood up abruptly and walked away.

"Seth, wait," Clio called, following him out of the stands. "Don't go."

Seth sighed and stopped when he got to the dark of the parking lot. He ran a hand through his hair and looked at her. "Clio, my life is very complex right now and you only make things more complicated."

She stood facing him with the stadium lights casting a halo around her and the low breeze ruffling her curls. "I could say the same about you. I have a lot going on right now and you don't exactly make things easy." Her voice sounded forlorn.

"I can't help liking you, but I can't seem to do much about that right now," he replied.

"Well, no one is asking you to," she bristled.

But words were irrelevant, it seemed. They moved towards each other as though compelled by forces larger than themselves. The crowd in the stadium roared for a touchdown. In the parking lot, Seth reached for Clio.

"My, my. Isn't this so romantic?" a low voice said out of the dark. Seth and Clio took a reflexive step back as they watched two figures in dark suits step out of the night. One was a very tall, very thin woman with her hair back in a severe bun. The other was a shorter Hindi man with an inclination towards pudginess.

The tall woman extended a hand. "Medea of Malsanto. And this is Shiva." She gestured towards her companion.

"Shiva? What on earth are you doing here?" Clio asked, totally shocked.

Shiva gave a smirking smile as his eyes wandered over her with insulting thoroughness. "Oh, we were just in the neighborhood, working on some local business." Clio bristled at the idea that there was any agribusiness in the area that would choose Malsanto over the Co-op. Shiva caught her look of disgust and smiled nastily. "We thought we might stop by and see whether Floracopia has come to their senses and reconsidered our offer."

Clio clenched her fist and realized that Seth was standing behind her in silent support.

"If they have, you'll have to discuss that with the Board," she replied smoothly letting her breath out.

"Oh we will tomorrow. We really are quite anxious to acquire some of your splicing techniques for the war effort," replied Medea. Then she turned to Seth. "I hear DARPA paid your company a little visit. How unfortunate. That sort of thing happens to those that do not enjoy the kind of trust and understanding that we at Malsanto have from the government."

Medea smiled nastily. "I've heard rumors that there are some specimens in the woods around here that are very unusual. Hard to believe such things can occur naturally. It's too bad the government gets so suspicious about things like that." She cut her eyes to Clio to underline her threat.

"We should go," Seth said. He pulled Clio away from the pair and into his waiting car. Shiva and Medea watched them drive away before turning towards the stadium.

"So that's the competition I guess?" Seth asked as they drove away.

"And our main suspect for our corporate espionage problem," Clio replied.

"Oh." Seth drove in silence for a minute. "Hey, I saw Joanna and Eric Guerrero in the stands. You don't think one of them came out to meet the Malsanto people, do you? A face-to-face meeting is one of the few ways to convey information encrypted by our software. They could be trying to pass on more of your trade secrets."

Clio's eyebrows shot up. "You know, that could be true. Nobody drops by unannounced any more, especially from wherever the heck Malsanto is. But I've moved everything to electronic files so they wouldn't be able to physically take notes out of the lab."

"Excellent," Seth nodded approvingly. He was glad she had taken his advice on that. Clio had done so grudgingly. To be fair, Seth knew it had been a huge pain in the ass to upload all her work and start using her handheld to take notes directly, even if he had helped her set up the software that made it easier.

"That doesn't narrow it down too much. I ran into Bob and Nancy earlier in the stands. All of our suspects are here so it could have been any of them," she realized. "On the bright side, I doubt any of them know enough about splicing to be able to describe the p-mod technique or any of our other proprietary methods. To be really dangerous, they'd need to be able to pass files. You are sure they can't do that?"

Seth shrugged. "As sure as a person can be. I went all out on the security at Floracopia. There are some very rich and very paranoid countries out there that would love to have that set up."

"Really? I don't see how we could afford something like that," Clio replied. Seth squirmed uncomfortably. "What did you do?" she asked suspiciously.

"Ah well, I needed a test facility for some of the software and equipment," he said.

It took a minute for it to click. "Seth, did you charge us what you would have charged a normal client?" she asked.

"Ah. Well. Possibly not." He mumbled. Then he gave her a pleading look. "Don't tell Gloria. She'll use my guts for garters."

"We aren't a charity case," she said with a scowl.

Seth swerved the car a little as he looked at her. Clio had a distinctly stubborn look on her face. Then he chuckled. He couldn't help himself. "You silly woman. I locked up your office tighter than Fort Knox because it helps me sleep at night. Nothing can get in and, more importantly, nothing can get out. That way I don't have to worry about what mad, hairy thing you've let loose in the woods this time."

"I told you the rabbits and the dogs were the only thing to escape," she said grumpily.

Clio would have much preferred he say that he gave them the deluxe security job because he found himself irresistibly in love with her. Men never act like they do in those romance novels she sometimes borrowed from Thalia. It really was a pity.

"Yes, I noticed you were very careful to say that," he replied. "But you might have let something out on purpose." He did not press that idea. He really didn't want to know if she had let things loose before.

*****

She watched the world whirl past the car windows for a minute before recalling her responsibilities. She ought to be doing something about Shiva and Medea. Clio pulled out her handheld and sent messages to everyone at Floracopia. When that was done, she got a message from Terpsi asking if Seth had explained what happened with his shoulder injury.

She opened her mouth to ask him as Seth turned into her driveway. Watching the moonlight play along his strong jaw, she closed her mouth. Let him keep that to himself if he wants, Clio thought. They had enough to deal with already. The stars twinkled overhead, unconcerned with their worries.

He stopped the car, but neither of them moved. The silence stretched awkwardly. Clio sighed and opened her door to get out. Seth quickly opened his door and got out too.

"I'll walk you in," he stammered.

"That would be nice," she replied.

They crunched up the gravel path to her dark doorway. There was more awkward silence.

"Wouldn't you like to come in for some coffee?" Clio asked finally. She was hoping that with some liquid courage, Seth might get up the nerve to kiss her or something. Otherwise she might be waiting on the porch for a long time. A mosquito bit Clio and she slapped at it.

"Yes, that would be nice. It's very late and quite a drive home,"

Seth said with relief. Then he paused.

"I guess Jason will go home?" Seth asked tentatively as she bent over to inspect the red itchy bite on her leg.

"Hmm? No, I sent him a message. He'll be over later," she replied, still examining the bite.

Seth stood there for a minute. Clio looked up and saw the frosty expression on his face.

"What? He won't be over for hours," she tried to explain. Seth turned and stalked down the driveway.

"Where are you going?" Clio cried.

Seth opened the car door. "You are obviously busy tonight. I will not impose," he said without looking back at her.

"Seth, wait!" Clio cried, not understanding what just happened. Seth's car was out of sight before she realized that he must have thought she was on a date with Jason tonight. How depressing.

CHAPTER FIFTEEN

"Are you serious? A few kisses and that's it? After all this time? Lordy, girl, there's something wrong with your hormones," Kalliope cried loudly. The other people in the room whipped their heads around to stare. Harmony gave them a scathing look and began getting up since the meeting was definitely at an end.

Shiva and Medea had left over an hour ago. This time their threats had been more direct. Shiva had not said much, but he acted as though he had them backed into a corner. He smirked at the Somata girls and went out of his way to make snide comments. It was disconcerting. They had no idea why he might think they had to comply with Malsanto's demands.

"Shut up," Clio muttered, turning red.

"Seriously. What is wrong with you? Of course Seth thought you'd called Jason to come over and give you some red hot loving after he left, you hussy," Kalliope continued loudly, grinning at her sister's discomfort.

"If there's a problem with your hormones, I'll be happy to run some tests for you," Terpsi said with a grin.

"Would you curl up and die, please?" Clio hissed, wishing she could still pound her sisters when they started acting like brats. Being an adult wasn't all it was cracked up to be.

"Oh come on, how hard is it to put on a tight shirt, pour a few drinks into a guy and then suck his tonsils out?" Terpsi asked. "I'll call my husband and we can give you a demonstration."

"Terpsi, don't be gross," Kalliope wrinkled her nose.

That gave Clio enough time to think of a reply. "You were the one who said I shouldn't get involved with him," she shot at Kalliope.

"Since when have you ever followed my advice?" Kalliope

asked. She had a point. “Besides, I’m not saying you should marry the guy. I’m saying you have the hots for him. He has the hots for you. Jump his bones and get it out of your system. It’s a foolproof plan.”

Clio could see several advantages to this plan. Her hormones were definitely working just fine. If anything, her hormones worked a little too well lately.

“Jump his bones? How is that a plan?” Clio said with disgust.

“Uncomplicated sex. Consensual relations between two adults. Get with the millennium, girl,” Kalliope said with a shrug.

Clio threw up her hands. “Sex is never uncomplicated! What if, afterwards, he doesn’t like me but I like him? Then I’ll look pathetic while he swans around with that cow, Gloria. Or afterwards, I don’t like him but he likes me and then it will be awkward because it’s a small town and I’ll see him everywhere. I’ll feel like a jerk. What if he thinks my bottom is too big or I fall asleep and drool all over? He’ll tell all his friends and everyone will laugh at me behind my enormous backside.” At this point, Terpsi clapped a hand over Clio’s mouth to get her to stop yammering.

“I agree with you. Intimacy in any form is complicated,” Terpsi said in a soothing voice. “But it’s so unattractive when you flip out, sister dearest.” She looked over Clio’s head to wave goodbye to the other Floracopia board members that were finding excuses to linger and listen in. Harmony ushered them out the door and then turned to her daughters.

“Anyway, after last night, he hates me,” Clio said in a small voice.

“There, there, honey. You are too cute to hate,” Harmony interjected as she patted her daughter on the head. Then her voice turned steely. “Now stop acting like a teenager. We need those Omerta people to be totally committed to our security here, especially after that awful meeting we just had. Get out there and smooth things over.”

“Mom!” all three daughters cried in shock.

“She can’t call him and apologize,” Terpsi was scandalized. “It’s against the rules.”

“Honestly, you girls make mountains out of molehills. Watch and learn.” She whipped out her handheld.

“Max? It’s lovely to hear from you too. Yes, it has been too long.

Oh, you big flirt, I'm sure you say that to all the ladies. Listen, I was wondering what you were up to tonight? The girls and I had a long day and we're looking to unwind a bit. Dinner maybe?" She paused to listen while Clio pantomimed strangling her mother. "How interesting. Well, we would love to. Wonderful. We'll bring drinks. Yes. See you then."

Harmony clicked her handheld off and put it in her pocket. "Come, girls, we must freshen up before we head over to the Omerta compound. Terpsi, do you still have that stash of Tito's vodka? I think we ought to take a few bottles over." Harmony asked as she headed for the door.

"Wait. What's going on?" Clio asked. Each sister grabbed an arm and started dragging her out.

"We're going to play dress up," Kalliope cried with evil glee.

An hour later, Clio was standing outside the Omerta compound, sullenly pulling at the plunging neckline of the shirt her sisters had insisted she wear. Kalliope leaned over and slapped her hand.

"Leave it," Kalliope threatened her. "And don't touch your face or hair. You smear that make-up and I will pinch you so hard you won't walk right for a week." Clio couldn't believe that she had let them dress her in the tight shirt and slinky skirt she was wearing. Especially since Kalliope was wearing jeans and an old tunic. The girl had washed her face but her boots were still dirty.

Terpsi had begged off to go home to her husband and kids, but not before coming up with an array of exotic underclothes than caused Clio and Kalliope to drop their jaws in shock. They had both thought of Terpsi as having a nice quiet, boring life. Clio had been so surprised, she agreed to a red lacy corset just to avoid saying something rude or prudish to her sister.

As they approached on the doorstep, the doors clicked and opened. When the lights flickered on, they saw Max coming down a corridor to greet them. He was wearing loose cotton pajamas, bare feet and a huge grin.

"Ah, to have such lovely ladies visit our humble abode," Max beamed. He ushered them down the hallway to an elevator. Harmony had changed from her conservative business clothes into a long summer dress. She had let her hair down and appeared more relaxed than the girls had seen her in years. Clio was glad her mother had found some new friends.

Max allowed the door's sensors to register them all before it clicked open and he led them down another hallway. "As you can see, our security is much improved. We actually turn it on now," he smiled, still embarrassed by the DARPA raid.

"This is our virtual conference area. We were playing a game so we set up in one of the better rooms," he told them. "I am further embarrassed that we have not invited you over before this. Unfortunately, we got behind in construction and we didn't want to invite you over to a dirty house," he grinned as he led them into a spacious room.

In the middle was a large round table with Seth and a half a dozen other men at it. Seth looked up at Clio. His eyes widened. When he realized that he was openly ogling her chest, he reddened and quickly looked away.

Clio was relieved to see such a warm and comfortable room after the impersonal hallway. Large couches and cushions were scattered around with an area for food and drinks to one side. An unusual, but entrancing, song played from hidden speakers.

Most of the large wallscreens were currently displaying the view from an underwater oilrig, with fishing swimming and seaweed gently swaying. Harmony walked over to a screen that showed a gently twisting pattern with colors that faded into each other.

"I always thought fractal mathematics were so beautiful. Are you using a chaotic process to map this dynamical system?" she asked.

Max reacted as though he had been electrocuted and shot over to her side. "Naturally a woman like you would recognize strange attractors when you see them." He almost danced with joy. "These equations depict an interesting thermodynamic phenomenon we have noticed in our server configurations. It mimics a *Poisson Saturne* system."

While Max talked math to her mother, Clio focused her attention on Seth. Kalliope had already poured a round of drinks for everyone and sat down. Kalliope poured the charm on thick, so the men enthusiastically explained their game to her.

"Clio, look! They are playing D&D!" Kalliope called to her. "We always wondered how you play this," she eagerly said to the men. Clio saw that the table was covered with little metal figurines on a board that could be rearranged for different scenarios. Clio noted Seth giving her a searching look as she walked toward the group.

"I thought you had to get dressed up in costumes and whack at each other with foam swords," Clio said, eyeing all the dice.

Seth laughed and gave her a lopsided smile. "What? No. That's SCA or Amtgard. They are 'live action' role-playing games. Dorks like us play those too. But this is traditional 'pen and paper' role-playing. No hitting each other with sticks or dressing up. The most exercise we get is rolling the dice. Although we have been known to talk in funny accents."

Clio desperately wanted to make fun of him right now, but realized this would not be the politic thing to do. She swallowed half a dozen jokes at his expense.

"Tell me more," she said with a smile, leaning over to look at the board. Any hint of mockery there might have been in her voice went unnoticed as Seth got an eyeful of what her shirt wasn't covering. Clio saw the odd expression on his face and quickly stood up. She only just managed to keep herself from tugging the top up.

The guys insisted on working the girls into their D&D game. After explaining a few basics they gave Clio and Kalliope pencils and paper. Then they told them to pick a character out of a book called "The Big Book of Monsters." After flipping through the book for a few minutes, the girls started giggling uncontrollably.

"What?" Seth asked, changing the music to a slow Brazilian tango with his handheld. Clio and Kalliope only giggled louder. Max and Harmony looked up from the couch in the corner where they had curled up.

"Oh come on! We are sitting in one of the most technologically advanced facilities in the world." Kalliope held up the book in disbelief. "You people have hologram projectors in your lunchroom and probably virtual reality plug-ins on your kitchen sink. And you are playing a game that involves pencils and paper? This is an actual book you just handed me. I thought Clio here was the only person left on the planet to use paper and even she uses a ballpoint pen."

From across the room, Max laughed. "We like to kick it old

school," he called.

Seth couldn't tell if they were making fun of them or not. "It's a time-honored tradition of our people," he said stiffly.

"What people is that?" Clio asked.

"Nerds."

"Oh."

Clio felt a change in subject was in order. She looked down at the book and pointed. "I'd like to play this character," she said.

Kalliope looked over her shoulder and read the description. "You want to be a vampire?"

"What? Isn't that what you are doing? Playing vampires?" she asked.

Seth and the other Omerta guys stared at her for a long minute before they started laughing so hard that one choked on a potato chip and had to be given the Heimlich maneuver. It was Clio and Kalliope's turned to look confused.

"What?" Clio asked, looking around blankly.

"We, uh, have a joke about vampires," Seth chuckled.

"Let's hear it," Clio said. Maybe she'd figure out why vampires kept coming up. She really didn't understand. She hated all that vampire and werewolf stuff. As a geneticist, she knew these things were all silly stories. Real monsters were much easier to make.

"No, it's stupid. Look here, why don't you play this character here?" Seth took the book from her and flipped to a different page. He sat close to her, discussing the game in a soft voice to show they had not been making a joke at her expense.

"Why don't we have some more drinks?" Harmony suggested to unanimous approval. "And Clio, I know you haven't eaten much today. Put something in your stomach before you have another drink, please."

Seth leapt to get her a drink and a plate piled high with food. "If I had known you were coming, we would have arranged for something better," he said, apologizing for the potato chips and other junk food lining the buffet.

"Don't worry about it," she said with a smile. She couldn't help the warm glow of joy she got just being around him. Then she realized she was starving.

As the guys resumed their game, Kalliope dove in while Clio was content to watch and eat. Seth explained what was going on until she had a fairly good idea of how the game worked. She had to admit it was quite interesting and she was looking forward to getting into the next part of the game.

Seth sat close to her and she could tell that he wasn't angry any more by the looks he was giving her. She took his hand under the table and they sat together, enjoying the moment.

Unfortunately, that's when the ceiling fell in. One minute they had been commiserating with Seth over getting maimed by a troll, the next minute the lights flicked to red and a loud siren began. Before she could react, there was the loudest BOOM! that Clio had ever heard. Then they were sprawled on the floor under a large chunk of rubble.

The world spun sideways for Clio as she choked on dust and pushed her way out from under the debris. She saw her mother climb out from behind a couch where Max had thrown her. Clio registered that her mother was coughing up dust, but seemed unharmed.

"The wall!" Max cried, pointing behind them. She turned around, trying to figure out what happened when Seth grabbed her and bolted for the door. She looked back to see the outer wall collapse. Fortunately, it fell outward so no one was beneath it.

She heard Gloria's voice floating through the terrible sounds of destruction. "We are under attack. Repeat. We are under attack. One incoming threat was neutralized before impact but resulting concussion has damaged a wall on ground level, northeast corner."

Seth swore angrily. "I programmed the defense missiles to launch too close to the building. I'll set them to go off much farther away next time."

Clio thought it was very cool and very scary that Omerta had defensive missiles.

Gloria's voice continued calmly, "One new threat approaching rapidly to the northwest. Repeat. Single external threat incoming. Everyone get to the lower levels and away from the northeast walls until we have assessed the damage."

"Seth, wait." Clio cried. "I have to make sure my sister and my mom are alright."

When he didn't stop, she began to struggle in his arms. She thought that, in a while, she would marvel at his strength and speed, but right now she had other problems.

"Seth, come on. We need to go back."

"No," he said grimly, without breaking stride. "I need to make sure you are safe." After racing down at least two flights of stairs and through a hallway with numbered doors, he shouted something she didn't understand that triggered one of the doors. When it didn't open fast enough, he kicked it, cursing loudly.

He gently put her on a soft couch and hovered over her with a worried look. She looked around at the room. Monitor screens lined the walls. Some of them displayed a jungle at sunrise. One screen was set up like a large white board with equations scribbled on it and a list of things to do: "Laundry, Lift weights, Call Clio." Another cycled through still shots from what looked like a family vacation with a smiling Seth in most of them. There were couches, random piles of computer equipment and a stack of dirty dishes on a table.

"Is this your room?" she asked, pushing away his hand after he'd poked her for the fourth time on what would definitely be a bruise later.

"I sleep back there," he replied, jerking his head to another doorway.

Clio wanted to explore, but she wanted to know her family was safe first. "We have to go back," she insisted.

"You stay here. I'll go back," Seth replied.

"No."

"I can lock you in," he threatened.

"Another explosion and we'll all be smashed to bits down here. We need to get out," she countered.

Seth shook his head. "It would take multiple direct hits by a Cold War Era nuke to affect us down here. Snipers could pick us off if we all trooped outside. Omerta protocol says to stay inside and get down low." Clio's eyebrows shot up. These Omerta guys took their security very seriously. Part of her mind wondered if the Co-op had ever even thought about any kind of attack like this.

Before she could protest, he was out the door. She got up to follow him and realized that she must have twisted her ankle. Wincing in pain, she limped to the door and looked out. He was nowhere in sight.

She'd been in such a daze that she really had no idea where they had come from and the hallway stretched out like a funhouse maze. She looked back into Seth's room, wondering if she should just stay put. A cracking sound and dust falling from the ceiling decided for her.

Clio limped along the hallway, wishing the doors had windows so she could see inside. When she got to the end, she decided this was the most likely spot for a stairwell and opened the door. What she found inside was straight out of a horror movie. She stuffed a fist in her mouth to keep from screaming.

CHAPTER SIXTEEN

Thalia was spending more time in Ambrosia Springs lately and not loving that at all. She had stayed late after the meeting with Malsanto to work up some projections. While they had no plans to turn over a powerful splicing technique to their biggest competitor, she had an idea about how to satisfy their requests without giving them anything too dangerous. It was uphill work though and usually her sisters would stay to help instead of flitting off to go flirt with those geeks over at Omerta.

When handhelds started twittering emergency alerts all over the Floracopia, she viewed it as a welcome change of pace. But when she saw that unknown forces had attacked Omerta, she started to panic.

Bolting out the door, she used her handheld to shoot off messages on the town alert system that her mother and sisters were in the building. When she got to the roadblock, she would have raced through it if she thought her scooter could do it. The sheriff walked up and gripped her handlebars as if he knew what she was thinking.

"The Omerta people asked us to set up this roadblock. You can't go in. They say they'll shoot down anything that approaches their building until they are sure they won't be attacked again," he said quickly. He switched his grip to her arm, anxious to get her feet on the ground. "You can't go in yet. They will shoot you," he repeated firmly.

Several more cars and trucks screeched to a stop behind her. "My sisters are in there. My Mom is in there," Thalia said desperately.

"I know," he replied. "And the calmer we can keep things out here, the sooner we'll be able to go in and find them. So help me keep these people calm." She looked at him and realized he didn't know if they were safe or not.

Terpsi and her husband strode past them with huge guns, but were stopped by the policemen. She saw Jason blaze through the field next to the road in his truck. A police motorcycle raced after him. Making him see reason took four more officers.

"This is going to get out of hand," Thalia said to herself as she sat down in the dirt to watch the mayhem. Then she heard a muted explosion.

*****

Inside the building, Clio heard the explosion too. The building shook slightly, it didn't seem like it had been hit. Although it could be that this explosion seemed milder because she was down in the basement and not sitting right next to it. She would much rather be sitting next to a bomb than down in this basement filled with blood. Clio really couldn't believe the room she was in. She had walked around twice looking for some indication that this was an elaborate hoax.

Blood banks lined two of the walls, motors whirring gently to keep a vast amount of blood preserved. Medical equipment lined another wall, along with several cots. The cots were set up just like they are at blood drives, except these had thick leather straps along the armrests. She really didn't want to know what that was about. One of the cots had equipment strewn about and a thin line of fresh blood across the headrest. Clio looked around. Someone had rapidly left this room recently.

Try as she might, Clio could not think of a rational explanation for a room full of blood like this. She could understand having a sick bay in Omerta's embassy compound with some blood on hand for emergencies, but this was way beyond that. She remembered Seth joking about a medical condition. Even if everyone at Omerta needed daily transfusions, it wouldn't account for this much blood.

Further ponderings were thrown from her head when a macabre figure appeared from behind one of the blood banks. She wasn't really sure she was looking at a human. Two dark eyes peered out of an impossibly scarred and wizened face. It looked as though someone set an old man on fire, let him partially heal and then did it again. Like a train wreck, the figure was terrible and fascinating.

"Are you alright?" she asked, watching him stagger towards her, clutching his stomach. It was a fantastically stupid question. There's no way this person was even remotely all right. He looked disoriented, but seemed keenly interested in her. Clio reached out to help steady him. He turned to her and groaned loudly. She saw blood dried around his mouth.

Clio decided the best course of action was to get the hell out of there. As she slammed the door shut behind her, Seth appeared at the end of the hall.

"There you are," he cried with relief. He flashed a quick smile that melted off his face when he realized what room she was just in. Clio turned and ran.

She knew her ankle was sprained but that wasn't going to slow her down. Her only thought was to get far away from that room right now. She'd had too many surprises for one day and none of them had been the good kind.

"Clio, wait!" he cried. She could hear him chasing after her, so she ran faster. She wished now that she'd attended a few of those martial arts classes everyone had been going to lately. She resolved to start doing some kind of self-defense training first thing tomorrow if a horde of zombies in Seth's basement didn't eat her today.

The Omerta complex was a maze. She gasped for breath and sprinted towards a doorway, Seth still calling for her to stop. Something tackled her and she let loose a bloodcurdling scream. She kept on screaming as Max elbowed her a few times, but then she realized he was just trying to roll off her. Clio ran out of air and paused to suck in a breath. Her mother shook her hard before she could start screaming again.

"Pull it together," Harmony said sharply. She looked disappointed in her daughter. Clio looked around and saw Kalliope right behind them. She was so glad they were alive and uninjured that she almost forgot the importance of leaving immediately.

"You were about to go right back up to the bombsite," Max said, apologizing for tackling her. "It's not safe up there."

"It's not safe down here!" Clio blurted out as she scooted away from Max. She leapt to her feet and began pulling her mother and sister down the hall. "We have to get out of here!" she cried.

She tried to explain, but her garbled account involving rooms of blood and tortured monsters did not instill the proper sense of urgency in her audience. They were attempting to make her lie down and breathe slowly when Seth caught up to her.

"Did she hit her head?" Harmony asked him anxiously. Seth shook his head as he bent over and gasped for air.

"Then what is she going on about?" asked Kalliope looking deeply trouble by the sight of her sister freaking out.

"She met Uncle Hester in the treatment room," Seth said slowly, looking at Max. Understanding flashed across Max's face. It was rapidly chased away by a stormy expression.

Max bent over Clio. Very slowly and clearly, he said, "I know you saw something that frightened you, but you are in no danger now. Tell us what you saw."

Clio cleared her throat and began to explain. As she talked, Seth slid behind her and folded his arms around her. Kalliope moved to stop him, but Clio shook her head. When she was done, Max sat down on the floor and sighed.

"Max?" asked Harmony, working to keep her tone neutral. When he didn't deny what Clio had told them, she seemed to harden. "I think the girls and I should leave now. We can worry about what Clio saw another day. Right now this building is under attack and we need to get out."

Clio looked at her mother. She wondered if anything could shake her mother's poise, but really didn't want to be there when something finally did.

Max shook his head. "I know this may not be what you want to hear, but we can't leave right now. The building is in automatic lockdown until the threat is gone. We can't get out. That's why we didn't want Clio in the stairwell. She'd get stuck in there until Gloria lifts the lockdown. And you know Gloria." They all smiled tightly at that.

"She sent out an update," Seth said, holding up his handheld. "That second explosion was our defense system shooting down a moving target. It was five hundred feet from the building. Nothing else is coming towards us right now. She's processing satellite, infrared, anything she can find. She thinks the two attacks were it, but until she's sure we are still in lockdown."

"So, we are stuck here?" asked Kalliope.

"Even if we weren't, I would do everything in my power to convince you to stay. It is very safe here. Out there, who knows?" Max said sincerely.

"So what was in that room?" asked Clio. She stood up and gave Seth and Max a stubborn look. She had never had anyone question her word before and she did not like it at all.

"She saw our Uncle Hester," Max said slowly, looking at Harmony. "He is horribly scarred, maimed and very old. He suffers from a rare disorder that we call Z-Factor Deficiency. It is like porphyria. He is missing certain enzymes required to correctly process hemoglobin. That's the stuff in red blood cells that transports oxygen. He requires blood transfusions to survive."

Max waited for a minute, but no one spoke so he continued. "Because of his condition, he is very sensitive to sunlight. The scars you saw were the result of exposure to direct sunlight for several hours on multiple occasions. So if he appeared confused and disoriented, it was because he is in a lot of pain right now and the explosion interrupted his treatment."

Kalliope pushed her sister. "Insensitive clod," she said. "You ran like a sissy and scared the crap out of some poor, sick old man."

Clio opened her mouth to protest. "If you were there in a room full of blood, you'd think differently. There's no logical reason for a room like that."

"Actually there is," said Seth quietly. "The Z-Factor Deficiency runs in our family. The Omerta family. One of the reasons we established the embassy here was because there is a blood bank close by that is willing to sell us the quantities we need to supply the ZFD sufferers back home."

Clio looked at him for a long moment until the puzzle pieces fell into place. "You have it. You have this Z-Factor Deficiency."

Seth nodded. "I think you can understand why we try to keep this condition a secret."

Clio couldn't believe that her initial reaction to someone with a debilitating disease was to run screaming like some sort of bigoted medieval peasant. If she had thrown stones and screamed witch, she couldn't have acted any more stupidly. She felt awful.

"I'm sorry," she said, taking his hand. He held her eyes and, for once, she knew he understood what she wanted to say.

"Z-Factor Deficiency? What does that mean? That sounds like something off a cut-rate science fiction show," Harmony said. The scientist in her was having a hard time with this.

Max shrugged. "That's what we call it. It's not in any medical journals. Because it's so rare and we've worked to keep it secret, there's no medical research. We're not even really sure it's a porphyria. We just know that if the victims go outside, they fry. And if they don't get blood transfusions every other week, they die. They die horribly and painfully. It's not pretty."

"Can I see your treatment facility?" she asked briskly.

Clio looked up from cuddling on the floor with Seth. "Maybe we should just wait for the lockdown to end someplace safe," she suggested. She really didn't want to go back to that room.

"Nonsense. Might as well use this time productively," her mother replied and began walking in the right direction.

"I don't understand why Omerta needs to cultivate blood supplies all the way down in Texas. Synth blood is freely available and much easier to maintain and ship," she said to Max as Kalliope followed in her wake. After a brief murmured exchange, Seth and Clio trailed behind them.

"Synth blood doesn't work. It has to be whole human blood. Most of us with ZFD require about 250 ml of whole blood every two weeks starting at puberty," Seth called out to her.

Harmony stopped and turned to him in disbelief. "Really? That much? But that amount requires two human donors giving blood regularly. Given the short shelf life of blood and all the other factors, I can see how this would be a very rare disease indeed." This was a nice way of saying that she couldn't understand how anyone, much less a whole family, could survive with this disease.

"Why doesn't synth blood work?" asked Kalliope.

"Again, we don't really know," replied Max. "We've tried. But the only thing that works is whole human blood. We can't even get by with plasma donors."

"You ought to put it up for inclusion on the list of acceptable human gene mods," Clio said. "Then we could work on a cure."

"Sometimes we talk about it," Max replied after a pause. "But most of the victims would prefer to keep it private. And it would take years to get it approved and even longer before there was hope of a cure. We'd be so far down on the list and you know how it is with a really rare case. Nobody would bother even if we paid huge sums of money."

"The UN Gene Council is very slow to add anything new to the list of acceptable human splices," Harmony agreed. "It's one of the reasons Floracopia tends to stay away from medical gene mods. There's just too much red tape."

They reached the room and Max opened the door. "Please wait here for a minute," he asked, holding a hand up. "Uncle Hester has had a very upsetting day and I want to get him calmed down before I introduce him to anyone. He doesn't see that many people."

While they waited outside, Harmony continued to quiz Seth. "How does ZFD manifest?"

"Usually it starts in puberty," he replied carefully. Clio could tell he was having a hard time talking about this. "For the most part it is passed genetically, but there have been occasional cases where the disease was passed through bodily fluids. That's extremely rare, though. When the disease begins, the victim begins to waste away, experiencing horrible stomach cramps and joint pain. Unless they are born into a family familiar with the disease or they get really lucky, they die quickly. With regular transfusions they can lead an almost normal life, but like I say, it has to be whole live blood."

"Interesting," Harmony replied. "What are some of the other side effects beside the photosensitivity?"

Seth hesitated a very long time. Clio nudged him a little before he said, "There can be dental deformities. Longevity is affected."

"That makes sense," Harmony replied. "Any disease that affects the skin will affect the teeth. And, of course, people requiring daily transfusions won't live as long as healthy adults."

Max opened the door and motioned them in. "This is Uncle Hester." He held the old man's hand and beamed at him encouragingly. The old man looked at the women anxiously. "He doesn't speak much English," Max said. "He's pretty embarrassed about running into you earlier and how he acted. You scared him, popping out like that."

Clio was mortified. "I'm so sorry," she told the old man. He smiled at her tentatively.

Kalliope prowled the room, looking at all the equipment and blood banks while Harmony gently examined the old man with ill-concealed fascination. Clio sat down next to Seth.

"You really need all this blood?" Kalliope asked. She was having trouble with the sheer scale of the thing.

"Most of it is shipped back to Queen Charlotte's Island," replied Max. "These large refrigerators are specially designed to preserve the blood as long as possible. Since people with ZFD die horribly without regular transfusions, we try to maintain a large back-up supply."

"How many people with ZFD does Omerta have?" she asked, still unwilling to believe the necessity of so much blood.

"Look here at this cooling system," Max said, by way of a reply. "I bet you could design something even more efficient." Kalliope's eyebrows shot up, but she allowed herself to be distracted by the inner workings of the blood bank.

"Any more news about what's going on upstairs?" Clio asked Seth as he tapped away on his handheld.

"Yeah," he replied. "We are almost out of lockdown. Gloria has confirmed that the two attacks are the only threat right now and they have both been contained. Apparently, it was two old trucks filled with your basic gasoline and fertilizer bomb and tricked out with a remote control. There's no clue yet as to who did this or why, but we are working with the local police to examine the wreckage and search the area for whoever was controlling the trucks."

"Great," she said. Seth avoided looking at her. As part of her new resolve to be better at communicating, she asked, "What's wrong?"

"Oh, you know," replied Seth, running a hand through his hair and then gesturing about him vaguely. "Everything."

After a short pause, he continued. "I didn't want to spring all this stuff about my condition on you. Terrorists tried to blow up my house. You were out with that guy last night."

"That's like three days of conversations in three sentences,"

Clio replied, trying to figure out what to say. "Which should we talk about first?"

Seth just shrugged and slumped against a wall. Clio took the initiative. "So you have a disease. Big deal. Before they cured diabetes, people had to give themselves injections and monitor their blood sugar constantly. That sounds like way more of a hassle than your thing. Transfusions every couple of weeks and you can't go out in the sun? It could be worse. ZFD, did you call it? What a funny name."

A smile tugged at the corners of Seth's mouth. "I always thought so too, but the Omerta Board came up with that name and they aren't so great at taking criticism. Z-Factor Deficiency. Sounds like something out of a comic book." They smiled at each other and Clio felt that maybe everything would turn out all right after all.

"From what you are describing, it sounds like it would be a fairly straightforward splice to fix this condition. You really ought to urge your Board of Directors to put this disease up for human gene mod list," Harmony said to Max as she probed Uncle Hester's shoulder joint.

"I will try, but they are very resistant to that idea," he replied. "Possibly if I tell them that Floracopia is willing to begin work, they will embrace the idea."

Harmony shook her head. "You would be much better served by a company that solely focuses on medical splicing. We really aren't set up for that. And we have a long list of vital projects. I would love to work on this, but we aren't the best for the job. And you deserve the best."

"Thank you for your refusal," Max said with a crooked smile. He stepped towards Harmony as though he would touch her. Seth watched him, waiting for the joke that inevitably came out of his uncle, but Max just stood there looking into Harmony's eyes.

"Yes, well, sorry," said Harmony briskly as she turned back to Uncle Hester. Now she began examining his eyes. The old man seemed to enjoy the attention, even if it consisted of impersonal poking and prodding. Over her shoulder she said, "I am really curious to know why synthetic blood won't work. Modifying synthetic blood for this condition *is* a project Floracopia could work on."

Max raised an eyebrow. "Really? That would be quite wonderful."

"We could?" Kalliope asked, giving her mother a quizzical glance. Harmony attempted to look in Uncle Hester's mouth, but here the old man pulled away. Harmony turned to Max. He shook his head but didn't explain.

"Seth said the disease causes dental deformities," Clio whispered to her mother. Probably why the old man is embarrassed to have someone look in his mouth, she thought. Clio didn't say that, though. She thought it would be rude.

Harmony looked even more interested as Uncle Hester edged away from her. "We may not be able to find a solution, but technically we could work on synth blood without having to obtain permission from the UN Gene Council. It's not human tissue," Harmony cautioned as Max did a little jig. "And it would still be a backburner project. We have starving people waiting for crops. We have to finish those splices first."

Max reached over and hugged Harmony who looked uncomfortable with human interaction but not displeased.

Seth looked at Clio. "I never thought about that. Most of your work involves splicing food for starving people all over the world."

She shrugged. "That's why it's so hard to go home at the end of the day. How can I sleep when people are dying for me to finish?"

Seth squeezed her hand. "That is a good reason for all that time you spend at work."

"Mother? Isn't that kind of a gray area? Legally?" Kalliope interjected doubtfully. "I mean, while we aren't disobeying the letter of the law, the spirit of it seems to suggest we ought to at least notify the UN Gene Council."

Harmony was patting her hair and smoothing her jacket after Max's hug. "It should be fine. If we can't wander into gray areas for our friends, then what's the point of running our own splicer shop?" she asked. She looked a little flushed.

It was the most rebellious thing they'd ever heard their mother say. So of course the girls were on board.

Turning to Max, Harmony said, "We will need samples—blood, skin, etc. Can you work on that?" He nodded enthusiastically.

"Gloria sent out another update," cut in Seth. "It looks like she is ending lockdown. They don't think anything else aimed at us. The evidence points to attack by the local terrorists."

Everyone cheered.

CHAPTER SEVENTEEN

"I should stay here with Uncle Hester until the nurse returns," Max said. They said their goodbyes and began heading towards the exits. Harmony walked ahead and was outside before the other three even reached the stairs.

"Why would these Texas terrorists what to bomb us?" Seth asked his voice heavy with rage. "I don't understand it. But I will. I will leave no particle of information out of my search for these terrorists. I will explore every byte of data ever committed to digital memory and I will find them."

"I doubt it was the terrorists. Probably someone else just making the attack look like the terrorists," Clio replied quickly.

"It's possible I suppose, but why would someone do that?" he asked as they reached the doors, his voice heavy with righteous indignation. "The simplest explanation is usually the correct one. But they made a mistake targeting us. I will root out these terrorists and make sure they can never attack people like this again."

"Still, you ought to seriously consider that whoever did this wants you to blame the terrorists," Clio said in a soothing voice. "Besides, if the US government can't find them, you probably won't be able to either."

Seth drew himself up. "I have resources the US government can only dream about," he declared. "I hacked into their satellite system six months ago and redirected their satellites so they don't fly over Ambrosia Springs any more. They still haven't even noticed. I can redirect India's defense system to shoot their nukes at anyone in the world. I can find these little terrorists and make them sorry they were ever born."

"Look, I'm telling you that it wasn't the terrorists," replied Clio, losing patience. "It was someone else. So don't go redirecting nukes at anyone until you figure that out."

"How would you know?" he laughed.

Clio was about to reply when Kalliope tripped her deliberately. Seth caught it out of the corner of his eye. Clio got up and yelled at her sister a bit while Seth frowned at them suspiciously.

"How would you know?" he asked, more seriously this time.

Clio looked at her feet. "I just know, alright? Let it go."

Seth gave her a hard look. "Are you in communication with these terrorists?"

Clio shrugged stubbornly. "The government calls them terrorists but they think of themselves as resistance fighters," she replied.

"Clio!" he cried, thoroughly scandalized. How could she risk herself like this? "What they think is not the point. You cannot have anything to do with these people. It is too dangerous."

"Your views on my friends do not concern me," she said mutinously.

Seth could almost hear his heart breaking when she said that. He tried to push his personal feelings aside and focus on the main issue here. He had to keep her safe. She was too important. After thinking for a minute, he countered, "I am in charge of Floracopia's security. How can I keep your business and your family safe if you associate with criminals?"

"Since when do you care whom I associate with?" she shot back.

"How can you ask that?" he replied, holding a hand to his forehead. "My head is still pounding from the bottle of tequila I drank last night after seeing you with that big oaf, Jason. If you won't spend time with me, I wish you would just stay in your lab where I know you are safe."

Clio wavered.

"You can trust me," he said lightly. Clio turned to him and her expression melted.

"No, she can't," said Kalliope, interrupting what was about to be a very tender scene. They both turned to look at her with shock. Seth had forgotten she was there.

"You guys were lying back there. I'm not totally sure about what, but I know you were lying," Kalliope continued, eyeing him beadily. "Max didn't answer when I asked him how many people have ZFD and you evaded Mom's question about the symptoms and side effects. What are you hiding?"

Seth was taken aback and floundered for an answer. While he groped for an answer, Kalliope grabbed her sister's hand and marched up the stairs.

"You be straight with us and we'll be straight with you. But for now, leave the terrorists alone," Kalliope called over her shoulder. "Come on, Clio. I'm betting there's a whole lot of people upstairs we need to talk to."

"Kalli, what the heck?" asked Clio.

"This is all too weird," Kalliope replied, dragging her through the rubble to the crowd waiting for them in the whirling lights of the police cars. "Tonight we should get out of here. Go home and think about all this. Don't make any decisions tonight."

Seth watched them go, standing in the shadows. Well-meaning friends and family surrounded Clio and Kalliope, hugging them tight. That was probably for the best. She should be with people who cared for her. He saw Jason appear in the crowd and wrap Clio in one of those blankets that they always seem to have so many of at emergency sites.

His chest tightened and he made himself unclench his jaw. Clio pulled away from Jason and turned to look for him, but Seth stepped deeper into the shadows. When she couldn't find him, he saw sadness pass over her face. Eventually she allowed Jason to lead her away.

Seth planned to linger in the shadows, feeling sorry for himself, but within minutes four joyfully yapping Pomeranians surrounded him. They were so proud that they found him. In their growling and stilted language, they gleefully boasted of their adventures through the rubble and insisted he reward them with liver treats immediately.

He sighed and patted his pockets, wishing they liked something less smelly. Then they announced that the other two dogs in Team Pom had captured a suspicious person in the woods with a funny box. *This could be the person controlling the truck bombs,* he thought. Quickly, Seth followed them into the brush.

It turned out to be that DARPA flunky, Stuart Littleman.

"What the hell is wrong with you?" asked Seth as he rummaged through the box of surveillance equipment Stuart had with him. Stuart moved to stop him and got his hand nipped by a Pomeranian.

"I don't think the guy with vicious fluffballs should be casting aspersions on the pastimes of others. One of your guard dogs just piddled on my socks," sniffed Stuart, brushing dirt off his black ops uniform. It was made of that camouflage that projects the scene behind it. Even this close, Seth would have had a hard time finding Stuart if the Poms hadn't helpfully chewed holes in the fabric.

Seth didn't find anything in the box that would defeat the Omerta security system. "So DARPA is behind the bombing tonight?" Seth asked, seething.

"No! Are you kidding me?" cried Stuart. He looked more offended by the suggestion than anything else. "If we'd bombed your building, it would have stayed bombed. We wouldn't have just dented a corner like these amateurs."

"So what are you doing out here then?" asked Seth.

Stuart shrugged. "My job. Keeping an eye on you guys."

"You expect me to believe that?" replied Seth. He made a brief hand gesture and Team Pom advanced on Stuart, growling and slavering.

That seemed to shake Stuart's confidence. "It's true! Look, you guys have the coolest tech around. What better way to test our equipment than to try breaking into yours? I've been out here a dozen times just beyond your surveillance limits."

"This is not convincing me to let you go," Seth said. He was just so tired. He really didn't want to deal with this guy tonight.

"If it makes you feel better, nothing works. So far." Stuart said grudgingly.

It did make him feel better, but what was he supposed to do with this guy? Was he supposed to capture him and torture him? Make him spill his secrets. Kill him and hide the body so Stuart couldn't pass on his knowledge of Omerta and Team Pom? It all seemed so dire.

"You don't know the pressure we are under at DARPA. They don't take failure calmly," Stuart whined. "If I don't come up with something for them, the military will skin me alive. And that's a best case scenario."

"Did you see who did this, at least?" asked Seth.

"Unfortunately, no. I tried, though," said Stuart, shaking his head. "The trucks were remote controlled and came from pretty far off. Probably someone controlling them with satellite, but it happened too fast for me to track the signal."

Seth sighed deeply. He was pretty sure that if he had been out here casing someone else's compound, he would have been able to lock on the signal off the bomb truck.

"God, you depress me," Seth said as he turned and whistled to Team Pom. They fell in line behind him, but they barked at Stuart as they left. They wanted him to know he got off easy.

"You are going to let me go?" asked Stuart, scrabbling to his feet.

"I am too busy to deal with you tonight," replied Seth as he stalked off.

CHAPTER EIGHTEEN

For the next few weeks, Seth only saw Clio at the weekly martial arts classes. So much had happened during the bombing of Omerta and its aftermath. But Seth hadn't called Clio. He felt Clio was better off without him there to complicate her life.

Seth felt too weird, too damaged to try to pursue her and what could he say after the bizarre bombing experience? When she didn't call him, he took that as confirmation that she wanted nothing more to do with him after that night.

These altruistic ideas did not stop him from bitterly downing enough alcohol to put an elephant into a stupor. It got so bad even Max told him to cut back. Seth didn't, but he threw himself into his work so no one could say he wasn't meeting his responsibilities. And if he occasionally redirected a satellite to pass over Clio's house? He told himself that he was just checking up on her and no one would be the wiser.

At first, they did no more than glance at each other longingly during class. Seth told himself to stop being foolish. She was watching him because he scared and confused her. Then, after a few weeks, she tentatively asked him about a move they learned that day. He was so happy that she spoke to him that he almost started dancing. Catching himself in time, he calmly explained it to her and then left quickly.

Over the next few weeks, they began chatting after each lesson. They kept their conversation strictly neutral, never straying on to certain topics. It was only a little awkward. Seth told himself this was enough. They could be friends. At least he'd still be able to enjoy her company. It was for the best that they don't get involved. Too complicated for everyone. This was enough.

The conversations grew longer and longer until one night, they were standing in the parking lot alone for an hour after class. Finally, he couldn't take it any more. "Would you like to have dinner with me tonight?" he blurted out.

Clio smiled wistfully and looked at her shoes.

"A nice boring date," Seth coaxed. Inside he was kicking himself. Things had been going so well and he'd screwed it up. But he couldn't seem to stop. "We'll have dinner and watch a movie. No monsters or crazy uncles or explosions. I'll bring boring food and a boring movie even."

Clio laughed. "Wow, how appealing. And what will we do when we get bored of the movie and the bland food?"

Oh, god. She thought he was trying to convince her to have a one-night stand. Seth was mortified. "Well, we could always just talk. We have so much to talk about," he floundered.

Clio nodded, the smile fading off her face. "You are right. We really should talk."

Seth sometimes wished conversations did not happen so rapidly. He really much preferred chatting digitally where he could collect his thoughts and take bathroom breaks during conversations. Now somehow he had invited her out to talk about all that stuff that they had been avoiding for months. There was no way he wanted to do that.

"Fine," she said at last. "Good. Great. Why don't we have dinner at my house? Can you pick something up and meet me? I want to get a shower first."

Seth agreed and sped off in his hovercar. When she was out of sight, he laughed triumphantly and turned up the music. He had a date with Clio. He sang at the top of his lungs all the way back to the Omerta compound.

He arrived at her house later with bags of food and the pack of Pomeranians. She laughed when she saw them.

"If I try to leave without them, they follow me. Or they sneak into my car. It's easier to just give them a lift," he said with a crooked smile. He watched the dogs hop off the porch, fan out, and disappear. They could hide in the tiniest of cracks.

"How is their language working out?" she asked as she poured them beers and began unpacking the food. She flashed him an approving grin when she saw that he had picked up barbeque and a strawberry pie from Bessie's.

He was glad she approved. "Pretty good. I'm getting the hang of their speech patterns. I've been walking with them in the woods around our building at night. Sometimes I feel like an early American explorer out of one of those cheesy old movies. The ones where the natives say things like '*How white man? Me name Tonto.*' That's how the dogs talk."

They ate and chatted companionably, gently bickering over what movie they should watch. They kept discarding movies as being too interesting for their boring date.

"Oh, I almost forgot," said Seth after they had eaten and were washing up the dishes. He ran out to his car and returned with a bottle. "I brought over this bottle of tequila. A client in Austin sent it to me after we set up some systems for him. Want to try it?" He passed her the bottle.

"Oh my God, Seth. This is pure blue agave tequila from before The Troubles." She gasped and held the bottle up like it was the Holy Grail.

"Oh really? Is that good?" he asked with interest.

"Good? Are you kidding? We mere mortals are not fit to be in the same room with this bottle. The blue agaves all died in The Troubles," she said, staring at the bottle in a reverie. "What we make tequila with now is the closest we could get, but this right here is the real thing. I didn't think there were any more bottles of this stuff left in the whole world."

"Awesome," Seth said, pulling out some glasses. "Lime and salt, you think? Or should we just sip it straight?"

"We can't drink this. It would be like drinking 'The Mona Lisa,' or something," Clio was scandalized.

"Why not? That's what it's for and I find myself with a powerful thirst," Seth replied, handing her a glass.

"You make a fine point. I'll get the lime," she said, rushing outside to grab limes off the tree in her yard.

They sat down and slowly sipped the tequila. Clio's eyes rolled back in her head. Seth let out a long slow breath.

"They should serve this stuff with a fire extinguisher," he said.

"That's the end of our boring date," Clio laughed. Seth looked at her with alarm. "No, I am not even remotely suggesting you leave. It's just that there's no way it will be boring anymore." Clio threw the bottle cap out a window.

Chronologically, only a few hours had passed, but for Seth and Clio it had been an epoch. The living room was strewn with pillows and socks. The kitchen was covered in globs of pie. Water dripped from the curtains and a washcloth was stuck to the ceiling. A boring movie played on the wallscreen, forgotten. They lay in each other's arms in Clio's front yard, staring at the spinning stars.

"I think I still have pie in my hair," slurred Clio sleepily.

"*Mmmm*, you smell good enough to eat," murmured Seth kissing the top of her head. He thought perhaps they should move inside before they fell asleep out here, but that would involve effort and he couldn't be bothered right now.

"Could you really redirect India's nukes?" she asked.

He almost giggled, but then decided that giggling was not manly. "Oh sure. India's are the easiest. There's practically no security on those things. Most security systems can't keep out anyone who really wants to get in. Except mine, of course. Most security systems are like a huge padlock on a flimsy door. You want to break in? All you have to do is bring a screwdriver and take off the hinges. If someone really wants to get in, they can usually find a way. No, the best security systems usually involve some misdirection."

"That's scary," she replied with sleep in her voice.

He shrugged slightly so as not to disrupt her head on his shoulder. "We have to protect ourselves. Omerta is a tiny country with no military. So we poke around in other people's systems to make sure no one is planning on bothering us. And we make sure we can borrow some weapons if we get in a jam. It's only theoretical. Plus, I get really bored in my office."

She laughed. "You get bored at work so you hack into India's missile defense system? Wow. And they complain about my experiments. What's a few ninja Pomeranians next to reshuffling the satellite network?"

He grinned with pride, but really didn't want to talk now. He wanted to smooch Clio and lie under the stars. She smiled at him and laid her head down on his shoulder.

"I'm not dating Jason, you know. Well, I did, but that was years ago. No interest in repeating that experiment. The results were conclusive," she said into his chest. "Not dating anyone."

Inside he did a little happy dance. He hadn't wanted to ruin the magic of the night by asking about Jason. "You are dating me," he replied, nuzzling her neck.

"I am?" she said with a smile in her voice.

"Oh yes, you definitely are." He playfully nipped at the nape of her neck.

"Well, alright."

A little while later, they paused for breath and Seth asked, "Then what were you doing with him that night at the football game?"

"What? Oh that. We are working on a little project," she replied.

"What kind of project?" he asked idly. Some sort of charity work, he thought. That Jason really wasn't such a bad guy. Just a bit too touchy-feely, Seth decided generously.

"It's a secret," she giggled.

"Oh come on."

"No really," she said more clearly. "I can't tell."

"Have some more tequila."

"Okay."

They happily discovered that the bottle, which Clio insisted she would enshrine above her kitchen sink, still had a few more drinks in it. Seth experienced a brief and unlikely moment of clarity.

"Wait a minute. Are you working with Jason on a project for that terrorist group?" He realized that he still hadn't gotten around to discussing her connection to that group. How dare that jerk Jason involve her with dangerous criminals?

"Resistance fighters," she corrected. She drew herself up and pointed an accusing finger at him. She staggered a bit as she did this, ruining the effect. "You can't deny that someone needs to resist the government. It's barbaric the way the US treats its citizens. Somebody needs to do something. Might as well be me."

"I don't deny that things cannot continue the way they are, but not you," he pleaded. "Anybody but you. You could get hurt. You could get arrested. Let the politicians and the government work this out. You need to stay safe."

Clio shook her head sleepily. "If you want something done right, you have to do it yourself. It's worth a little risk," she said, absently picking grass out of her hair.

"You can accomplish these things without risk. I did," he countered triumphantly. "I wrote a script that hacks into the US government, pulls out the names of all the foreign nationals they have kidnapped, and let's their governments know where they are being held and how they are doing. Now the US takes fewer people because they know that they can't do it secretly. Lots of change for very little risk." Seth watched Clio's eyes go round as her mouth formed an 'O.' He had obviously made his point. Perhaps they could get back to the kissing soon.

"You did that? I always wondered who was behind that. Pure genius. That was really you?" she asked breathlessly. "All by yourself?"

Under the force of her gaze, Seth was powerless to resist the urge to brag. "Well, most of it. Max helped a little although he made me swear never to tell."

"You are a resistance fighter too," she declared, hugging him happily.

"What? Me? Oh no. Just patching a faulty system. What use would a resistance movement have for a guy like me anyway?" he said modestly, hugging her back and running his hands through her thick hair. He was pretty sure they were headed in a more hormonal direction soon.

"Are you joking?" she cried, pulling him up off the grass and into the house. Seth complied happily. "The Resistance desperately needs a guy like you. Come see what you've already done."

When they got into the house, Seth tried to start kissing her again, but she pushed him away and began fumbling with her handheld. "Just a second, sweetie, I want to show you this."

Seth did not wish to appear overly anxious, but by his calculations, they were very close to her bedroom right now. That knowledge was driving all coherent thought out of his head. He sat down and watched her. She turned on a little box that he recognized as a scrambler. He had hardwired scramblers into the wall at Omerta, but why would she think she needed to block spyware right now?

After a few muted curses, the wallscreen flickered on. "Look," she declared.

"It's your Revolution World game," he said, confused.

"No, it's my terrorist cell," she said with a flourish. "We've used your in-game security function to organize a resistance movement."

Seth frowned through the haze of hormones and alcohol that had been so thick all evening, trying to concentrate on what she just said. She couldn't possibly mean what it sounded like. Clio entered the game. The wall screen showed a little room that used every security feature he had built into the game.

The game balked at the virtual door sensing Seth in the real life room, but Seth gave his override access code and it let them both in. He nodded approvingly. The game would not have let her access to this room with someone sitting next to her that wasn't allowed. He was glad that feature worked, but also glad he had the override code. That didn't stop the sinking sense of impending doom.

"See? We started with just a little extra security so we could gripe about the government without worrying who was listening. Then we got organized," she was telling him. "First, it was just funny to start rumors about a Texas terrorist group that was targeting government buildings and foreign businesses. You know, 'Yankees go home.' That kind of thing. Then we thought it wasn't such a bad idea. We'd get rid of all the carpetbaggers by encouraging them to move away someplace safer."

"You are using a game called Revolution World to plan a revolution," he said with disbelief.

He waited for her to tell him not to be silly. The whole thing was ludicrous. She laughed and he slumped back with relief.

"Oh, not a revolution," she said. "No, that would require the whole state to be in on it, the Texas legislature, the governor and just everybody. Even then, I don't think a revolution would be possible. No, we are just aiming to be a vocal minority for change."

That was not at all what he had been hoping to hear. "You bomb people? You take part in terrorist bombings?" he thought maybe his voiced cracked a little there.

"We don't really," she beamed at him. "That's the beauty of it. Usually someone has a building they wanted to demolish anyway, so we blow it. Or else we blow up a truck in someone's parking lot and say the terrorists were demonstrating their hatred of some business or another. There's this group of guys that specializes in faking 'terrorists accidents.' So that it looks like they made a mistake and the bomb didn't go off. You'd be surprised how well that works."

"That's great," he said in a strangled voice. "So you've never hurt anyone?" She nodded, pleased that he'd grasped that.

"Wait a second," he suddenly had a thought. "The Texas terrorists kidnap people all the time. Is that you guys? Why would you do that?"

She opened her mouth and then stopped. She gave him a hard look. "I'm telling you things that could get me and a whole bunch of nice people killed."

"I know," he said, totally overwhelmed.

"Do you ever get the feeling that you are locked into some crazy destiny? And no matter what you do, you can't escape where fate is taking you?" Clio asked him.

"Yeah," Seth replied. "I've felt that way ever since the Board of Directors mentioned scouting Texas. Like I've just got to be here in the thick of all this stuff. I don't seem to have a choice in the matter."

"And we are getting washed away by events that are greater than us," replied Clio.

She sat next to him on the couch and they stared at the wall, both feeling the tingling joy of inebriation drain away.

"Why can't we have a boring date?" Clio asked the wall plaintively.

Seth threw his head back and laughed. As he did it, he realized he had never performed that specific action before. A hopeful smile played at her lips while she toyed with the almost empty bottle of tequila. Well, he thought, change can be good.

"I suspect boring is impossible when we are in same room," he mused. He took the tequila bottle and tossed what was left in it straight down his throat.

"Ok, I'm in. Sign me up for a heaping helping of resistance fighting," he said after the tequila stopped burning his throat. "Do you want me to swear a blood oath or something? Or hey, I bet I could write a blood oath script into the game." He paused to consider that.

Clio let out a squeal and launched herself at him. After thoroughly smothering him in kisses to which he did not object, she sat up. "Are you sure?"

He was really sure he wanted nothing to do with all this, but if the line was to be drawn in the sand, then he wanted to be standing on the same side as Clio. And this way he could keep an eye on her. He gave her the most confident grin he could muster up and nodded.

There was more squealing and more smooching. After a bit, Seth insisted on full details of Clio's resistance group.

"Well, the thing you see the most is the 'Terrorist attacks,' but much of our time is spent spreading disinformation about the conditions in Texas," she said as she proposed Seth's inclusion to the group. He raised an eyebrow.

"Actually I guess I don't really have to submit your name for approval,' she said. "Since you made the system, you can probably set that up yourself."

He nodded. "Yes, but it's better to go through the normal route. We don't want any of your terrorist buddies to get twitchy trigger fingers."

"Good point," she countered. "Anyway, we do things like alter geological surveys of water or other natural resources to make it look like we have less than we do. For example, we alter records to make it look like a mine was depleted when it's not. Things like that. If the government doesn't think you have anything, they won't try to take it away from you."

Seth scratched his head. What she said implied a fairly large conspiracy with people placed inside several government bureaucracies.

"We've also been reporting huge increases in crime and poverty, but it's all fake," she continued as she idly played through a skirmish in Revolution World. "We want the rest of the world to think Texas is a worthless cesspit. We want them to leave us alone. So we make it as unpleasant as possible to come here. Remember how they treated you when you and Max came to survey sites? Our plan almost worked too well that day." She grinned at him impishly and squeezed his hand.

"Local government offices have always found ways to hide

money they need from the nationals, but now we are ramping up big time," Clio continued. "The national government wouldn't give us enough for police and fire stations so there's a whole group of accountants juggling the books so that we look broke, but we have what we need."

Seth shook his head. "How is it possible for your group to accomplish all that? You'd need top hackers working night and day."

"Well, we've been at this almost six years now," she said with a shrug. "It started as small acts of rebellion. Myrna at the county office spills a drink all over the server that stores all the mineral rights data and then makes sure that the new data doesn't contain any information about oil deposits or water reserves."

"I see. It sounds like you are trying to keep the government from arresting people with the kind of money or resources that might attract their attention," he replied. "That's kind of a roundabout way to do it."

"We have more direct methods. We operate an underground railroad for people trying to escape military detention or flee the country. That's our 'terrorist kidnappings.' They've been taking up quite a bit of our time and money the last two years. The government is totally out of control with these arrests," her voice rose.

Seth stared out a window as he turned it over in his mind. It really was astounding how quickly you adapted after you found yourself down a rabbit hole with mad hatters and tea parties.

He was impressed at how much they had done and terrified at how swift the US government's vengeance would be if they ever found out. He doubted being a foreign citizen would slow their hand even in the slightest. "You really need my help."

"Oh God, yes," Clio replied. "We need so much help."

"I don't think it's a good idea to involve Omerta," he said at last. "But I think Max might like to join. If your family is involved, he'll want to play rebel too."

"Not all of them are," she cautioned. "We don't involve Terpsi because she's got the kids and the town needs its doctor. And my Mom has refused to even hear anything to do with it."

"Really? This sounds like the sort of thing you mother would be running. It's so organized," Seth replied, typing in some calculations into his handheld. He was already planning out some possible applications.

Clio took his comment as a compliment. "Well, we try to be organized. After we lost a few people to the prisons, we were pretty motivated to save as many as we could."

"You really need to think about defense. By which I mean weapons," he said, pointing out the glaring hole in their plan.

"Oh we do," she replied. "Jason is on that committee. He thinks it's hilarious that they keep sending money and weapons down to help us control the 'Terrorist Threat.' All the guns and ammo go right out of the government warehouses into our hidden safe houses. It's a lot easier to be a terrorist when you get all your bombs from the military for free."

Seth snorted. He would have laughed, but he still wasn't ready to like Jason.

"That group started before the resistance group did, really." Clio bustled around, cleaning up the evidence of their earlier tequila-tinged antics. Seth watched her sadly. Someday, he would get to just spend a quiet evening at home with her. But not tonight, apparently.

Clio explained, "They got worried that with all the wars the US was fighting abroad and all the ill will our foreign policies were creating, the US was making itself a huge target for foreign attack. And they didn't have to look around too hard before realizing that the US wouldn't be able to protect Texas if that happened. So they started doing it themselves."

"How? Local militias would be one way I guess, but that would be pretty obvious," Seth said.

"Not if the local militias are just rednecks playing a stupid computer game," she grinned. "And they have other irons in the fire. I don't know what all, but they have plans." She answered the next question she could see forming on his lips.

He blew out a slow breath. "This has been an overwhelming evening."

Clio sat next to him and held his hand. "I know. I'm sorry. I wish things were easier."

He pulled her into his arms. "I'll take what I can get."

Clio made a happy noise. "So you still want to date?"

"Are you kidding? Hell yes, I want to date. I'm now a member of a vast conspiracy to undermine the government. Without love, I'll turn into an alcoholic for sure."

She gave him a steamy look. "Well, we can't have that."

CHAPTER NINETEEN

The senator was already waiting when the governor arrived at the Elephant Room. He waved him over to a different table than their usual.

"Does that not look like the shiftiest little weasel you ever saw?" the senator growled as soon as the governor had turned on his scrambler. He pointed to a man slumped in their usual booth. He was a singularly unimpressive specimen.

"He's probably just depressed about this current attempt by our totalitarian regime to destroy all that is good about America. I know I am," replied the governor, dismissing the unfamiliar man with a wave of his hand.

"What's got you in a snit?" asked the senator, pushing a beer into his hand.

"Oh, not much. Just the federal government trying to requisition the Texas oil reserves," the governor said after a healthy gulp.

"They've been doing that forever," the senator said.

"No, not stealing from private citizens. They want our public oil reserves. The ones we use to fund the university system," the governor said. He just barely stopped himself from bellowing. Only the look of horror on the senator's face kept him leaping up and pacing about. "Did you turn off your handheld or something? It went out two hours ago."

The senator dove into his coat pockets and pulled out his handheld. "Are you sure?"

"Of course I'm sure. They are probably trying to keep Senate and Congress from finding out until it's too late to do anything about it," the governor replied darkly. "They can't think they will get away with this."

"How will we fund the universities?" asked the senator,

bewildered. "This can't be right. They wouldn't do that. The right to our public lands and mineral rights is the basis of our membership in the United States at all. It was in our annexation agreement back in 1845. Texas retains all rights to public lands. That includes mineral rights. They can't try to take that away."

"This isn't the time for a history lesson, Joe. We need solutions and we need them now," cried the governor.

"Screw the beer, I need something stronger." The senator suddenly looked like the old man that he was. "How did it come to this? How can we protect ourselves?"

"I have some ideas," replied the governor. As they mapped out their plans on bar napkins, Shiva and Medea entered the bar. They made straight for the unimpressive man sitting at the governor's normal table.

"Why don't you have the information for us yet?" Shiva hissed at him.

The man looked startled and began to shift away from her as though she were a poisonous insect.

"What are you doing here? I can't be seen with you," he replied as Shiva slid into the booth with a shark smile. He looked around quickly, and then asked in a low voice. "Are you people crazy? When I said to create a distraction so we could break into the lab again, I did not mean blow up a building. An embassy, no less."

"We will do whatever is necessary to finish the project. Right now you are not helping us, even though we gave you quite a lot of money to do so. Please don't make us try to think of ways to get our money's worth out of you," Medea hissed.

"Maybe we should just take you back to our labs and start yanking out your fingernails until you are properly motivated," said Shiva with an evil glint in his eyes.

"Shiva here made some truly horrific mistakes using the notes you took," Medea chimed in. "Maybe we'll stick you in a cage with one of them at feeding time."

"Now, wait," replied Eric in a panicky tone. "You can threaten all you want, but there's nothing I can do. Really. What could I do?"

"Think of something," hissed Medea. "Impress us."

"And do it soon," said Shiva. The man bolted for the door. After a moment, Shiva and Medea slithered over to a table close to the stage. There was a short man with a fiddle and a tall woman with an accordion setting up on the stage.

The governor looked up, realized their usual booth was now empty and turned to tell the senator they should move. The senator was busy glowering at a loud group in the corner. The governor noticed the musicians and realized they were in for another night of experimental jazz. He made a mental note to order a round of scotch. He found that was the best anesthetic for experimental jazz.

"Those fools are obviously lost. They belong in one of the shot bars on Sixth Street," said the senator as someone from the loud group threw back a shot and the others cheered. "Not here where people are treating the business of drinking with the proper level of..."

"Sobriety?" finished the governor. The senator gave him a wry grin and flourished his empty glass by way of reply before he lurched off to the bathroom.

The governor turned his gaze to a table close to the loud group. He thought that the two people at the table were those Malsanto folks he'd overheard a few weeks ago, but he couldn't say for sure. His eyesight was going again and he hadn't had time to go get it fixed. They were obviously arguing about something. He wondered if they had given up bothering those Floracopia women.

After overhearing them, the governor had been interested enough to look up their company, Malsanto. If he had to guess, he'd say these two were under a military contract for something that they weren't able to provide. He almost felt sorry for them.

The military was not forgiving to those who didn't give them what they wanted. Not forgiving at all. Most of the military research facilities were staffed with scientists who were little better than indentured servants. That's what happened when you failed to fulfill a military contract.

After observing these two bickering away for the last hour, the governor thought the world would probably be a better place if the military threw them in a hole somewhere. That would keep them from bothering normal people who were just trying to get through the day.

"There must be a way to get access to their notes," Shiva said to Medea, though his eyes never rose above his feet. "Maybe we just need to go to Gordon and tell him everything? Maybe he'll have a way out of this mess?" Shiva proposed.

Medea rolled her eyes. "Go to the CEO and tell him we utterly screwed up? What a great idea. I'll be sure to bring a sword so we can commit ritual suicide in his office right afterwards. He'll find that amusing."

"He's got to suspect something is up with all the trips we have been logging down here," Shiva pointed out.

"Are you kidding me?" Medea croaked, choking on her drink. "I had to seriously shuffle the numbers to hide all the fuel expenditures. He thinks we are locked away in some lab too deep to get globenet signals for the weekend."

"We have to tell him something. What else can we do?" said Shiva. "If only we could actually call up our powerful military buddies and send them in to bust heads."

"I know, believe me," she replied, tapping her foot unconsciously. "But to do that, we'd have to admit that we don't have anything for them. And it's off to the salt mines for the both of us, best case scenario."

At this point, someone from the loud group was standing behind Medea and telling a story that involved wild hand gestures. He stumbled backwards right into her chair, spilling beer all over her. Medea leapt to her feet with a shriek. The group was all apologies. Medea fumed at them for five minutes before they soothed her with free drinks.

"What brings y'all to Austin?" one of them men asked after Shiva and Medea said they were from out of state. He was a soldier. Something about the way he carried himself would never let him hide that.

"We're trying to do some business in Ambrosia Springs," Medea said.

"And failing miserably," Shiva added.

"At least we aren't the only ones," replied the soldier man. The rest of his group groaned and ordered another round.

"What do you mean?" asked Medea.

Some of the group shouted that they didn't want to talk business on their day off, but the soldier answered her. "We were dispatched from our unit to help DARPA test surveillance equipment out in Ambrosia Springs. I never heard of the place before."

Medea raised an eyebrow. Encouraged, he went on. "Well, come to find out, there's this group there that makes security stuff for the private sector. Omerta? Something like that. Apparently, they ate DARPA for breakfast a few months ago. DARPA's hot for payback and wants us to catch these guys with their pants down."

Shiva leaned forward to make sure he missed nothing. The soldier continued, "And after working down there, I can understand why DARPA's so pissed at these guys. Everything we come up with, they catch on immediately and they are such jerks about it. There's this snotty little nerd with his freaky girlfriend," the soldier said. He demonstrated his frustration by taking a violent swig of beer.

"I sure would like to get some dirt on those guys," the soldier man said. "It would be a real pleasure to haul those jerks off to a dark prison. But we can't just raid the building or haul them off for questioning on account of them being some sort of diplomats with powerful friends in the UN."

"Why don't you raid the girlfriend's office?" Medea suggested, as though the thought just popped into her head. "Involved with a guy like that, she's bound to be up to something."

"Lady, you're alright," the soldier said, slapping her leg in what might have been a flirtatious gesture if Medea looked and acted less like something that might kill and eat you after you mate with it. "That's the kind of thinking that's going to win this war. If I only had some kind of evidence I could take to DARPA's colonel. He'd love it. He's not too fond of those Floracopia women either. Of course, he's not too fond of anybody."

"Did you say Floracopia?" trilled Medea.

The senator had bent to tie his shoe on the way back from the bathroom and stopped right next to Shiva. He was considering giving them all a good telling off. But after listening to them, he hurried back to his table.

"That pack of hyenas in the corner there is some sort of military group for DARPA," the senator hissed to the governor. The governor returned his gaze and appeared massively unconcerned.

The senator continued with ill-concealed excitement, "I bet they're the same bunch of hotheads that caused that fiasco with Omerta a few months ago."

The governor nodded. "And they are getting friendly with those Malsanto people. The ones who were trying to steal from that Floracopia group down in Ambrosia Springs," he supplied. "It is such a small world we live in, isn't it?"

The senator couldn't agree more. His mind wandered around these facts but arrived at no unifying conclusion, so he moved on to the topic he most wanted to discuss this evening.

"So, I took your recommendation and spent some time relaxing," he said with an overly casual tone. "Decided that since so many of my constituents like playing that Revolution World game, I should try it out."

That drew the governor's attention away from the drama unfolding on the other side of the bar. "Really?" he said. "And how did you find it?"

The senator leaned forward. "I liked it quite a bit."

The governor nodded gravely. "I quite enjoy playing that game myself. I find it calms my mind in quite interesting ways." The governor reached into his pocket, turned on the scrambler, and set it on the table.

"If that thing doesn't actually work, we are totally screwed," observed the senator.

"Then let's make sure we are doing something worth getting screwed for," replied the governor.

CHAPTER TWENTY

Gloria burst into the break room and collapsed in a chair behind Max in a huff. She was having very trying day. She had spent all her energies trying to motivate the employees to have a more positive outlook and no one appreciated her efforts.

Max turned to look at her with a mildly inquisitive expression. "I hear you have spent the whole day screaming at everyone in the building. What's going on? Are you having female troubles?"

Rage boiled through her veins. The fact that Gloria was, in fact, having female troubles made it so much worse.

"You are all trying to slack off on your work and undermine my authority here, but I won't let you," she thundered. "Even if I have to chain you all to your desks, I will make this facility a success."

Max twisted his face in a way that strongly suggested he was choking back a chuckle. Gloria seriously considered backhanding the man. But even confidence in her position wouldn't overcome her ingrained respect for her elders. Max got up quietly and left Gloria alone in the break room. She felt like crying, but refused to allow herself to wallow in such weakness. Other women cried. Fluffy blond women with no self respect. Not her.

Max returned with a bowl of chocolate ice cream and a stiff shot of rum. He set these before her and sat down. Gloria considered them. He might be trying to suggest that she was in a bad mood and taking it out on others. Or he might be offering her tokens of alliance in the manner of a vassal, swearing fealty to his lord.

Yes, she decided. *Probably that second one.* She drank the shot and began eating the ice cream in what she hoped was a dignified manner.

"I can never believe you are so young," Max said into the silence.

"The weight of responsibility ages a person," she replied gravely.

Max chuckled. "That's not really what I meant, but it doesn't matter. Why do you let it bother you that Seth has left early to have a picnic date with his girlfriend?"

Gloria sucked in her breath before she could stop herself. "It doesn't bother me at all," she said in a clipped tone. "I couldn't care less, except he is falling behind on his work. He's letting the company and our family down. If this little relationship of his causes him to forget his responsibilities, it is my job to force him to his senses."

Max studied his feet for a moment. "Why don't you just go back to the island? You are miserable here."

Gloria shrieked indignantly. "And blow my big chance? Drag back home with my tail between my legs and admit defeat?" she cried. She couldn't believe he would even suggest such a thing.

Failure was not an option. If this Texas facility didn't work, another shot at moving up in the company might never come along. If she had to personally imprison every terrorist in the state, this facility would be a success.

Max shook his head. "Seriously, Gloria, let's be honest for a minute. Why are you so obsessed with Seth? If you gave anyone else a chance, you'd have your pick of the men."

Again, Gloria was strongly tempted to sob like a little girl. She didn't know why she wanted Seth. She just did. She would have him eventually and then he would regret making her wait like this. But he was not leaping at this opportunity to be with someone fabulous like her.

Why didn't he realize how perfect they would be together? How could he prefer that blond with her stupid Texas twang? Didn't he realize that he fulfilled all of Gloria's main requirements for a significant other? Gloria blew out a frustrated sigh, but did not speak.

"I suspect your interest mainly stems from his lack of interest," Max said gently. "But, really, you just aren't right for each other. You should find someone else."

"I don't need dating advice from the world's oldest bachelor," she snapped. Gloria would have really given him a piece of her mind, but her handheld started beeping its alarm.

"Is there no such thing as a lazy day in Texas?" muttered Max.

*****

Leaning against a tree with a gentle breeze wafting along his face, Clio knew that life inside the cloud of bliss she'd lived in for the past few weeks couldn't last. She knew that eventually she would have to resume her grueling work schedule. She knew the demands of Floracopia and Revolution World would force him back to reality sooner or later. She didn't care.

They cooked dinner together and watched movies on the couch. They talked about politics and made plans for the future. They stayed up late plotting for a better world. This evening had felt like something out of one of the sappy movies Thalia and Terpsi sometimes made her watch.

They'd gone out just after sunset. The last rays of daylight dappled through the trees as Seth lay with Clio's head in his lap. The wind played with the wildflowers as they idly ate fruit and sipped wine.

They had their picnic on a large hill that looked out over the Floracopia buildings. Clio was gently dozing when Seth saw the first of the DARPA vans roll to a stop in Floracopia's parking lot.

"Clio, we have a problem," he said.

"Are we out of wine?" she asked without opening her eyes.

"DARPA is invading your lab," he replied as he began fumbling for his handheld. Clio shot to her feet. She stared at the soldiers streaming out of the vans and into the Co-op with her mouth wide open. She started to bolt down the hill, but Seth grabbed her.

Dragging her behind a tree, he said, "We really don't want to go down there."

"My lab," she cried.

"I know, but better your lab than you. What do you think they will do with you?" whispered Seth. Clio sat down hard.

If they were raiding her lab, they would take her to an interrogation facility. A torture prison. She jumped to her feet again.

"My mom is down there!" she cried.

"And you cannot help them if you are down there getting roughed up by those idiots," replied Seth, pulling her back down.

Clio shook her head to clear the panic out. He was right. She pulled out her handheld and joined him in firing off cries for help to anyone and everyone.

Working her handheld furiously, she watched as soldiers dragged specimens, equipment and people out of the building. It was agony.

"Oh my god, they are taking the Chinese mushrooms. Six months of work are in that vat. And they've got my mother on her knees in the gravel," she sobbed.

"But they don't have any of your notes or other data," Seth said grimly. She whipped her head around to look at him. He held up his handheld.

"I moved it all someplace they will never find. Whatever else they do, they won't get any of your real data," he said. Then he immediately went back to work. She wanted to kiss him for that. She wanted to curl up in his arms and pretend this was a bad dream. Instead, Clio continued firing off messages.

"Thalia is out of town and safe. Terpsi grabbed her kids and took off for the hills. Folks will hide her until we know what's going on. Kalliope got my message, but god knows what she will do," Clio reported mechanically to Seth as they both frantically tried to save Floracopia.

"I doubt Kalliope's plan will be to run and hide," Seth chuckled grimly.

Clio prayed to whatever gods may be that she didn't hear any gunshots. She did hear a lot of smashing sounds and a few gut wrenching screams. She hoped everyone was all right down there. She wondered how much of her lab would be left at the end of this day. If only she knew what was going on.

"Here comes the cavalry," Seth said. He stopped working on his handheld to watch. Clio tore her eyes away from Harmony and the man pointing a gun at her mother's head.

A cloud of dust was the first sign on the horizon. Within minutes the parking lot was filled with cars, trucks, and scooters of every description. The soldiers tried to stop them, but it was like trying to hold back a tidal wave. When the lot filled, the vehicles jammed the roads, pulling off any which way. Hundreds of people raced out of the night and over the hillside, streaming towards the building like ants on their way to a picnic. All of them were armed.

"Wow," whistled Seth. "People sure do feel strongly about Floracopia here. I didn't know Ambrosia Springs had this many citizens."

Clio stared at the angry mob. "If the government shuts down Floracopia, Ambrosia Springs is out of a job. It could end up a ghost town. There are enough of those around here to get people pretty worked up."

"This could go very poorly," Seth murmured.

Clio saw her mother stand up and dust herself off under the parking lot lights, despite the loud objections of the man with the very large gun pointed at her head.

Harmony kept her hands over her head and moved slowly. She seemed to be talking to the man, who only became more agitated. As the crowd forming pressed closer and got louder, he shot wildly over their heads. People screamed and hit the dirt. Harmony flinched, but remained standing. Clio could see that people were filming all of this, including several local reporters for the major globenet news stations.

And every single head turned when gouts of flame began shooting out one of the windows. Soldiers burst out of the doors, screaming. A fireball followed them out. At first Clio thought DARPA was blowing up the building, but the obvious agitation of the soldiers ruled that out. They were cowering behind the van, totally ignoring the crowd as they aimed their guns at the door. Another fireball shot out.

"Oh dear," said Clio. Her stomach sank like a stone when she realized what it was.

"Wow," said Seth. "That's definitely a security feature I did not add to your building. Did Kalliope do that? She really does have a scorched earth philosophy, doesn't she?"

"No, this one is on me," Clio said.

A flaming cow bolted out the door. It opened its mouth to bellow in outrage and a plume of flame shot ten feet. It scorched the front of one of the DARPA vans. The cow looked as surprised as everyone else. Pandemonium ensued as the cow charged wildly. People alternately leapt out of its way and tried to smother the flames on its back.

The soldier with his gun on Harmony lowered his weapon uncertainly. His training clearly hadn't covered this eventuality. People in the crowd hit the deck. Seth laughed out loud, and then looked embarrassed.

"Sorry, Clio. I know this is serious, but that right there is hilarious," he said. "You made a self-barbecuing cow."

"No, that's not what it's for. They are for methane recapture," she began, but gave up. "Stupid DARPA."

They heard a man shout, "Bubba, get some sauce! This cow is cooking itself!"

Seth smirked. Clio punched his arm.

"You really do create miracles, don't you? When this is over, I'll take a whole herd," he said. She turned to punch him again but Seth stepped back.

Eventually, the crowd extinguished the cow. Their attention was returning to the DARPA crisis when another burst of flame erupted from the building. As more soldiers burst out of the building, a soldier panicked and let loose another stream of bullets. Harmony fell to the ground, clutching her shoulder. Blood sprayed down her arm. Clio screamed.

Seth tightened his grip as she lurched towards her mother. The soldier who shot Harmony almost dropped his gun, but didn't fire again. There was total silence, like the calm before a storm. The building continued to burn, but nobody cared. The crowd lurched towards Harmony, but the soldiers suddenly remembered their job and turned their weapons on the mob, stopping their advance. Another man in uniform strode forward and grabbed the quivering soldier's gun before he could fire off another round.

"There's your friend, Colonel Crazypants," Clio said without tearing her eyes away.

"He's doing the sanest thing possible right now," replied Seth. The colonel was obviously screaming at the soldier who fired. No one moved to help Harmony, who sprawled in the gravel, bleeding.

The crowd was now massive and more kept coming. They held a collective breath as the soldier turned and entered one of the vans. Several older women with large bouffants edged slowly towards Harmony. When the colonel gestured impatiently, the women ran to Harmony. After a moment, they helped her to her feet.

"It can't be that bad," Clio said, a breath away from hysteria.

"That's Millie standing next to her. She's Terpsi's head nurse. She wouldn't let my mom get up if it was really bad."

"It's going to be alright," Seth soothed her without letting go. "Everything will be alright." Clio found comfort in his words, even if neither believed them.

Harmony leaned on a woman and began speaking. Clio couldn't make out what she was saying, but the gathered masses aimed their weapons right at the colonel.

"I had no idea the Junior League target practices were so popular," Seth said. Clio choked on a laugh.

"I think the colonel does not appreciate an armed populace," Clio replied. "You'd think a military man would be in favor of that sort of thing."

The colonel raged and bellowed as the soldiers formed a defensive line around the vans. Other soldiers ran back and forth from the labs with cages, boxes, and equipment. The mob advanced upon them with unmistakable menace while Harmony held her arms out to the colonel.

"Your mom is really scary sometimes," Seth said.

"The colonel doesn't think so," Clio said, trying to keep the quaver out of her voice as the colonel strode towards Harmony. Clio thought he might strike her down.

"He hasn't tried her waffles," Seth replied. "Those things will put the fear of god into any man."

Clio smacked him on the arm. "Stop trying to make me laugh. This is possibly the most horrible night of my life."

"Let's hope not," murmured Seth. She was grateful that he did not name the thing she feared. That this would be the night she watched a man kill her mother.

Now another soldier started pushing a line of Co-op employees out of the door. The people in their work clothes shuffled along slowly with their hands over their heads. Clio saw Harmony stagger forward, but couldn't make out what she way saying. Whatever it was sent the colonel into fresh bouts of rage. He gestured to the soldiers and they began pushing the people towards the vans.

Clio doubted that anyone within three miles failed to hear Harmony.

"Stop." she said in a terrible clear voice. Clio thought that if God ever objected to something, that might be what it sounded like.

The armed mob advanced. Clio could see the telltale motion of gun safeties flicking off. This was going to be very bad. She wanted to turn and hide her head in Seth's chest, but she couldn't. She thought about medical cases of hysterical blindness.

People who saw something awful would go blind, even though medically there was nothing wrong with them. They saw something so horrible that the only way their brain could cope was to turn off their eyes. They saw something so terrible that they didn't want to see any more, ever. Clio suddenly understood how that could happen.

Then the colonel stopped raging. He seemed to slump his shoulders in defeat. He barked at the soldiers. They immediately shouldered their weapons and raced to the vans, leaving their prisoners in the gravel of the parking lot. Harmony held up her hand and the mob stopped their advance. Clio thought it was rather like watching a silent horror film.

"He's giving up!" cried Seth. "They are leaving!"

The colonel slowly and belligerently got into one of the vans. He yelled some parting shot and the DARPA vans sped off. It would have been a very dramatic exit if the road were not completely blocked with cars.

As it was, the vans had to slowly pick their way through a ditch and drive on the shoulder. As people put down their weapons and began milling about, the vans finally disappeared over the horizon. Clio let out a breath she didn't realize she had been holding.

She pulled away from Seth and raced down the hill towards her mother just as Kalliope roared up on her steamcycle, armed to the teeth. Clio realized that her sister had mounted some sort of cannon on her cycle. That's probably what took her so long to get here, Clio thought. She thought about making some snide comment, but was too busy pushing her way through the crowd around her mother.

Harmony was white as a sheet. She stumbled as gracefully as she could towards the building. Blood soaked her shirt. Clio fought to her side and began guiding her to the building while trying to keep the crowd back. She didn't want any enthusiastic friend to accidentally bump her mother. Kalliope was close behind her, cutting a swath through the crowd with tears streaming down her face. When she saw the blood on her mother, she snarled. Dropping a few guns, Kalliope picked up her mother and strode quickly to the building, leaving the crowd behind.

The building was in shambles. Anything that had not been taken was ruined. Injured animals cried piteously. Glowing fish flopped on the floor, their tanks smashed. At least someone had put out the fires caused by the cows.

"We need to keep everyone out until we can make sure it is safe," said Clio as Kalliope gently laid her mother down on a lab bench. She grabbed a lab coat and wadded it up for a pillow.

"Get Terpsi here," Kalliope replied.

Clio shook her head. "She took the kids and ran. I'm not calling her until we are sure those DARPA guys are gone and not coming back."

Kalliope looked like she might hit Clio for a minute, but instead pointed to Harmony. "Then you fix Mom," she said, her lower lip trembling slightly. "Do it now."

"Girls, girls, no fighting," Harmony whispered.

"Get me a first aid kit. Over there, in that cabinet," replied Clio.

Clio could see that he sister would seriously lose it if she didn't do something soon. So she bent over her mother. Kalliope could never understand that genetics and medicine were two totally different fields. Now was not the time to educate her.

Clio took her mother's vital signs and began gently peeling off her bloody shirt. There was a bullet wound in her shoulder, close enough that it may have shattered a bone or torn the joint, but far from the major arteries that would mean death.

Clio poured rubbing alcohol over the wound. Harmony sucked in her breath sharply. As gently as she could, Clio pulled Harmony's shoulder up to see the other side. Harmony cried out in pain. Kalliope began cursing at her sister, the military, and the world. She did it thoroughly, leaving no one's parentage or personal appearance untouched.

"I have to check for the exit wound," Clio snapped when Kalliope moved to stop her. "We are in luck. The bullet went all the way through. Keep gauze on the wound and let's get her to the hospital."

Clio suddenly realized there were other people in the room. Joanna was in one corner, directing platoons of volunteers to get animals back in their cages and plants in their pots. She made sure the reporters were there, filming every detail of the destruction.

Clio looked around. She found Jason at her elbow and Seth standing anxiously by the door. Turning her head made her temples throb.

"My truck is right outside," said Jason. "Let's go."

"The closest hospital is an hour drive away," Seth objected. "We can take her to the Omerta facility."

Harmony shook her head feebly. "Public," she whispered. "Need to be in public."

"Mom wants to go to the hospital," announced Kalliope. "Jason, let's move her. Now."

Clio and Seth followed them out the door. Harmony reached out to lay a cool hand on Clio's arm. "Need you to stay here," she whispered to her daughter. "Since I can't."

Clio wanted to object. She wanted to go with her mother. Instead, she squared her shoulders and stepped back to let them go.

Jason carefully bundled Harmony as Kalliope hopped in behind them. Jason paused to squeeze Clio comfortingly and then leapt to the driver's seat.

"That guy is always around," Seth commented. He almost laughed as Max appeared out of the crowd and slipped into the truck before it roared off. Seth wondered when Jason would notice the extra passenger.

"Who?" Clio asked. She had responded without thinking, her mind on her mother.

"Jason," replied Seth, his mind on her lab. "He never leaves. Even without the, uh, other project you two are working on, there's really no excuse for him to be around all the time like he is."

"Jason is a family friend. He's always around when I need him," Clio said, bending to pick up some broken glassware.

Seth studied her for a minute. "He was around this time because you called him, didn't you? You needed help and you didn't think I could do it so you called him."

"Oh, for the love of God, Seth. I can't bicker with you about my ex-boyfriend right now," she cried, thoroughly annoyed. She stood up to look for a trash bin that wasn't already overflowing with a fortune in broken equipment. She heard police sirens.

"I could do with fewer sirens in my day, that's for sure," Clio sighed. She set down the broken glass, dusted off her hands and walked out to meet the police.

Seth caught her by the elbow. "Maybe you shouldn't go out there. What if this is round two? What if they are here to arrest you?"

Clio pulled away from him. By this time, her head was throbbing from a monumental headache. She was almost surprised other people couldn't hear the pounding in her skull. "Then they arrest me. If that will stop more shooting, then that's what I'll do." She walked to the door with Seth trailing behind her. Actually, a nice quiet cell sounded appealing right now.

Any ideas about preventing more shooting died at the entrance of the building. The sheriff and his men were lined up behind their cars, guns drawn and pointed at the hundred or so armed people in the parking lot. The mob had their weapons drawn and were pointing right back. The mob began shouting and shuffling towards the police cars. The police pulled out tear gas canisters and held them aloft in an unspoken threat.

"Everybody take it easy!" shouted Clio over the sirens. The impending doom paused. Clio walked out, but Seth held her back so she couldn't walk between the two groups. The sheriff edged over to his car and turned the lights and sirens off.

"Clio, what the heck is going on out here?" the sheriff shouted.

"Military men just left, sheriff. They destroyed our lab and carted off everything they could find. They shot my mom," Clio's voice broke for a moment, but she continued when she heard gun safeties switched off and muted cursing from her mob of protectors. "They would have taken a bunch of our people, but these nice folks here convinced them to leave." She gestured to the mob.

Joanna pushed her way out of the building to stand by Clio. "They had no warrants, sheriff. I asked to see some identification so we'd know they were really military and not terrorists. A soldier hit me over the head. Bob asked them to get the police. Legally, they should at least call you so someone would know we were taken. They hit him in the face with a gun."

Everyone looked at Bob and the crusted blood down his shirt. His nose was swollen to twice its normal size. Clio turned to look at Joanna and saw the blood crusted on her neck and the matted lump behind her ear.

Joanna leaned over to Clio and whispered, "I made sure the

reporters filmed every disgusting inch of it." Clio almost smiled, but she almost started crying too.

The sheriff absorbed this information. "Nobody told me anything about the military having business here. Definitely no one told me that they would be raiding your lab today. I don't know what's going on here, but I think all these folks here need to put down their guns so we can figure it out."

"You aren't taking anyone today," shouted a voice in the mob. There were a few cries seconding that notion.

"I have no orders to arrest anyone," the sheriff declared loudly. "And if I did, I would wait until I was one hundred percent sure that they were legal and above board before I acted on them." His voice hardened and he took a step towards the mob. "But if any of you hotheads fires a single shot, I promise you are going to spend months in a hospital, wishing I arrested you today."

"Please lower your weapons," Clio called. "The sheriff is here to help." There was a little grumbling, but the guns came down. A collective sigh of relief went up.

"Now y'all get out of my way so I can do my job," the sheriff roared. He strode into the building with every policeman in the county following in his wake.

Clio's headache continued for the next hour as she went over everything with the sheriff. Then she needed to check to see how much of her lab remained. If anything, her headache got worse as she realized the full extent of the damage.

"I just don't understand why this happened," the sheriff said. "Maybe tomorrow they'll be back with a warrant to arrest everyone in town and Bigfoot Wallace."

Joanna put a hand on his shoulder as he looked around in a daze. "Sheriff, you are a good man in a troubled world. You need a hobby to relax you," she gently steered him towards the door. She felt that the sooner the police and everyone left, the faster the cleanup would go.

"I like fishing, but you know how the rivers are these days. If there's fish in them, chances are you don't want to be antagonizing them," he said, taking his leave.

"Can I suggest perhaps starting an online game like Revolution World?" Joanna replied. "I play it myself and find it quite soothing. Very easy to play."

"A lot of my deputies play. I may give that a try," the sheriff commented. Then he turned and began directing the removal of the mob and the police.

"We may have to lay some people off," Joanna said when she returned. She punched calculations into her handheld. "It's going to be very tight, trying to replace all the equipment and start over on the research that was destroyed. Thank God Seth was able to move our data so they couldn't destroy it. If it weren't for that, we may not be in business at all."

Seth gave her a small smile. He had been a ghost, shadowing Clio all night.

"And your other security features worked like a dream. Everyone was on alert the minute they kicked in the doors and the network snapped shut like a steel trap," Joanna continued. "It's a cold comfort, but they didn't find anything here they could use against us. Nothing to incriminate us and not a shred of our research protocols to steal."

Clio was on a call with Jason. He reported that her mother was stabilized and resting after having a few stitches and a synth blood transfusion.

"Kalliope is camped out in front of her door, glowering at everyone who walks by," Jason told her.

"Great. I will try to get over there as soon as I can," Clio replied.

"I can come get you if you want," Jason offered.

"No, Seth will give me a ride," she said, looking to see Seth nod his assent as he continued restoring some security equipment.

"Is that guy still there? It's his fault those DARPA guys were at the Co-op to start with," grumbled Jason.

"It is not!" Clio hissed, dropping her voice and moving away from Seth.

"Why else would they bother you, if not because of him?" asked Jason. "Foreigners are bad news. I don't know why you are seeing him."

"Who I see is none of your business," she replied. "I'll be up to the hospital as soon as I can. Call me if there is any change, ok?" She ended the conversation and flicked off her handheld before he could go any further.

Seth gave her a hug. "After all I've done to help out with

Revolution World, he still doesn't trust me?" he guessed. They had decided to refer to his involvement in Clio's rebellion as 'doing some consulting for the Revolution World game.' That way they could discuss it in public.

"He says DARPA attacked us to get to you," Clio replied, resting her head lightly on his shoulder.

Seth's expression sobered. "He may be right. Those DARPA guys are Class A Crazy and we have no idea why they targeted your office. I don't know what I've done to get them so focused on me either."

"Still, it's not your fault that this happened," she said, gesturing to the wreckage of her life's work.

Seth tightened his arms around her and wished they were someplace more private.

"Speaking of perpetual pains in the ass." Clio nodded towards the sight of Gloria striding through the crowd like the queen at a garden party.

"She's helping to organize the volunteers," Seth replied, pointing to the tables of food and beverages set up by the door. Gloria was directing a line of trucks waiting to take away equipment that couldn't be salvaged.

"She's just doing it to irritate me," Clio said sourly.

Seth adopted a mock-frustrated tone. "I can't bicker with you about my cousin right now." He grinned at her to show he was teasing.

Clio didn't think that was very funny. But right now she didn't think anything was very funny. She was about to go in search of medicine for her headache when Bob the Money Guy appeared at her elbow.

"Bob, you look much better," she said, welcoming a change in conversation. "I guess your nose isn't broken after all?"

"I need to talk to you," Bob said, ignoring her question. "It's important."

He led her into an empty lab, motioning for Seth and Joanna to follow.

"First off, if I had known what would happen, I would have come to you much earlier," he started. Then he went on to detail his meeting with Shiva and Medea earlier in the year.

"They tried to buy you off? While doing that, they told you that they had already bought off someone else in the company," Clio summarized to make sure she understood what he was saying.

"Why on earth didn't you tell us this before?" asked Joanna. "Just knowing Malsanto was behind that burglary would have been a huge help for us."

Bob hung his head. "Look, I know you probably suspected I was involved with the break-in. I figured that if I came to you with this story, you might think it was all made up to get you to stop suspecting me. I mean, it sounds fishy right? They said that whoever was helping them before couldn't do anything more for them, so I figured that meant they would give up. I told myself there was no sense getting everyone stirred up if the danger was past."

"But today it was DARPA," Seth pointed out. "How does knowing Malsanto was behind the raid months ago help us now?"

"This brings me to my second point," Bob said, pulling out his handheld. "Look at this. I went through the video files that those reporters shot, looking for anything that could help us."

He played some footage of the DARPA raid, and then skipped ahead. Clio involuntarily winced when they passed the part where her mother was shot. Bob zoomed in on soldiers throwing equipment and specimens into the vans. Then he stopped the tape and focused more tightly on one of the vans.

"Look who was waiting to get their sticky mitts on our stuff," he said, pointing to a grainy but distinct shot of Shiva and Medea sitting in one of the vans, grabbing what the soldiers brought.

"Ha! So this had nothing to do with me," crowed Seth.

"That is true, but not the main point here," said Clio, studying the image.

"Wow, if Malsanto and DARPA are working together, maybe my troubles with DARPA might actually be a result of your problems with Malsanto," Seth continued. "My problems are all your fault, not the other way around. I am so throwing that in Jason's face the next time I see the big jerk." He smiled at the idea of scoring a point off Jason.

Clio turned to look at Seth with astonishment. She couldn't believe he was smirking at her at a time like this. Her headache made her whole body throb. She didn't need him irritating the crap out of her right now.

"Seth, I think now is a good time for you to go. I'll finish up here and then head out to the hospital in Austin," she said icily. She pitched her voice so the others couldn't hear.

"Don't you want me to give you a ride to see your mother?" he asked, bewildered.

"No. What I want is for you to go away now," she said, turning away from him pointedly.

He stared at her for a long minute but she continued to ignore him. He left with a perplexed shake of his head.

After he left, Clio dropped her head into her hands. "Joanna, my head is killing me. Can you get me something to fix it? An aspirin? A hammer? Anything."

Opening the door, Joanna solved the problem with a wave of her hand to her underlings. "And I will give you a ride to the hospital myself," Joanna added. "I need a nice long car drive to clear my head and I won't be able to sleep until I see your mother with my own two eyes. When I think how close we came today to getting thrown in one of those awful prisons or shot in the road like dogs." She shuddered and left the room.

Much later, Clio sat in the lounge at the hospital. It was like all hospital lounges. Old sofas, stale coffee and the smell of despair soaked into the carpet. She flicked through the channels on the wallscreen. On the news, she recognized the Texas governor, his face almost purple with rage.

"We demand to know why the military attempted to kidnap Texas citizens earlier today," he cried. "Reports indicate that the military invasion of a small business caused massive unnecessary damage. This damage is not just to the business itself but also to the local community. We demand reparations be made. If the government if going to act like a natural disaster, they should help our citizens recover from their onslaughts. Just like they would after a hurricane."

Clio was glad she had voted for this man. She hoped that his obviously elevated blood pressure did not keep him from continuing to be governor for at least a few more years. He was getting older, after all.

The news screen split to show the Texas governor and the Admiral in charge of the United States armed forces.

"How dare you demand anything from your country?" the admiral fired at the governor. "My reports indicate that our troops were performing an important security maneuver when they were accosted by an armed mob. Some reports indicate that this was some kind of local militia. A local militia setting itself up against the United States military? That's another name for terrorists, mister."

A vein in the governor's forehead began throbbing. "People simply try to defend themselves from military tactics that Cold War Era communists wouldn't sink to and you label them terrorists? Your troops shot an unarmed woman in front of her daughter."

The admiral blustered. "She was resisting arrest. And anyway, that woman is apparently going to live."

The wallscreen cut to images of the destroyed lab. There were a few clips of witnesses shouting angrily before it cut back to the governor.

"Your troops didn't have a warrant. When they were asked for a warrant, they responded by breaking a man's nose and causing another woman injuries that required stitches. How could she resist arrest if there was no warrant?" the governor asked. His voice had become monotone.

It was as if he knew, and wanted everyone watching to know, that there was no point in talking to the admiral. The admiral was beyond listening. But still the governor tried. "Your troops did not alert the local police to their presence. The police assumed that your troops were a terrorist group and further bloodshed was only narrowly avoided."

Close-ups of Joanna and Bob, before they had been cleaned and stitched up, replaced the governor's image. It was not pretty. Jason came in and sat next to her, watching the wallscreen. He had brought coffee and some donuts. He passed her the chocolate ones because he knew she liked those best. When she sipped her coffee, she found he had already added cream, just the way she liked.

"The United States military is doing what it must to protect itself. I mean, to protect the nation," the admiral was saying. "There will be no reparations paid to those who get in our way. Furthermore, armed citizens prevented us from doing our jobs. We have allowed Texas to have their lax gun controls laws long enough. There will be stricter laws coming soon. Texans cannot keep arming themselves against their government."

"That's not for you to decide," shouted the governor, losing his temper. The wallscreen began replaying the footage of Harmony's shooting again. Even though she knew her mom was doing better, she didn't want to see that again if she could help it. She switched the screen off.

"The doctors say she can go home tomorrow," Jason told her. She was so happy to hear it that she impulsively hugged him. He held her a little too close and a little too long for friends.

She pulled away and studied him. They had a lot of history, she and Jason. Whatever else their relationship had been, being with Jason had been easy. At least, it was easy in the sense that her family had not objected and their dates were not interrupted by military attack or mutant outbreaks. Their relationship had not been punctuated by long pauses brought about by monumental miscommunication.

On the other hand, she remembered feeling slightly uncomfortable all the time. She would never have dozed with her head in Jason's lap. She had never been able to relax that much around him. And she always felt like they were so alike that they kept running out of things to say. She never felt that way around Seth.

With Seth she never ran out of things to say and she always felt comfortable telling him anything. Maybe a little too comfortable, she thought ruefully. Looking back, she couldn't believe she told him all about the resistance the way she did.

She sighed and shook her head. Why does all this romantic stuff have to be so difficult? Surely there are better ways to ensure the survival of the species?

Clio smiled to herself. This is the sort of existential nonsense that you always end up pondering in hospital waiting rooms and on long car trips. It never seems to change anything. She patted Jason on the arm and left to go check on Kalliope. Her sister was still stubbornly guarding Harmony's door. She had repelled the advances of several nurses and attendants who might have otherwise disrupted their mother's sleep.

After intense negotiations, Kalliope had allowed Max to sit inside with Harmony. Clio wondered what Max had promised Kalliope. His first-born child? Canada? At any rate, he had been sitting there, still as a statue, for hours.

When she got to the room, Clio found Kalliope snoring. Clio tucked a thin blanket around her sister and sat down on the floor next to her. Her mind wandered over her lab, the events of the day, and what tomorrow would be like. She found she couldn't deal with problems that large and instead focused on whether there was anything in her fridge that would spoil and where she might find a toothbrush. It was going to be a long night. They all seemed to be lately.

CHAPTER TWENTY-ONE

Gloria stormed into Seth's private room to find him moodily constructing rotating lightform sculptures.

"Oh, that's pretty," she said, momentarily distracted from her righteous indignation. She recalled herself. "So, what have you discovered from that girlfriend of yours? Had she started any research into ZFD? Did DARPA steal any of it? Will the American government be coming to kidnap us all for experiments?"

Seth balled his hands into fists, but did not look away from his handheld. He forced himself to relax. "I have checked my data logs," he said patiently. "She started some preliminary studies, but nothing that would catch the eye of the government. And, as I have told you several times now, DARPA didn't get any of their data. That's because when I secure a network, it stays secure."

"I would never doubt you," Gloria replied. "But what did Clio say about it?"

Seth blew out a breath, and turned to look Gloria in the eye. "I don't know. I haven't talked to her since her lab was raided."

Gloria perked up. "Really? But that was almost two weeks ago. What happened? Did you two break it off?" Max walked in and overheard this last part. Gloria scowled at him. Every time she came to find Seth for a little private conversation lately, Max appeared. She found it disconcerting.

"You should call her," Max said as he made himself comfortable on Seth's couch.

Seth turned back to his sculpture, tweaking the colors to get a more realistic hologram of a fluffy little dog. "The last time I saw her, she told me to go away. As a gentleman, I complied with her request. I feel it only courteous to wait until she initiates contact. I don't want to burden her with my company if she does not want it." That sounded good, he thought. It should. Seth had practiced that little speech a hundred times in his head.

Max laughed. "It sounds good, but a little too stuffy. You'll want to phrase it less bitterly when you talk to Clio." Seth gave him a dirty look. Sometimes he wished his uncle didn't know him so well.

"Why are your making a hologram of such a repulsive little dog?" asked Gloria. Dimly realizing that what she just said was insulting, she added, "It's a beautiful sculpture though."

"Yes, why don't you just scan in the original?" Max smirked, hinting at the number of times he observed Seth out for walks with a little dog in the forest.

Seth sighed. The stupid sculpture was something to pass the time while he sulked in his room and programmed a massive assault on the American military intelligence databases. Also, he thought it would give him something to show Clio if she ever called him again. It kept his mind off calling her first. He had, in fact, scanned in the leader of Team Pom.

"Why are you two in my room?" Seth asked.

"Because you haven't left your room in four days," replied Gloria.

"I'm working from home," Seth said defensively.

"We wouldn't know. Whatever you are doing is taking up substantial bandwidth and covered with impenetrable security," Max explained. "Naturally, I was curious. You wouldn't leave your uncle out of anything exciting, would you?"

"Just catching up on some stuff," Seth replied, wondering how he could turn the conversation. He really did not want to get into a discussion about Revolution World or what he was working on now, but he could see no way out of it. Out of sheer desperation, he asked, "So I guess you know about the dogs?"

Max laughed and then stopped. "Wait, dogs? Plural? I just saw the one? Aw, do you have two itsby bitsy cutesy little dogs?" He started laughing again. Seth took joy in realizing that Max had only ever seen one dog. That meant Team Pom really was quite good at their stealth maneuvers.

Gloria looked irked. "Dogs? Is this another one of your stupid codes?" She had never seen any dogs anywhere. She wasn't a big fan of pets. Too messy. She squinted at Seth's hologram suspiciously. "Have you coded some sort of security feature into your dog hologram?"

"What? Yes!" Seth briefly entertained the idea of creating a lie so incredibly crazy that they would never question it. Then he remembered that this plan had never worked for him before. And he tried it many times. "No, not really." He hung his shoulders dejectedly.

"Did Clio give you some stupid fluffballs that you hide in the forest out of shame?" giggled Max. "You big sucker. God, no wonder you have problems with that girl. You act like she walks on water and she sticks you with poofy dogs."

Gloria's face soured at the mention of Clio. She flounced over to a chair and sat down. She made a big show of inspecting her nails.

"Shut up," Seth mumbled. Well, it was sort of true. Clio had stuck him with the stupid creatures, even if they were interesting company and he was growing quite fond of them.

Maybe he was too needy? He'd have to pull up some psychological research on this and see what better tactics he could use. He was discovering that it was best to treat love like war. He would have to rethink his infiltration strategy since the last big push had failed so miserably.

"Sucks to be you," said Max as he collapsed on the bed and idly flicked on the wallscreen. "I'm glad to see you aren't working on a Saturday night. Want to watch a movie? I queued up a bunch of great kung fu flicks."

If Seth had known how easy it would be to distract his uncle from finding out his deepest darkest secrets, he'd have done that a long time ago. "Sure, why not? Gloria, are you in? Want me to go get some food from the kitchen?"

Gloria leaned forward and smiled nastily at Max. "Kung fu movies? And what brought on your sudden lust for that genre? Perhaps certain Somata women suggested them to you? Who's the bigger sucker here?"

Max glowered at her. "That is totally different. You are a sad, vindictive woman and I pity you." Gloria scowled right back. Evidently, that had been Max's goal because he grinned cheerily. "Now, I'm going for drinks and something to munch on. Want do you want? Wine? Mixed drinks? Tacos? Ice cream?" Gloria put in her order and made herself comfortable.

"I'll come with you," Seth said as he flicked off his hologram dog sculpture.

"Fine," agreed Max. "Gloria, you pick out the movie. Anything is fine as long as it has Michelle Yeoh in it. That woman is smoking hot." Max sighed appreciatively and Seth followed him out the door.

As they walked down the hall, Seth endured several minutes of his uncle studying him with an air of speculation. Finally, he couldn't take it.

"What?"

"Do you really not know that Gloria is choking to be your girlfriend?" Max asked. "Really? You haven't noticed the five hundred times or so she crawled into your lap and practically started chewing on your boxer shorts?"

Seth stopped and stared at him. "What are you talking about?"

Max grinned. "Oh come on. Cut the innocent act for a minute. You know all about it, right?"

"What?" Seth sputtered incoherently for a minute. "Have you been drinking? Or huffing paint? Gloria does all that 'licking my ear' crap because she wants to annoy me. Not because she actually wants to do anything physical or romantic or whatever."

Max clapped him on the shoulder. "I never understand how you can be so smart and so clueless at the same time. But you do manage it, don't you?"

Seth pushed him away and walked down the hallway to the kitchen. "Delusional. That's what you are."

"Nope, I'm really not. I wish I were," sighed Max. But he didn't bring it up again as they collected goodies and drinks and went back to Seth's room.

Seth, however, spent quite a bit of brainpower on that topic. He eyed Gloria in a way that bordered on paranoid. Was she really interested in him? Surely not. Yet she laughed and flirted with him. She edged closer to him on the couch. Normally he would edge away, but this time he let her. He was shocked to find she didn't spit popcorn at him or put ice down his shirt.

He'd never considered Gloria as a possible date and his mind couldn't really grasp the concept now. She was Gloria, not a girlfriend.

Yet when he thought on it, he could see how dating Gloria might be a good idea. They had much in common. Their views were the same and their backgrounds were similar. In short, they were very compatible. If he hadn't met Clio, who knows?

"Look, I know you are rummaging through the American government's networks looking for answers," Max was saying. "What I don't understand is why you think you need to hide it. Do you think the rest of us here want to wait around for DARPA to get up the guts to come bother us again? We should be working together."

"Oh." Said Seth. He hadn't thought of it that way. But how could he do that without getting into all the Revolution World stuff? "You are right. Let's work on it tomorrow though. Tonight we should relax."

Max looked satisfied and turned back to the movie. Seth congratulated himself on dodging that bullet, at least for a few more hours. He would come up with something tomorrow.

"You forgot the chocolate milk," sulked Gloria playfully. It was one of life's minor miracles that cocoa trees adapted easily to the Texas climate with only minor splicing needed.

"We are out," replied Max. Gloria continued to pout until Seth offered to go get some for her.

Gloria looked thrilled, but shook her head. "Oh no. I wouldn't want you to go to all that trouble just for me."

"It's no trouble," Seth replied. "We are also out of my favorite beer. I'll just go down to the market. It's after dark and they should be open for a little longer. Keep watching the movie without me."

Gloria gleefully waved him goodbye.

"See you soon," he said cheerfully.

But it was a long, long time before Seth saw anybody he wanted to see.

CHAPTER TWENTY-TWO

"Seth disappeared? What do you mean?" asked Clio. She sat down in her new lab chair and clutched her handheld.

"He went out for chocolate milk and beer three hours ago and didn't come back," Max told her. "He isn't there?"

"No, he's not with me," Clio responded. "I haven't talked to him since the DARPA raid."

He hasn't called me, she thought. *Not once. I was rude to him that day and he was mad at me and now he's missing and it's awful.*

She almost confessed all her pent-up angst to Max. But she realized now wasn't the time to get emotional about her maybe-boyfriend like some sort of pathetic teenager.

"Have you gone to the market to see if he made it there?" Clio asked Max.

"Yes, I'm standing in their parking lot right now," Max replied. "They say Seth came in, bought a few things and then left. I had Gloria review the recordings of our parking lot and he definitely did not return there."

"So, he didn't make it home," she said. "Maybe he just went for a drive or something?"

"We were watching a movie and he went out for snacks. If he changed his mind, he would have called," answered Max, fear edging his voice.

"That's true. Seth is a very conscientious guy. He would have called," said Clio. She was glad Max wasn't there to see her wince. Whether or not Seth called was a tender subject for her just now. "I'll get the police."

"Clio, I think the market has surveillance cameras out here. Can you convince them to let us look at the recordings?" asked Max.

"Good idea. I'm on it," said Clio. That was something she could do. She ended her call with Max and began firing messages to her mother, her sisters and the owner of the market.

Ninety minutes later, seven people crammed into the market's tiny office to peer at a dingy little wallscreen.

"I can't thank you enough," Harmony was saying to the owner of the market as he hovered over a young man sitting in front of the wallscreen.

"Oh, it's nothing, Miss Somata. Always happy to help, especially when someone is missing," the manager replied, wiping sweat off his forehead. The room had gotten hot. "Just wish I was better at figuring out all these digital doodads. But my nephew here will get us squared away right quick." There was a note of warning in his voice for his nephew. He could see Max was itching to push the boy aside and get at the controls.

Harmony noticed too. She slipped her hand into Max's and squeezed gently. "It's going to be alright, Max," she told him softly.

Max looked at her with anguish in his eyes. "I seriously doubt it."

"Why don't you call Gloria?" Harmony suggested. "I'm sure she is anxious to know what is going on."

"I wanted to wait until we had something to report. Anxious is a mild way to describe Gloria right now. She's working herself up to Category Five Hurricane Gloria," replied Max, glad that he was here and nowhere near her. "The only thing keeping her happy is tearing through Seth's work for the last two weeks. I don't think he has slept a minute, trying to figure what is behind the raids and DARPA's acute interest in all of us and how to make it all stop."

"So he's been really busy," commented Clio as Terpsi and Kalliope jostled her to get a better view of the wallscreen. "Too busy to call."

Max had been looking for a reason to vent his frustrations and Clio just gave him the perfect opening. "You two are such a train wreck. It's a wonder the species survives," he sighed. "Honestly. He wasn't calling you because you weren't calling him. Look, all you two have to do is make a decision. It's really easy. Either you are together or you aren't. Just pick one. But don't change your mind or second-guess yourself or wonder if your lover is as into you as you are into them. Just decide to be in love and then do it. You kids give me a headache."

"Hey," interrupted Kalliope, "Let's try to focus on what's important right now." She pointed at the wallscreen, which was now playing scenes from earlier that night. Everyone turned to the screen and pressed closer.

Clio hung her head. Apparently, she was pretty bad at focusing on what was important. That was something she vowed to fix as soon as they found Seth.

The images jumped around as they tried to find the right time. "There," cried Terpsi. "That's Seth going into the store." They let the tape play.

Seth came out of the store with a bag in his hands. He opened the passenger door and bent over to put the bag in. Two men dressed in black appeared and grabbed him. Everyone in the little room gasped.

Seth struggled, but they had a firm grip. Another man dressed in black appeared in the shot. He shoved a bag over Seth's head and slapped a set of magnetic cuffs around his wrists as they dragged him off. A few seconds later, they could make out the front end of a vehicle as it kicked up gravel and sped off.

No one spoke. The nephew backed up and played the whole thing again. And again. And again.

"Breathe, people," said Kalliope. They let out the breath they had all been holding.

They stopped the tape and Max finally pushed the nephew out of the way. He connected his handheld to the wallscreen and fiddled with it for a minute. The resolution got much better. They could see that the clothes were military uniforms. Max zoomed in on a small patch on one of the men's shoulder. You could just make out a blurry insignia.

"DARPA," spat Kalliope.

Harmony rubbed her shoulder. Her bullet wound itched like hell, but that was part of the healing process. "I am so very sick of these damn DARPA guys."

The way she said it sent chills down her daughters' spines. They knew that voice. That voice meant doom. Mom had officially lost her patience.

CHAPTER TWENTY-THREE

Seth marveled at how long his patience was lasting. There really was nothing like being kidnapped by military thugs to teach you the art of sitting and waiting. The whole thing would be quite Zen, he thought, if it wasn't so uncomfortable. And boring.

They had been bouncing along in a dismal twilight fugue for hours before someone roughly pulled him out of the van and yanked the hood off his head. Seth showed his appreciation for this change in circumstance by immediately vomiting all over the nearest pair of shoes. The following five minutes of cursing brought a cracked smile to his face. He briefly considered urinating on himself just to annoy them, but decided it wasn't worth it.

After forcing some water down his throat and giving him a brief, humiliating opportunity to urinate, they shoved him back in the van and began driving again. They didn't untie him or let him clean the vomit off. Seth sat crouched forward with his hands going numb behind him while the soldiers around him sat, fondling their weapons and pretending to ignore him.

"So, where are we going?" Seth asked.

Total silence.

"What did I do?"

Nothing.

"Are you really with DARPA or is that patch on your uniform a clever ruse?"

They didn't even look at him.

Seth was getting cranky. He considered starting to scream for help, but figured that would lead down the path of pain. He really wasn't keen on pain.

"Off to one of your lovely prisons? Not enough puppies in the world for you guys to kick so you thought maybe you needed me?" One of the soldiers cracked a smile.

"Shut up," the man in the corner said. Seth turned to look at him. He was surprised that he hadn't recognized the weasely face of Stuart Lineman, DARPA's cryptographic pocket monkey. Seth considered and rejected several fabulously nasty things to say to Stuart.

"Why can't you just do your own homework, you little jerk?" was what he ended up with.

Stuart's features took on a haughty expression. "You are the idiot that started moving American satellites around. Did you think no one would notice? Not even your precious Omerta can save you now. You'll spill your guts or we'll spill them for you," the little man sniffed and utterly failed to look menacing.

Seth snorted. He was tempted to start spewing curses at the little toad, but decided it would be immature. Inside he felt the cold knot in his stomach unclench just a bit. Of all the things the Americans could grab him for, the satellite shuffling was small potatoes. Kind of silly, really.

Seth had spent years rifling through the American government networks, installing software and editing files to keep Omerta safe. He's spent the last few weeks doing some hardcore hacking for Clio's Revolution World guerrillas. But he moves around a few satellites so he can keep an eye on his girlfriend and they pop him in a black van with a bag over his head. That right there is the definition of irony, he thought.

Seth closed his eyes and slumped over. If they wanted to know how he moved the satellites, then they probably didn't know about Revolution World so Clio was safe. And they probably didn't know about the Omerta hacks so his family was safe. At least he hoped. In that case, he was exhausted and a nap was in order. He acted accordingly.

After a while, he felt a booted foot nudging him awake. He woke without opening his eyes or altering his breathing. He was oddly thankful to the many times Max tried to sneak up on him to play pranks. Now he was well trained in the art of appearing asleep.

He heard one of the soldiers mumble. "Well he won't sleep that good where we're taking him."

"We ought to wake him up, the snotty little nerd," said another.

"For all the trouble we've had down in Ambrosia Springs. I'm glad we'll be out of Texas."

"We'll probably have to go back if this guy gives it up," said the first soldier gloomily.

"At least that Floracopia raid wasn't a total loss," the second one said. "It put us on to the nerd here." He dug his boot into Seth's ribs viciously.

Seth rolled over to look at the soldier. The man smiled at him nastily and kicked Seth hard. As Seth coughed and twisted away, the soldier said, "I hope you like pain, nerd. We're tossing you in the darkest hole we can find and I doubt we'll ever let you out."

Seth couldn't help it. He laughed. He laughed because he remembered that his last blood transfusion had been five days ago. If he didn't get another transfusion within two weeks, he would die a slow and agonizing death. Reportedly the pain drove ZFD sufferers insane before the end. Seth wondered if he would find out for himself.

Unfortunately, the soldier interpreted Seth's smile as bravado and smashed Seth across the face with the butt of his gun. Seth decided this was an excellent time to black out.

CHAPTER TWENTY-FOUR

The Texas Omerta Facility was a madhouse on speed. Pandemonium on crack cocaine. Insanity in an Elvis suit mainlining caffeine. Max was holding court in the main banquet hall. People streamed in an out as he and Gloria fired off commands and pleas. A parade of outraged politicians and Omerta leaders flickered through the holograms. Max could tell Gloria was close to completely snapping. He briefly imagined her commandeering the world's satellites and armaments and blowing up landmarks until someone gave Seth back. He probably wouldn't stop her.

"What good are you people if you can't find him? We already know who took him!" Gloria cried. A moment later she threw her handheld down. "We should have installed a tracking device in his skull like I wanted to do in the first place."

Max remembered the brief, but highly emotionally charged debate over the tracking device idea Gloria had last year. He was still glad they voted her down.

Rubbing his eyes, Max wandered out of the room to find coffee. He passed Clio in a room covered in wallscreens. There was no one else in the room with her, but he could see hundreds of game avatars milling around in the wallscreens.

Clio had buds in her ears and was talking to the avatars like it was a town hall meeting and she was the mayor. "Alright, now where is the Fredericksburg militia? Someone get them out here on the double. This is a five-alarm fire, people."

All the avatars were dressed in what looked like old military uniforms, perhaps from the Civil War Era. He wasn't sure. American history wasn't something that interested him. Then Max remembered that Seth had been spending a lot of time on the Revolution World game with Clio. He wondered why she was playing a game at this point in time. It was weird. But he was too shell-shocked to ask.

"Speed is of the essence in this maneuver, folks. This is not a drill," Clio ordered as he wandered off. "This game has a high likelihood of live rounds. Repeat. This is not a drill."

Harmony was in the next conference room, surrounded by people. She was like a queen bee marshaling her workers.

"Sheriff, since these DARPA guys seem to be able to roam the countryside like banditos on a spree, I don't really know what you can do to stop them. But you need to try," she commanded, sweeping past the poor man. In the last six months, the sheriff seemed to have lost what little hair he had. He'd gained a whole new set of worry lines, though.

Max admired the seething competence Harmony exuded, but watching her made him tired. He briefly considered sneaking down to his room and hiding under his bed. But he knew that wouldn't help, so he kept walking towards the kitchen.

Max pondered whether or not to start poking around in Seth's private work. Seth had given him all the access codes, but Max had never used them out of respect for his nephew's privacy. There was probably something in there that might shed light on what was going on.

On the other hand, DARPA may have tagged one of Seth's programs and poking around might set them off again. Max couldn't be sure. He decided his time was better spent convincing politicians and bureaucrats to press for Seth's release. It didn't matter so much why Seth was taken so long as he was returned quickly and in one piece.

Max recognized the hulking frame of Jason as the man came barreling down the hall. Jason had a smaller man in a headlock and was dragging him down the hall.

"Hello, Jason," Max greeted him. "Need help with something?"

Jason stopped. The man in the headlock let out a squeak. "Nope," drawled Jason. "I got this particular situation under control. Found Floracopia's rat, you see." Jason nodded at the man in the headlock. Max bent to peer at the man.

"That guy looks familiar," said Max.

"This is Joanna's husband, Eric Guerrero," Jason replied. "You know Joanna, right? The woman who runs the business side of Floracopia? And the Junior League and all that other stuff?"

"Oh yeah," Max remembered.

"Well, I got a buddy down in Austin who bartends at this little dive bar on Congress Avenue called *The Elephant Room.* I'm down there keeping a barstool warm last night and who comes in but Eric here? He doesn't see me, but I watch him have a nice cozy chat with two people from Malsanto." Jason gave Eric's head a squeeze. Eric made a pained sound. Jason looked pleased about that.

"How did you know they were from Malsanto?" asked Max, eyeing Eric with disfavor.

"Some guy at the bar told me. My buddy the bartender says he remembers them coming in pretty often for little chats. He says the first time was probably six months ago, before the Floracopia break-in. The first one," Jason explained as he resumed dragging Eric in the direction of Harmony. Max followed.

After a brief flurry of activity, Max found himself in a small room with Eric Guerrero seated in front of Jason, Harmony, and Clio. They kicked everyone else out, including Joanna.

Joanna looked ten years older after Jason's explanation. After a brief look at Eric's hangdog expression, she left without a word. For once, her shoulders slumped. It was as though all the life force had drained right out of her. Max had made the executive decision to kick Gloria out too.

"We need you out there calling in favors and pulling strings and finding out everything we can. I'll take care of this while you do more important things," Max told her as he pushed her out the door. Max was actually concerned that she might kill the man before they found out anything useful.

"They made me do it," Eric was babbling. "They're crazy. They threatened me." Nobody had even asked him any questions yet.

"Why would you do this, Eric?" Harmony asked softly.

Eric babbled wildly about being threatened and how it was not his fault.

"Eric, calm down," interrupted Max. "Right now, we just need to find Seth and get him returned as soon as possible. Is Malsanto in some way involved with that? Do you know anything at all about his kidnapping?"

"It was all those Malsanto people," Eric cried. "Shiva and Medea. It's all their fault."

Max began to see the attractiveness of torture in a way he never had before. He didn't think it would make this man stop telling lies. But Max was angry and Eric was grating on his very last nerve. Even if it didn't get them any information, it might make Max feel a little better. He sighed and stepped away from Eric to avoid the temptation to slap the little worm.

"They were the ones who blabbed to the DARPA guys. Shiva and Medea," Eric said.

Max sat up. "What are you saying?"

"Shiva and Medea wanted that p-mod technique and they were crazy to get it," Eric gasped, his eyes darting around the room. "They said the military guys would throw them into a labor camp if they didn't get it, but they were just evil. Yeah. They tried to break in that first time. I got the access codes out of Joanna's handheld. I told them it was stupid but they made me." Sweat rolled down his face. The last sentence was so manifestly a lie that even Eric didn't look like he believed it.

"I knew it. I knew it wasn't Joanna or Nancy," exploded Clio. Her mother looked at her reprovingly. Clio shrugged. "But now we at least know."

Eric looked like he thought he might be able to talk himself out of this situation. "Yeah, I'm helping you. See? It all works out because I'm helping you now. And anyway, I thought they were just going to take a few papers. Hardly stealing at all. I didn't know you'd be in the building that night or I never would have given them the access codes."

Jason clenched his fists and took a step towards Eric, but Harmony restrained him.

Eric noticed the movement and started babbling again. "Then they wanted me to go in and get some more notes, but the notes weren't there any more. It was all electronic files after that. I told them I couldn't do it. Not without getting caught. So they said they'd create a distraction. How was I to know they were going to bomb the Omerta compound?"

"Why would you people do that?" choked Max.

Eric's voice started to take on a whining tone. "Well, we needed everyone away from Floracopia so we could try to break in again.

The security system was recording everything and sending it to the Omerta computers, so we needed to disrupt the computers. Also, some of the security stuff they installed after the first break-in tripped alarms at the police station. So we needed for the police to be distracted as well." Eric whined, reminding Max strongly of a rat in a trap. "It wasn't my idea."

"They were in town that day meeting with us," said Harmony. She was trying to fit it together. "So that night they sent remote controlled car bombs into the Omerta compound so they could break in to Floracopia?"

Eric just shrugged. Harmony gave him the kind of look usually reserved for escaped mental patients or very ugly children.

"And did you succeed? Did you get what you wanted from Floracopia?" asked Clio.

"No," said Eric with a scowl. "We couldn't get the data off the computers. They got some, but apparently that didn't help enough. Medea was always riding Shiva about some failed experiments. They had a deadline, see? If they didn't produce what they promised the military, they'd get tossed in one of those prison labs the military has."

And it went on like that for over two hours. Eric rambled and pleaded and told them everything he knew. Nobody even threatened him but he begged for his life, all the while insisting that Shiva and Medea had forced him to participate. Presumably in the same way Max and the others were forcing him now.

"But how did Malsanto get involved with the DARPA guys?" Harmony asked again.

Eric gave an irritated shrug. "I don't know. I thought they were done after the bombing failed. The next thing I know, I get a call from Medea saying if I want to redeem my failures, I'll help them out on the DARPA raid."

It turned out that Eric had again snuck in at night and helpfully shut down some of the security features to make sure there was little resistance or help when the DARPA vans arrived at Floracopia. Fortunately for them, he was as incompetent at that as he was at everything else.

"You mean that, if you had managed to turn off all the alarms, everyone in the building would probably be locked up in a military cell right now?" asked Max.

"They made me," whimpered Eric.

Max had to leave the room for a little while after that.

Harmony studied this man that had brought so much ruin into her life. Putting aside the injuries to herself and potential harm to her family and friends, Harmony thought of the massive amount of damage done to the labs and the huge loss that the destroyed and confiscated experiments cost them. She took a few deep breaths and considered leaving the room for a break as well.

Jason remained in his chair, examining Eric. He leaned forward. "And what does all this have to do with DARPA kidnapping Seth tonight?"

Eric licked his lips. "Well, DARPA got so much bad press for the raid on Floracopia that they really needed to come up with evidence for some terrible terrorist plot to justify shooting Miss Harmony and breaking all that stuff. But they didn't find anything on Floracopia. Made them real mad. They were looking really hard. From what I hear, they got some kind of dirt on that Seth guy so they decided to pick him up."

Clio stared at Eric for a long minute. "What you are saying is that DARPA found something about Seth that they used to justify taking him. So we know how it is that DARPA came to kidnap Seth. But that still doesn't help us get him back," she said slowly.

Max looked around and everyone just shrugged. He shook his head to get the stupid out, but it just wouldn't go.

CHAPTER TWENTY-FIVE

Seth shook his head to clear away the groggy sick feeling that was wrapped around it. Then he realized that it was actually a hood. He had a brief but sincere discussion with his stomach over the importance of not throwing up with a hood taped over your head. Just as he felt that he and his stomach had come to an understanding, the bag was roughly pulled away to reveal to foul faces of the crazy DARPA colonel and his flunkies.

"Are we really going to do this? Really?" asked Seth in a uninterested voice. Honestly, he hadn't expected to be bored like this, but he'd been sitting around for hours with nothing to do. He was hungry and his back was killing him. Seth realized that real life happens at a much slower pace than James Bond movies and the villains are much less interesting.

"Boy, you fail to understand the seriousness of your situation," began the colonel. He went on at length, but Seth's attention wandered around the room. He noticed a variety of sharp and wicked-looking implements.

Two men in white coats bustled around in a very efficient manner. That did not bode well. The room looked exactly like what he envisioned a high tech torture chamber would look like.

Seth interrupted the colonel to ask, "Don't you have one of those really bright lights to shine in my eyes?"

"What's that, boy?" barked the colonel.

"We're in here so you can torture me, right?" Seth asked, nodding to the equipment. "That's what all this stuff is? So where is the bright light?"

The colonel appeared somewhat taken aback by Seth's attitude. "I don't think we have one of those." He looked around the room for a minute.

"Why don't you just tell me what you want to know?" suggested

Seth in a reasonable tone. "Who knows? You may not have to torture me for it."

Seth began to feel that the colonel had some speech prepared in his mind that he was determined to get out. Perhaps the best thing to do was to let him get through it so they could move on. Seth shut his mouth and looked in the colonel's direction. His mind wandered off, but he tried to nod occasionally to make it look like he was paying attention.

Seth had asked about the bright light primarily because he worried that a bright enough light would have the same effect on him as the sun. It would burn his skin and then the colonel here would know there was something wrong with him. Seth would much prefer that didn't happen.

"What if they decide to torture me by cutting me up? They'll notice when the cuts heal too quickly, won't they?" he wondered.

Seth looked back to the two men in lab coats. He wondered if they were doctors or just DARPA guys in white coats. He could only hope that doctors who participated in torture were not very good doctors. Perhaps they wouldn't notice his medical anomalies.

"You better listen to me, son," growled the colonel.

"What? I'm sorry. My mind wandered there for a minute," apologized Seth.

The colonel turned red. Seth thought that if ever there was a man in need of anger management classes, the colonel was it. He wondered how such a man came to a position of power like this. Perhaps he had been a reasonable and calm person and had cracked under the strain. Who knew?

"Well, I think we have a few ways to make sure you take our time here seriously," the colonel said with a nasty grin. He nodded to the two men in lab coats.

Seth felt incredible pain coursing through him. He looked down and saw electrodes attached to his feet. Seth had never been electrocuted before. Honestly, the experience wasn't all it was cracked up to be. After the pain stopped, the colonel grinned.

"Get used to that kind of thing. You are going to be here a very long time. Maybe for the rest of your life," the colonel announced before he swept out of the room.

"Drama queen," mumbled Seth.

The men in white coats began attaching electrodes to various other parts of his anatomy and all of them were places he would rather not be electrocuted. They also set up a table in one corner with several vials and syringes.

The pain began. In a corner of his mind, Seth was glad that all the equipment he had seen would not involve cutting him or anything else that might show them how different he was. That was a minor blessing, at least. He did not want them to find out about his disease and give him a transfusion. It was strange sort of comfort to know that, one way or another, he would be done with all of this in two weeks.

"Son, I think you are holding out on us. All we want is some information," the colonel said much later. He seemed somewhat subdued after two days of Seth's torture. Seth wondered if the colonel had ever done this before.

"So, come on. Level with me," Seth replied. "Why do you guys do this? Torture, I mean. Of all the scientific studies to be done about interrogation techniques, none of them have ever concluded that torturing people yielded better information than other methods. Like just asking them."

The colonel looked at him blankly.

"Seriously. Torturing people doesn't work. They proved it scientifically a long time ago. So why do it?" Seth asked as he spit blood on the floor. It made him sad to do this. He had dry mouth for hours and even the salty taste of blood was welcome.

"What do you mean it doesn't work?" blustered the colonel. "The United States of America wouldn't do something that didn't work. You hook a man's scrotum up to a car battery and he talks. Everyone knows that."

"Oh please," laughed Seth. "And they put you in charge of the science division of the military? That's pathetic." He was beyond caring. "You electrocute a person's gonads and they talk, sure. They'll tell you anything. Anything at all. Anything they think you want to know. That's the key. Anything they think you want to hear. But that won't be the truth. Maybe they don't know anything and they make up a lie just to get you to stop. Maybe they do know something but they tell you whatever they think will make you stop. Maybe that's the truth and maybe it isn't."

The colonel gestured to the men in white coats to continue. And Seth talked. He talked about video games he hated and his favorite kinds of clouds. He talked about Clio and every girl he'd ever dated and his favorite algorithms. Seth spun incredible tales about dragons and security systems and Japanese animation. Actually, he was fairly sure they were lame stories, but it passed the time. He had analysts working around the clock to find the meaning in his madness.

"Science shows torture is pointless. If it doesn't work, why do it, Colonel?" Seth asked between jolts of pain. "Do you just like being the kind of guy who tortures people? Are you just a cruel sadistic jerk who can't find enough butterflies to rip the wings off of?"

The colonel gave up and stalked off. The men in white coats turned off the machines. One of them brought Seth some water. Seth sipped at it gratefully.

"I think it has more to do with the past than the future," the man said. Seth looked up at him.

The white coat continued, "They never try to get information out of you to prevent some future terrorist attack. They say they do, but that's not it really. They are trying to get you to confess to something. They want revenge and they want you to be their scapegoat. The truth never seems to have much to do with it."

Seth thought about asking him why he was involved in this, but decided the answer was bound to be unfulfilling. They moved him to his cell. Seth had to admit that this cell was a pretty impressive piece of torture technology. The ceiling was just slightly too low for him to stand up straight and the walls were slightly too snug to allow him to lie down comfortably. It was cold and dank. The lights were dim and flickered. There was a nauseating static sound that faded in and out. In short, it was like every airplane toilet in the universe.

If he'd been in a mood to crack and tell them everything, this cell would have had him talking on the first day. But Seth wasn't in the mood. He wondered if the program he wrote would do its job and alert Omerta that he had been taken. He wondered if any one would come for him.

Over the next few days, Seth spent quite a bit of time thinking about Clio and Gloria. At least he thought it might be a few days.

He couldn't be sure. He thought about the kind of life he wanted to have and how he might go about getting it. Seth thought about what was really important to him. He thought about what he would do differently if he ever got out.

Seth frequently chuckled to himself in a less than lucid way. Other people paid buckets of money to life coaches and psychologists and gurus to help them figure out how to live. He got all of that for free plus more electricity than any sane person could want, courtesy of the American military. What a bargain.

Sometimes, Seth allowed himself to hope that his family would negotiate for his freedom. He spun luxurious fantasies in which he would be released and go on to live a long and peaceful life. As the days passed, Seth tried to keep those thoughts out of his mind. They just made it worse. The pain that began in his stomach and joints served as a distraction. Seth's body was breaking down.

Sometimes in the torture room, Seth almost cracked and told them that all their equipment couldn't come close to achieving the level of pain that his body was in already. Whenever he thought about doing that he laughed maniacally. The men in the white coats told the colonel that his mind had broken and there was no point in proceeding.

Seth wondered if that was true.

CHAPTER TWENTY-SIX

The governor had never seen The Elephant Room so packed and he'd been drinking in that bar for more years than he cared to add up. He still managed to secure his usual table, although he suspected the bartender had moved some folks to accommodate him.

As he waited, he watched the wallscreen show the news. He wasn't the only one. The screen showed the Texas capitol earlier this week when the military had announced stricter gun control laws for Texas to be enforced immediately.

The governor winced as the image of himself filled the screen. He hated seeing himself on the screen. He always looked so old and angry.

"This amounts to nothing less than the forced disarmament of a peaceful country," he was shouting out of the wallscreen. "The right to bear arms was so cherished by our forefathers that, when they founded the United States of America, it was the second amendment. The second one. The only thing they thought more important than the right to defend themselves was the right to freedom of speech. They crossed an ocean and fought a war for those rights. How can we be expected to just give them away?" The crowd assembled on the capitol steps roared.

The screen switched to the image of a little old Texas lady in lavender pantsuit with a fluffy white bouffant. She was clutching a shotgun and screaming, "You can take it from my cold dead hands!"

That clip still made the governor smile. He smiled every time he saw one of the thousands of shirts, bumper stickers, and yard signs that had sprung up in the last week. The ones with the slogan "Come and Take It" written across the Lone Star Flag.

Lord knows he needed something to smile about these days.

The whole world had gone crazy.

The senator slid into the booth. "Don't you feel like a jerk, sitting in this booth alone when this place is packed?"

"I just thought that's what it felt like to be you all the time," the governor shot back, passing his friend a beer.

"I've arranged for some people to meet us later. I think you'll find their conversation to be very stimulating," the senator replied.

The governor nodded. "Any luck getting that Omerta ambassador freed?"

The senator shook his head. "Those military jerks are like a dog with a bone. I don't know what they think that kid is going to tell them, but they're all excited about it. Now that they've done the unthinkable and snatched a foreign dignitary, they refuse to admit that it was a mistake and turn him loose. Honestly, I think we'll get him out eventually, but it's going to be a while."

"He doesn't have a while," said Jason appearing from the crowd. "He has another week at the most."

"Governor, this is one of the men I wanted you to meet," said the senator, moving over to make room for Jason in the booth.

"Seth has a medical condition that will kill him in less than a week if he does not receive treatment," said Max as he slid into the booth next to the governor. A short man with flame red hair followed behind them. This man dragged a chair over and sat down without comment.

"And you vouch for these men?" the governor asked the senator.

"I do indeed," said the senator. The governor removed the scrambler from his pocket and turned it on. Max leaned over to pick it up.

"Sir, I am flattered that you have one of my inventions, but please allow me," Max remarked as he pulled up his sleeve and tapped a button on his wristband. The wallscreen immediately went dead and a cry of disappointment went up from the crowd. "My personal scrambler is a little overzealous, but you can't be too careful these days."

"Governor, may I introduce Max," said the senator. "He's the other programmer-ambassador from Omerta. It was his nephew who was taken."

The governor shook Max's hand vigorously. "I'm very sorry about your nephew. We are doing all we can to secure his release."

"Not to doubt you, sir," replied Max. "But we are meeting today because I feel there is quite a bit more we could be doing. And I am not just talking about Seth. Texas has quite a large number of problems lately. Some of which we are involved in. All of them affect us. I can't help but feel this is an excellent time to cooperate on a dramatic gesture."

The governor started to reply, but the senator cut him off. "Let me introduce Jason here. He's the man who brought us Revolution World. All of it. Particularly the parts of the game that you and I have found so interesting lately," underlined the senator.

Jason cleared his throat. "I think you gentlemen need to understand exactly how popular Revolution World is. At this point, at least sixty percent of Texas plays the game. More than half of those players are members of the secret rooms that you gentlemen have been exploring lately." Jason paused to let that sink in. "So if you want to make a dramatic gesture, governor, your people stand at the ready."

The governor raised his eyebrows and sat back in his seat. The senator grinned. This was the most fun he'd had in years. Jason continued after sipping his beer, "Seth was doing valuable work for Revolution World. We need him back, sirs. We need him badly. And even more important, we cannot have him telling anything he knows to the military."

"Amen to that," said Max.

"But what can we do?" asked the governor, blowing out an angry breath. "If they won't give him back, we can't exactly send the Texas Rangers in to Idaho or wherever it is they have him. And you tell me the boy only has a week."

"Well, now there is a chance," answered Max. "It's a slim one and a long shot and a wee bit complicated. But it's better than nothing. We've been doing nothing for far too long. The American government is a big bully and it's time someone stood up to it."

The governor gave the men in front of him an appraising look. They grinned like fools. "What are we talking about here?" he asked them. "What do you boys have in mind?"

The senator leaned forward once more and gestured to the

unnamed man sitting with them. "This gentleman here is Linus Marceux, the owner of SpaceTex. You know, that astronaut company out in Houston in charge of all the Texas satellites? Turns out he and Jason here are drinking buddies from way back in the day. They've been working on a little project that I think will come in handy very soon."

Linus nodded and began speaking with a thick Cajun accent. "Well sir, first off I want you to know that all them satellites we put up work just fine. It just doesn't suit us to let the big government man know all our business. They think I am an ignorant coonass who can't get a satellite working any better than a Yankee can do a keg stand? I let them keep thinking that. And let me just tell you, our satellites have a few extra bells and whistles that you boys might find useful. So there's that."

"Tell him about the trash," said Jason gleefully.

"I hadn't heard about trash," said the senator turning to look at Linus.

The man chuckled and scratched his red goatee thoughtfully. "Well, we come up with a way to clean up all the space trash out there, see? All them countries been dropping stuff in the thermosphere for decades and they want it out of the way for their shiny new toys. So we clean it up for them and we get *lagniappe*. We find a funny little use for all that trash."

It took a while to explain what they had in mind. The governor gasped. The senator roared with laughter. The other bar patrons slowly filtered out to find someplace where the wallscreen worked and they could use their handhelds. The five men called for the bartender's best whiskey, rolled up their sleeves, and began to plan some serious naughtiness.

CHAPTER TWENTY-SEVEN

The last time Seth told Clio he was a vampire, they were fighting their way out of a military research facility. Clio dragged a groggy Seth down a series of corridors while alarms sounded.

"I'm so happy to see you," he slurred. They'd used a combination of sensory disorientation, electrocution and sedatives to try to get him to comply. It didn't work.

Seth would never, to his dying day, forget the sight of Clio kicking down that door. The light from the hallway filtered in behind her and a rush of cool air tossed her curls. She looked like an angel in steel-toed boots. A seriously pissed-off angel who was about lay down some vengeance. He was glad she was on his side.

He wanted to ask her where they were, how she found him, how long he'd been there, and how they were going to ever get free. But this first thing out of his mouth was: "Why did you shove cotton balls up my nose?"

"I'm soaked in synthetic pheromones. Any one who gets a whiff of me immediately takes a nap." That would explain all the soldiers curled up on the floor.

"I see. And what is this you handed me?" he asked.

"Laser gun. On second thought, give that back. You don't look too steady. Better takes some of these marijuana grenades. Just pull the pin, toss it at the bad guys and all they'll want to do is give peace a chance and feed the munchies." She smiled ferociously as she kicked open a door.

If she wasn't so afraid that she wanted to vomit up her spleen, Clio might almost enjoy this. Since they started playing Revolution World, she and her sisters had built up quite an arsenal and she was finally getting to use some of it.

They encountered plenty of resistance. Seth threw the grenades and Clio fired off laser bolts and taser pellets. Over the bodies of fallen soldiers, they finally made their way to the door out.

Seth stopped at the door and squinted at the sunlight. Behind them he could hear muted explosions as well as what sounded like small dogs barking and gun fire. She must have brought Team Pom or else he was just hallucinating.

"How far will we have to run?" he asked.

"Just over there. I brought your hovercar. I got as close as I could." She looked him over and winced at some of his injuries. "Come on, we've got to get out of here."

As they made the final run, time seemed to stop when Seth saw the two gunmen. He saw that they had on masks to filter out Clio's pheromones and smoke bombs. He saw that they had their guns pointed at Clio. He forgot about Clio's grenades.

Whenever Seth tried to remember those moments, it always came back to him like flipping through a series of photographs. First, he was leaping between Clio and the gunmen. Then, he was ripping the mask from one of the men, his retractable fangs fully extended. Next, he was sticky with blood and turning to the second gunman. Last, he was standing over two bodies, watching his skin burn and sizzle as he felt Clio's hand on his shoulder. That's when he noticed one of the nose plugs had come out.

Seth woke up later in the passenger seat of his car as it raced along much faster than he'd ever driven it before. Clio was clutching the wheel, staring at the road.

"Don't you have the autopilot on?" he rasped.

"Yes." She still didn't look at him.

"Then why don't you let go of the wheel?" he asked. Clio scowled at him but didn't reply.

After a moment, she handed him a jug of water. He drank it and took stock of his various injuries. Although it hurt like hell, the sun damage was not too bad on his face. He peeled back a bandage and examined his hand. That would definitely scar.

"I gave you a blood transfusion while you were out," she said stiffly. Seth flexed his fingers experimentally. The joints didn't scream in pain. He would live.

"What happened?" he asked.

Clio took a breath and let it out slowly. "They took you over a week ago. It took us a while, but Max and your cousin finally found you. Kalliope and your uncle made some modifications to your car. I came alone with the poms."

Seth looked back to see a bunch of singed fluffballs lolling their tongues at him.

Clio gave him a short smile. "We lost one back there and I had to leave another at home. Apparently, you're going to get puppies soon."

"Oh," was all he could think to say at first. "Where are we?"

"Halfway home. You've been out for about five hours," she replied, gripping the steering wheel tighter. "You grabbed the guns from those soldiers like you were plucking grapes."

"Endorphins. And I've been working out," Seth muttered feebly.

"You tore those guys' throats out with your teeth," Clio replied tersely. "I didn't even see them until you were shredding their masks! And then you ripped them apart. You have fangs! You drank their blood." She screeched and threw up her hands. And there it was.

"I told you I was a vampire," he said quietly. He couldn't resist adding, "Twice."

"Oh don't start with me, mister. First I thought you were joking, as you well know. And that second time, I thought you meant you were doing a vampire LARPing game. But no! I examined you while you were out, you know. You have retractable fangs." She pointed at him accusingly.

Seth frowned, distracted. "LARPing?"

"Oh, you know, 'Live Action Role Playing.' LARPing. It's what you nerd boys do. I thought you were just letting me know you are extra-special dorky, not that you are a member of the undead."

Seth thought about that for a minute.

"No, I still don't get it. People actually go pretend to be vampires together? What do they do, exactly? Sneak around trying to bite each other with fake fangs?"

"I'm not really sure. I looked it up on the globenet. It seems to involve hand signals and costumes." Clio had gotten sidetracked.

Seth arched an eyebrow. "You thought I pretended to be a vampire as a hobby? You must think I'm really weird."

"Well, of course I thought you were weird," Clio said softly. "But that's why I like you. I'm really weird too. But you really are a vampire."

"Yes," he replied. She said nothing. She didn't even look at him.

So this was it. She'd finally realized his true nature and was repulsed. Seth felt a wave of despair as he watched her frown silently.

"So, how does that work exactly? You can't be undead. That's just stupid. I'm a geneticist and I refuse to believe in the undead," Clio said, deep in thought. "Obviously you have some sort of genetic abnormality that causes you to burn in sunlight. That would make a lot of sense with the glowing eyes and teeth thing. Some kind of porphyry or an alteration to the kidney function? Maybe it's a strange permutation of lupus."

He couldn't believe her. He'd gone from being a monster to an interesting science project in fifteen minutes. There really was no one quite like her. If he could convince her not to dissect him, he was going to marry this girl some day.

"Of course, I am not undead. This isn't a fairy tale. It's just some weird medical disorder," Seth said. "I should tell you this, though. While very few of us that survive to adulthood and almost no one survives if they are not from a family that knows how to deal with the disease, we do live a long time. Not forever, but under certain conditions there are some that have lived over three hundred years."

"Really?" she asked, with interest. "How is that possible?"

Seth shrugged. "I'm not really sure, but there are people at Omerta who are over two hundred and look like they are in their fifties. We almost never catch diseases."

"Very interesting. Perhaps the constant transfusions retards the aging process," replied Clio. "I wonder why. Think of the medical applications. Got any other neat tricks up your sleeve? Can you fly or something too?" She was only half joking.

He rolled his eyes. "No. I can't fly or turn into a bat. Some of us do have enhanced senses. Better hearing, better eyesight, that kind of thing. Most of us are a little faster and stronger than your average guy, but nothing super. Like me. I have great night vision, but I'm still klutzy."

"Aw, really? You can't turn into a bat but you live forever and have a rock star immune system? Bummer." Clio whistled. Then it occurred to her to ask, "So how old are you then?"

"Sixty-four."

Clio gave him a disbelieving look.

"I'm not counting in dog years either. I was born sixty-four years ago," Seth continued.

She reached over and smacked him on the head. "You jerk. You should have told me this a long time ago. Man, I can't wait to get you back in the lab and get some samples."

Great. She'd want bone marrow, a brain sample or something involving huge needles.

Clio had another thought. "No wonder you guys don't put yourselves on the UN list for gene modification or get the disease officially recognized. I bet a lot of you don't want to be cured."

"Exactly. It's not a great life. No sunlight. Lots of secrecy. But it has its benefits." He swallowed and then said quickly, "You don't mind being with an old man like me?"

"Ick. Old guy." Clio wrinkled her nose playfully. "Like I care about that."

Seth pushed her. She giggled and then had a revelation. "Wait. How many people have ZFD at Omerta?"

Seth hesitated, and then sighed. "All of them."

Clio almost jumped out her seat. "All of them? Your uncle! Your whole family. Gloria?" She was floored. "Your uncle is a vampire? Oh man, my Mom is going to freak out."

"We can't tell her," Seth said quickly.

She gave him a withering look. "Yeah, sure. You keep telling yourself that. See who she breaks first."

Things on the dashboard began to light up. Clio began tapping at various consoles.

"So when we were together, you were thirsting for my blood, like in the books? You were keeping yourself from tearing my throat and drinking me dry?" She had stopped looking at him again.

Seth snorted in disgust. "Bah. That's the worst part of the vampire mythos. I mean, in the heat of lust that you'd want to start drinking someone's blood? Gross. When we are passionate together, do you want a ham sandwich? When you get hungry, do you think about roasting and eating your dog? No, it's ridiculous. We are rational humans. We don't suddenly become cannibals at the first hunger pang. If we are sick, we take medicine. That's what blood is for us—medicine."

She laughed so he continued. "And those movies! They make it seem as though the victims of vampire attack get some sort of sexual thrill from the whole thing. It's just silly. Do you find it sexually thrilling to cut your hand or bump your knee? No. Foolishness."

Clio laughed again and tapped away some more at her handheld. "Well great, because that would be a little too weird for me, quite frankly. But right now we have a problem. Those idiots at DARPA appear to want you so bad that they've sent some actual diesel-burning armored cars after us. Barbarians."

"How far are we from home?" he asked.

"We've got another five hours until we pass the Texas border," she replied. "I don't know how we're going to make it."

"I've made some alterations to this car myself," Seth said as he quickly tapped away on the dashboard. A whirring noise made the dogs whine. The hovercar shot forward at a speed that Clio would have previously assumed impossible. The armored cars faded into the horizon.

"They'll probably send more," she said. "They know where we're going so I would also expect a road block."

"True. Well, we're in a hovercar. We don't have to stay on the road, but off-roading will slow us down," he replied. "It will give us some time to make a plan, though."

"Fine, let's do it. But we have get across the Texas border by eight p.m. tonight or we are totally screwed," Clio said, like this was a totally reasonable thing to say.

"That's going to be tricky. They are jamming my satellite connection. We can't call anybody or access the globenet," he replied.

"I stored detailed maps on my handheld before I left because I figured they would do that." Clio passed him her handheld and his plugged it into the dashboard so the autopilot could access the maps. "Actually, I had hoped that getting you out would be a quiet maneuver and they wouldn't notice so much. But the situation got out of control." This was a huge understatement.

Seth reprogrammed their course in the autopilot and they shot off the road and through a field. Then he looked at her mournfully. "Clio, my love, what's to stop them from taking me again even if we make it home?" he asked.

"Don't you worry. We just need to make it to Texas. And we will." She smiled that fierce smile of hers again and it comforted him.

"I love you," he sighed.

Clio melted like a teenage girl getting her first bunch of flowers. "Really? You love me? Even with the vampire thing and the age difference?"

"Yes. You are the woman for me," he said firmly. He wanted to hold her in his arms and smother her with kisses, but he was pretty filthy right now and the cab of his car was tiny, so he settled for holding her hand.

Her smile could have lit the world. "I love you too."

They smiled like fools for several long minutes.

"So how are we going to keep the government from arresting me the minute we get home?" he asked to distract himself from a lurid daydream he was having in which he pulled over the car and ravished her thoroughly.

"Well, I can let you in on the secret now," she whispered. "We have an army of werewolves ready to overthrow the government."

"What?!" He was stunned.

Clio just looked at him and grinned.

"Vampires are so gullible."

CHAPTER TWENTY-EIGHT

Harmony was cursing. She did this fluently, thoroughly and with great imagination. This did not stop her from working with single-minded focus to get Seth and her daughter home. It didn't even slow her down. For the last two days, she had been a whirlwind of activity. She had not slept a minute. Pausing only to recharge with coffee and protein drinks, she had coordinated a massive plan to get them home and keep them safe.

The problem was that there was nothing she could really do now but wait. Harmony had never been good at that and she saw no need to start practicing now.

"You have an impressive command of the English language," Max remarked without looking up. He was tapping away on the wallscreen so quickly his hands were almost a blur. She gave him a sharp look.

Max held up a hand, "Now don't start in on me too. I'm helping you, remember?"

"Then help faster," she grumped, sitting next to him so she could watch. He moved satellites and rummaged through the American military network like it was a yard sale and he was looking for cheap socks.

He had been monitoring Seth and Clio's escape through the sensors in the hovercar and by intercepting military communications, so he knew they had made it out in one piece. But getting Seth out had taken Clio a lot longer than they had planned. He could see that they were now headed to Texas, but they'd be coming in very close to the deadline. From what he was intercepting, the military planned to stop them before they got there. All this worry and frustration was going to give Max an ulcer.

He spared Harmony a small smile, but didn't stop working.

"How could I refuse such a gracious command by so beautiful a woman?"

"I'm not in the mood for your flirting," Harmony snapped. "Save it for women your own age."

A smile quirked at his lips. "Let's just say I prefer women of a certain age and that is whatever age you are."

"I'm sure all the other women you used that line on thought it was charming," Harmony replied, getting up to pace around the room.

She did not see Max's shoulders slump. He stopped what he was doing and watched her pace. "I have, in fact, said charming things to hundreds of women. That is true. But I moved hundreds of miles from my very comfortable home just to hear your witty banter. Believe me, I've never done that for anyone." He sighed and rubbed his forehead.

Harmony stopped pacing and looked at him incredulously. He returned her look with a level gaze. "When are you going to take me seriously?" asked Max.

Harmony frowned and looked at him for a minute, then shook her head and went back to pacing. "Don't be ridiculous."

Max let out a shout of pure frustration and shot to his feet. Harmony was startled. Max stalked across the room, pulled her into his arms and kissed her roughly. Once she realized what was going on, Harmony couldn't help but kiss him back. Enthusiastically.

"I am quite willing to demonstrate the seriousness of my attraction for you," Max growled into her ear without releasing her from his embrace. "In a variety of ways. Over the course of several hours. I have spent quite a bit of time alone at night thinking about how best to do that." His sprinkled kisses down her neck as Harmony tried to collect her wits.

"Yes," she said finally, struggling to put some distance between herself and Max. "That, ah, sounds quite nice actually. Obviously, we have some sexual tension that should be, ah, diffused. After Seth and Clio are safe at home, I will be happy to, ah, do that."

Harmony pulled her clothing back into place and buttoned her shirt. It was like her clothing was trying to leap off her the minute the man looked at her with lust in his eyes. She tried to smooth her hair as Max caught her in his arms again.

He scowled at her. "Woman, you aren't going to get rid of me by screwing my brains out." A lecherous smile crossed his lips. "Although I'd love for you to try."

Harmony pushed him away. "Please Max. I'm a mature woman. You don't have to pretend to want some sort of serious relationship when we both know you'll be out tomorrow with a girl your own age. I don't have time for a serious commitment and I doubt you are capable of such a thing."

Max threw up his hands and collapsed on the floor. "Harmony, you are going to be the death of me. I haven't touched another woman since the day I met you. And would you please stop harping on my age? I'm thirty years older than you, for pity's sake!"

Harmony was moved, but still wary of him. "What are you talking about?"

Max sighed. "I am every bit of eighty-five years old."

Why not? Why not just tell her everything? From what he could read in Seth's private files, his nephew had already revealed the full extent of their little problem to Clio. So it was only a matter of time until Harmony found out anyway. And the world was ending out there anyway. If the US was crazy enough to retaliate with nukes, they could be vaporized at any minute and this woman would still be dismissing him as a lightweight. What the hell.

She raised an eyebrow.

"Seriously," he said. "And madly in love with you."

She narrowed her eyes, but sat down on the floor next to him. She turned and started to speak, but then stopped with a frown.

"I'm a vampire," he said miserably.

Harmony started laughing.

"It's all true," he continued. "Horribly, depressingly true."

"That makes sense," Harmony said, still chuckling.

"What? No it doesn't," he protested. "I've been a vampire for my whole life and it still doesn't make sense to me." He ran a miserable hand through his hair. She must be teasing him.

"Oh, no, I knew about the vampirism. Very interesting genetic anomaly you have there," she chuckled. "No, I meant your age. It hadn't occurred to me that the retarded growth rate I saw in my tests meant a slower aging process and longer lifespan. I'm such an idiot sometimes."

"Tests?" he choked.

"What did you think I would do with the samples you gave us?" she asked.

"I thought you would give them to Clio to make synth blood. You said you didn't do medical splices. I didn't think you personally did much splicing at all," he said, fumbling for understanding.

She explained, "From what I saw at Omerta and the way you were acting, I felt it was better for me to handle those samples personally. I was curious." Harmony paused for a minute and looked embarrassed. "And I ran black market medical splices for years. How do you think I came up with the capital to start Floracopia? I don't any more. But I don't want anyone connecting Floracopia to my shady past." She took his hand and a ray of hope lit up his face.

"Oh." That was all he could think of for a minute. But then he had another thought. "Perhaps you handled those samples personally because you care for me?"

Harmony leaned over and gave him a smoldering kiss. When she broke away, Max had to work to keep himself from tearing her clothes off right then and there. They were in one of Omerta's conference rooms. It lacked the proper ambiance.

"Interesting," she said. "I can't feel the retractable fang teeth with my tongue."

"Are you sure?" panted Max. "Want to try again?"

Harmony did.

After a few more minutes of that, she had to take a break. "So, I believe you said that occasionally this disease is transferable by fluid contact?"

"What? Yes. Very rarely," said Max, taking deep breaths. He got up and straightened his shirt. "We've only seen a few cases. Those have occurred with repeated exposure."

She gave him an inquiring look, so he said, "Transfusions are obviously the best way to handle the blood requirements, but it was not too long ago that we had to use the fangs and bite. Most of us made some kind of arrangement for blood donors. A servant or a lover. Like that. Some of them turned after several years."

She coughed. "I assume that a long-term sexual partner would be at the most risk from a fluid-born vector." Max moved towards her again with a devilish gleam in his eye. Harmony did not object.

"I can't believe you people have managed to conceal this condition for so long. And I assume a large portion of Omerta has this disease?" she asked.

"Yes. Actually, that's why we started creating the privacy software," he replied, tenderly tucking an escaped lock of hair behind her ear. "We needed to hide our longevity and blood requirements when all the records started going digital. Then we decided to start selling our privacy system to everyone else. That was the best decision we ever made. It enabled us to create the settlement on Queen Charlotte Island. We don't do well in cities. We're very sensitive to carbon monoxide levels."

"Then life here in Ambrosia Springs should suit you," she said.

"Quite a bit," he replied.

They were too busy for talking for several minutes after that. Then alarms began going off on the wallscreen and Max's handheld.

"What's going on?" cried Harmony, instantly on the alert.

"It's Seth and Clio," Max replied. "They are on their way, but they will be cutting it very close to the deadline."

"My daughter," she whispered, covering her mouth with one hand.

He gave her a grim look. "And they have half the armed forces trailing behind them."

CHAPTER TWENTY-NINE

"How close are we?" asked Clio.

"Fifteen minutes closer than the last time you asked," Seth replied, his eyes glued to the road.

"No need to get testy," she snapped.

"Other than the roadblock ahead and the six helicopters behind us?" he snapped back. "Look at that. They have tanks out there. Real live tanks. I should be at home playing D&D or something. How on earth did we get here?"

"Fate. Karma. Maybe we offended the gods and they are punishing us. Who knows? Let's just focus on getting home," she said, tapping away at her handheld.

"Look, maybe we shouldn't try to blaze through this like action-movie commandos. Maybe the way to win this is to pull over and let them take us," Seth said, groping for the reasonable solution.

One of the helicopters fired a missile. It shot over the hovercar and exploded in the road in front of them. The autopilot swerved to avoid the crater. They managed to miss most of the damage, but the car fishtailed as they were struck by fallout. It set off a chorus of yips from Team Pom.

"Yeah, I don't think turning ourselves in is the best option right now, honey," replied Clio. "They seem pretty pissed off."

"Fair enough," replied Seth. "So, let's think about this. How will we get past the roadblock and away from the helicopters?"

"The EMP pulse?"

He shook his head. "It doesn't have enough power. They'd have to be really close and we would have to stop. We wouldn't hit enough of them."

A spray of bullets erupted from the closest helicopter. They lurched to the side as the autopilot threw the car in a tailspin.

"How bulletproof is this thing?" asked Clio in a strangled voice.

"Not that bulletproof."

"Got any other tricks up your sleeve?" she asked.

"Just one. I've got a missile launcher."

"Hot damn!"

"It only has four missiles."

"Oh."

The car lurched again as one of the tanks at the roadblock fired at them. Seth got a face full of Pomeranian.

"So how close are we?" she asked.

"Clio!"

"Look, I'm not asking just to annoy you. I have a plan. But we need to get past this roadblock and make it to the border in the next fifteen minutes," she replied. "The hovercar doesn't need a road. Find us a way around."

Seth obliged, frantically programming an escape route. "Even if we get past the tanks, we can't outrun the helicopters," he growled at her.

"Are you sure? This thing is pretty fast," she said as they shot off the road and over the terrain.

"Not that fast," he replied. The helicopters were gaining on them. Team Pom expressed their feelings for the helicopters by snarling and chewing on the seat cushions.

They flew through a field and over a stream, then cut back to the road past the roadblock.

Seth whipped his head to look at the tanks that were now lumbering after them. "Here they come!"

Two helicopters blocked his view. They swooped so close to the hovercar, he was surprised they didn't bump it.

"Missile launcher?" screeched Clio. "Didn't you say you had a missile launcher?"

"I'm already on it," he yelled as the rear window cracked under a spattering of bullets. A missile shot out of the back of the car and hit one of the helicopters. It spun down to a fiery crash.

The hovercar raced down the road, bobbing and weaving like a heavyweight champ. Seth fired off two more missiles. Two more smoking helicopters were forced to land.

Seth was thankful that he hadn't let Max talk him out of putting in this missile launcher. His uncle had told him he was insane. Seth was glad he'd sprung for the guided missiles too. If you are going to be insane, you might as well commit to it. From his experiences in the last few days, sanity was highly over-rated anyway.

"The autopilot in this thing is amazing," gasped Clio as she held on to her seatbelt for dear life.

"It's got an AI. I didn't train it for military combat, but it's adapting remarkably well," replied Seth as he fired off the last rocket. "If we make it out of this alive, remind me to brag about that."

The last rocket missed.

"Never mind," he said.

"How close are we?" asked Clio, checking the time yet again.

Seth swallowed his irritation with visible effort. "Almost there. Two miles."

"Ye gods, this is going to be close," she cried. "Ok, stop here."

"Are you crazy?" he yelled.

"Use the EMP!" she yelled back.

He knew this was suicide, but he could see the border now. It was empty. There was no one there to help them. From the way Clio had been talking about getting to the border, he assumed there would be reinforcements there. Something. Anything. But he saw nothing.

"Oh well," he sighed. "It will be over soon. Why not go out with a bang?" The hovercar spun dramatically and screeched to a stop.

The remaining helicopters sped closer and closer. Clio found herself crawling back in her seat to get away from the sight of them.

"Now? Can you do it now?" cried Clio.

"Not yet," replied Seth.

"What if they blow us up before they are close enough?"

He turned to look at her.

"Did you just think of that NOW?"

Two helicopters hovered over them as the third landed next to the car. They could see the line of tanks approaching on the horizon. The sun had just passed over the horizon and they watched the military in the fading twilight.

Seth turned and traced the line of her jaw with his finger. "I love you," he said. He hit the button.

The pulse rocked the car. The landing helicopter sputtered and died.

"Go, go, go!" Seth screamed at the hovercar as a falling helicopter scraped along the side of it. The hovercar shot off, narrowly missing the other helicopter as it smashed to the ground.

They sped away with the line of tanks hot on their trail. As they crossed the border, Seth searched the horizon for some sign of help. There was nothing. They were doomed.

"Alright, stop here," said Clio cheerfully.

"Why not?" Seth replied quietly. The sun had gone down so at least he wouldn't burn again.

They got out of the car. Seth watched the approach of the military. Clio watched her handheld.

"I've got a connection again," she laughed. "It is 8:01 p.m. and we are on the right side of the border." She punched a fist in the air triumphantly. Seth wrapped her in his arms. Her brain had obviously cracked under the pressure.

"Now we'll just see if Jason can deliver," she said, snuggling in to Seth.

"What?" he asked, looking around. Then he saw tiny streaks in the air, like the smoke trails that follow jets. But the angle of their flight was all wrong.

He heard a high whistling noise. One of the tanks exploded. Shrapnel flew everywhere. They both stepped back even though they were far from the blast.

Clio laughed. More smoke trails shot through the sky. More tanks exploded. Clio crowed and danced around. Seth just stared. Team Pom filed out to form a hyperactive barrier between Seth and the explosions.

"What's happening?" he asked stupidly.

"Welcome to the revolution, baby!" laughed Clio, shoving her handheld in his fingers.

He looked at the device as if he had never seen one before. The tiny screen showed the governor of Texas on the capitol steps, giving some kind of press conference. Behind him were hundreds of people. Seth recognized a few faces and realized this must be almost everyone in the Texas government.

The governor was in rare form. "In the words of the great Thomas Jefferson: 'We hold these truths to be self-evident: that all men are created equal. They are endowed with certain unalienable rights. Among these are life, liberty and the pursuit of happiness. That whenever any form of government becomes destructive of these ends, it is the right of the people to alter or to abolish it, and to institute new government, laying its foundation on such principles and organizing its powers in such form, as to them shall seem most likely to effect their safety and happiness. But when a long train of abuses and usurpations, pursuing invariably the same object evinces a design to reduce them under absolute despotism, it is their right, it is their duty, to throw off such government, and to provide new guards for their future security.'"

Here the governor paused to clear his throat. "The greatest fear of the people of Texas is the government of America. That government should be protecting us and helping us. Instead they imprison and torture at their whim. They destroy our livelihoods and take our loved ones. Now they seek to remove the one last security and right we have—the right to defend ourselves. Enough! No more! America, we are done with you. Texas would like to officially tender their resignation from the United States."

Here he had to stop for the roaring of the crowd. Seth realized from the sound that there must be thousands of people around the capitol this night. The governor held up a hand for silence. "We have had enough. Quite simply, America, you do not get to oppress Texas. And if you care to object, I have only one thing to say to you. Come and pry it from my cold dead hands!" Here the mature and stoic members of the Texas government totally lost it. They roared their support and threw the governor on their shoulders.

"Um, Clio?" asked Seth. "What's going on?" He looked from the handheld to the smoking wreckage of the tanks.

"The border closed at eight p.m. for the revolution," she replied, like this was the most sensible thing in the world. "We made it to the right side. They didn't." She pointed at the smoking tanks.

"They waited this long to give us a chance to get back, but they had to do it tonight. They received intelligence that military convoys would be coming tomorrow to put Texas under martial law and start forcible de-armament. Speaking of which, I better let people know we made it," she took the handheld out of his limp fingers.

"They fired missiles at the tanks? How did they know?" asked Seth, still trying to make sense out of what just happened.

"Naw, it's the satellite swarm. Pretty cool, right? It's on remote for the next little bit. They warned everybody who lives along the border. I expect there will be some casualties until they get the kinks out, but you can't have a revolution without taking out a few cows, I guess," she said as she tapped away. Seth heard screaming and hooting from the handheld. He guessed she had called her sisters to let them know she was all right.

"A satellite swarm?"

"Yeah. Remember I told you that Jason was working with some guys on defense weapons? This is it. Apparently, one of his drinking buddies is the guy who runs SpaceTex," she replied. "The got their start cleaning up space junk. Originally, they slapped guidance systems on everything they found and just sent it into an orbital path so it can burn up in the atmosphere. Then, being rednecks, they started making a drinking game out of crashing space junk into targets on the ground. That's how they got the idea for a satellite defense system for Texas."

Seth looked back at the smoking tanks. He could see men milling around, loading things into the undamaged vehicles. "So they are pelting the border with space junk?"

"Yep. I guess they've been launching millions of these little satellites up there for the last couple years," Clio said. "They sent them up as communication satellites. Then they would tell the government, 'Gee, we must have screwed up. It broke into a bunch of little pieces that spread out above Texas. Guess we'll have to send up another one.' I can't believe they got away with that." Clio shook her head. "Those Yankees really do think we are a bunch of inbred idiots down here."

Seth thought that over. "So it's not like the United States can target your satellites because if they take out a few, there will still be thousands more. And they work on remote right? So they just target anything incoming?"

She nodded. "They can pick up anything larger than a dog,

but they also track the way it moves and looks so the US can't send dogs with bombs strapped to them over the border. Also, I believe they already sent out a wave of drones to take out the US military tracking satellites. Your software helped them with that," she said, giving him a squeeze. "They are desperate to get you back. That SpaceTex guy is crazy smart, but they need your programming expertise."

"Did Jason program the tracking system?" asked Seth, looking up to the sky again. Clio nodded.

"Should we be standing this close to the border?" Seth asked, edging towards the car.

Clio's eyebrows shot up as she scanned the sky. "No, probably not. Let's get of here."

They sped home, holding hands the whole way. On the handheld, they watched the news as the governor pounded the senator on the back, both of them grinning like fools.

"Well, I hope this all gets sorted out in time for football season," laughed the senator.

"Joe, that don't matter," said the governor into the cameras. "We already got all the important teams on our side of the fence."

"Clio, darling," said Seth as they watched the impromptu street party on the handheld. "I hate to be a spoilsport, but this could all go horribly, terribly awry. From what you are telling me, they planned this revolution in three days. The satellite swarm is a really neat piece of technology, but I don't think that will win a war."

Clio kissed him gently. "Have a little faith, Seth. Everything will turn out the way it is supposed to turn out."

Seth kissed her back. "Well, I hope this mess is over in time for the wedding."

"What wedding?"

"Ours, of course. My parents will want to come."

Clio gave a very unladylike squeal as satellites streaked through the sky behind them.

And that's how love can start a revolution.

ABOUT THE AUTHOR

Katy Stauber has degrees in Biochemistry and Mathematics from Texas A&M University. She currently lives with her husband and two sons in Austin, TX. This is her first published novel.